HOLIDAY HEARTS

Visit us at www.boldstrokesbooks.com

HOLIDAY HEARTS

by

Diana Day-Admire and Lyn Cole

2021

HOLIDAY HEARTS

ISBN 13: 978-1-63679-128-9

This Trade Paperback Original Is Published By
Bold Strokes Books, Inc.
P.O. Box 249
Valley Falls, NY 12185

First Edition: December 2021

CREDITS
Editors: Victoria Villaseñor and Cindy Cresap
Production Design: Susan Ramundo
Cover Design By Inkspiral Design

Acknowledgments

We are forever grateful to our families and friends, the number of which constantly increase with our blessings. The members of MRW (Midwest Romance Writers).

Dedication

We dedicate this to Joshua C. and Patti A.

CHAPTER ONE

December 20th, Logan Brady, drunk, killed in plane crash. Logan could see the headlines now. *Holiday Tragedy: Broke, jobless, homeless local woman has one last drink before boarding plane to visit her family.*

Logan mentally shook herself. The plane hadn't crashed—it had touched down safely. She tugged the handle of her purple carry-on luggage, a gift from her parents when she'd graduated college eons ago. Why had she packed so much? Surely, she could have made do with less.

The trek up the ramp seemed to last forever, and the impending reunion with her family played across her mind's eye like a Coen Brothers farce. She could see her parents—her color-blind, homespun mother with her thick glasses and bunchy sweaters; her paunchy, couch potato father. Behind them were her extrovert, gay brother, Donavan; and her self-righteous, nose-in-the-air, older sister, Doreen. Whatever had possessed her to *want* to spend the holidays with any of them?

The answer was immediate. Comfort in the familiar, the security of home, even if home was the weirdest place on the planet. At least there'd be plenty of food. Why hadn't she eaten before boarding in Dulles? Why the hell had she downed those three drinks on an empty stomach during the short flight from DC to Kansas City?

Because you just got laid off, because you're scared, because Marcus Dupree, your ex-best-friend and fake fiancé, just bailed on you, and because you're a dumbass. She grimaced at the brightness of the airport's interior.

This wasn't Kansas. She blinked against the overhead lighting. *Crap.* Her muddled mind, combined with alcohol and sleep, had confused her. Snowstorm. Emergency landing in Chicago. Overnight at the airline's expense in some hotel.

Ah, the turbulent flight into O'Hare International Airport, one of the reasons she'd had those last two drinks.

"Here. Let me help with that." The velvety female voice caressed the back of her neck and grated against her last nerve. Then strong hands steadied her and retrieved her luggage as it slipped from her hands.

"Thanks." Logan offered what she hoped was a grateful but not pitiful smile. Then her body shook. "I'm gonna be sick." Logan fought a violent retch, and her rescuer stopped for a moment.

Unable and unwilling to chance raising her head, Logan studied the Italian loafers in front of her own waffle-stompers as her mom called them. If she died, at least she would spend her last moments with someone who had good taste in shoes. Salvatore Ferragamo, if she wasn't mistaken. She'd admired a pair while window-shopping one day outside Saks Fifth Avenue. She cocked her head, examining the sturdy but definitely female footwear. Embarrassed beyond belief, with no warning this time, she retched again. Thank God she hadn't eaten anything and she mostly had dry heaves, but still.

To her companion's credit, she remained stock-still, didn't even appear to inch back.

Oh shit. "I am so...ugh...sorry!"

Wordlessly, the woman released her hold on their luggage and held Logan's hair back from her face as another spasm slammed her. The Good Samaritan—Logan still hadn't seen her face—turned her counterclockwise, which only served to make Logan dizzier and sicker, but at least this time there wasn't clothing for her to target, only the polished airport floor.

Mortified, she clutched one of the woman's arms, her fingers digging into the jacket's fabric. Logan wanted to pass out and felt more than heard the irony-intoned voice above her.

"Clean-up on aisle twenty-seven. Anybody got a mop?" Logan's rescuer thrust a crisp white handkerchief in front of Logan's face.

Don't get me tickled—this is so not funny. Wouldn't Donavan enjoy this little scenario? The silly queen would never let her live it down if he knew. *Then let's not tell him.* She took a shuddering breath, belched, and felt better. *Great, Logan, just great. Why not fart while you're at it? Charm the nice lady so that she can say good-bye without remorse.*

"I am so sorry!" Logan tried to rise, but the woman held her in place. If Logan weren't afraid of being sick again, she'd have snorted with laughter. "It's okay," she said from between her own legs. "You're safe now. The storm has passed."

The woman clasped Logan's arms and helped her to an upright position. "Well, not quite. We still have to get to the hotel. Think you can make it?"

Logan saluted by raising her hand and forming a circle with thumb and index finger. Her mock bravado froze as she stared into the most luscious amber eyes she'd ever seen. "Just lead me to baggage claim, and I'll be on my way," she finished weakly.

Did she chuckle? Is she laughing at me? Even in her condition, Logan still had *some* pride and dignity. She'd find her own damn way to the rest of her luggage. She struggled to wrest her arm from the grasp then swiped the hankie she'd been offered across her face and squared her shoulders. All Logan saw was her new friend's backside since she'd turned away and appeared to be looking for someone.

Logan's tongue stuck to the roof of her mouth. *Nice ass.* She craned her head so that her gaze could travel from narrow hips and the small of the back, all the way to the woman's shoulders, graceful neck, and dark hair. That was one yummy, classy businesswoman. As memory of what she'd just done pricked her, she quickly glanced toward the floor and wrinkled her nose. Broke or not, once she found her voice, she'd feel obligated to pay her rescuer's cleaning bills. She only hoped nothing had to be replaced. If it did, the woman would be waiting a while before she got her money.

The woman—who looked to be a few years older than Logan—didn't appear to be concerned about her attire. Composed and all business within seconds, she'd flagged down an airport employee, talked him into giving them a lift to their baggage claim on an indoor shuttle, and tipped him enough to make the man gush like her rescuer was a billionaire. Then she'd positioned Logan, their carry-on luggage, and herself within the confines of the shuttle.

Words escaped Logan. For a woman used to giving orders to others at DC's now-defunct Book Boutique, she couldn't manage a simple thank you, a protest, or an apology.

She observed Miss Italian Loafers' hands. Salon-perfect nails. Tanned skin, no wedding band and no jewelry on either wrist, not even a watch, which prompted Logan to check for a cell phone.

The flat pockets in the other woman's pants told Logan that she definitely wasn't carrying her phone there. *Hmm. Nice-looking form.*

"Looking for anything in particular?" Her voice dripped amusement.

Could this day be any worse? Logan didn't even attempt denying that she'd been caught giving the crotch a once-over. "Cell phone."

"It's in my jacket pocket—you were looking a little too far south. Need to use it? The phone, I mean."

"I know what you mean." Logan ground her teeth on the words and shook her head. "I was just thinking that I need to buy a new battery for mine. I've been dropping calls from my family. I need to tell them that I won't arrive until tomorrow."

"Well, you're welcome to use my phone when you're ready." She patted Logan's knee.

The action made Logan jump, not from the electrical charge that connected them, but from the realization that eventually she'd have to glance upward and meet the woman's gaze again. *Shit. Might as well get it over with.* She crunched the handkerchief in her hand. "I'm afraid I've ruined your shoes, your pants, and your hankie. Any chance you could trust me with getting back to you for their cleaning costs?"

"Nope."

Great. She didn't fancy giving Logan her telephone number or a way to reach her. Not that Logan could blame her.

The irritatingly rich voice continued. "But I'll let you buy me a drink once we get to the hotel."

"Not unless it's water." Logan immediately clamped a hand over her mouth. "I'm sorry. I seem to have diarrhea of the mouth today."

For the first time since they'd met, she heard the other woman belly laugh, and Logan couldn't resist seeing what the rest of her looked like.

Those warm amber eyes met hers and held contact. The woman seemed genuinely at ease, despite the situation. Logan thrust out her free hand. "Thank you for helping me. Seriously. I'd have been in a world of hurt if you hadn't been there." She looked at her feet again. "Sorry about the shoes. And pants."

"Stop apologizing." She shook Logan's hand, and her fingers held a strange comfort. The look on her face was one of amusement coupled with irritation.

"I didn't wipe my mouth without the hankie, so the hand is clean." Logan grinned wryly.

Logan's rescuer released her hand and took the handkerchief. "I'm Mick, short for Michaela."

Another M name. Logan sighed in resignation as she thought of Marcus, her roommate and closest friend. He was supposed to accompany her to her parents' home and pose as her fiancé. Now Logan would have to ward off the usual battery of questions alone. And even though she kept in touch with all of them, her well-meaning but meddling family members would ask the same things they always did. Why wasn't she at least engaged? When would she settle down?

Mick asked, "And yours?"

"Logan."

"Is that your first or last name?"

She was used to the question. "My first. Irish on both sides. What can I say?"

"Enough said. My last name is—what?" Mick halted when Logan held up her hands to stop her.

"Please. Don't tell me. Let's just keep this as casual as possible. I'm already embarrassed to death. If I knew your last name, I'd be obliged to tell you mine, and right now I want to disappear into the walls of this airport without you knowing *anything* else about me."

"If it makes you feel any better, I once did the same thing to a date. Blame it on the roller coaster. I'd warned her that fast motion made me ill."

Logan smiled at Mick, happy her gaydar still worked. "You're just saying that."

"God's truth." Mick held up her right hand like a Girl Scout saying the pledge.

"How old were you? Ten?"

Mick shook her head with mock seriousness. "Fifteen."

By the time they'd collected their luggage and ridden to their hotel, Logan felt relaxed, not as sick to her stomach, and not as horrified at her behavior. Must be the cold air blasting me, she thought as their driver apologized for the umpteenth time about the passenger window that had frozen stuck before reaching the top of the doorframe.

Mick suggested that they spend the next hour or so having dinner. "The airline comps our meals while we're here," she reminded Logan.

Logan grimaced as she glanced at the long lines in front of the hotel's front desk and agreed. By the time they finished eating, the lines would be much shorter. It didn't make sense not to have dinner to get something in her stomach to help with the alcohol she'd consumed on the plane.

"You're right, and I'm starved now." She offered what she hoped was a friendly smile that didn't seem flirtatious. Jeez. It wouldn't do for Mick to think that she was hitting on her, not after Mick had rescued her and knew that she had no other way of paying her back just yet.

"Look, I'm not saying this to embarrass you or get you to apologize again, but…" Mick looked down at her pants and shoes. "I need to visit the lobby restroom and get cleaned up a bit before we go into the restaurant."

Logan bit her lip then waved. "Please. Be my guest. I'll wait with the luggage. When you return, maybe you could give me a few minutes to freshen up?"

While Mick took care of the mess Logan had caused, Logan looked about their hotel lobby and got her bearings. At the far end of the open-spaced area lay a bistro that looked as if it were closed. Another eatery was nearby, with a polished bar, intimate tables, flowers, and soft lighting. The sophisticated surroundings served to remind her that she hardly looked as if she belonged there. Or felt like it.

She could use a toothbrush. And a bath and a comb. She slid her tongue over her teeth and ran her fingers through her hair. She knew she looked frightful.

Thankfully, Mick didn't take long, so she was able to tend to her own needs before she sat down to a meal with her. The first thing she did was track down a member of housekeeping and request a toothbrush and toothpaste before she darted for the restroom.

A porter touched Mick's arm briefly when Logan returned to the lobby. "Want me to grab one of the trolleys for you, so you can leave your luggage while you eat?"

Mick turned to Logan. "Everything should be fine here while we eat, don't you think?"

Logan glanced worriedly at their surroundings. Nobody seemed interested in stealing—all of the hotel's visible staff appeared busy helping their unexpected guests. "Sure."

Mick helped the porter stack their suitcases then turned to Logan with a grin. "I'm famished. Wonder if they have steak?" She cleared her throat. "Earth to Logan."

"Sorry. Just wondering if maybe we shouldn't take our things with us."

Mick took a deep breath and blew a stream of air in a low whistle. "We may struggle for a place to stow it is all."

Logan looked longingly toward the restaurant, praying that their table would have crackers and complimentary water soon after they were seated. At this point, she was ready to eat the tablecloth. "I suppose it'd be too much to ask that they'd have a mocha Frappuccino." She glanced toward their luggage again.

Mick seemed horrified. "I saw you on the plane. You never ate. So you want a milk-based drink on a stomach that has only had alcohol during the past few hours?"

Logan shrugged. "Fraps calm me. Chocolate, whipped cream. What can I say?"

"If you're worried, we can take our suitcases with us," Mick told her.

"Nah. You're right, and the porter said it'd be fine." Logan shrugged off her doubts. "I tend to worry too much."

It was all Mick could do to keep a straight face and contain her laughter. She didn't want to embarrass Logan, but damn, she was funny without trying. Mick had spotted Logan on the plane and sat a short distance away on the other side of the aisle, her seat perfect for glancing back at her and watching the copious amount of alcohol she drank. At first, it had been amusing. After the first thirty minutes, however, Mick became alarmed. She felt compelled to follow closely once they deboarded to make sure her object of interest was capable of navigating the airport on her own. She wasn't.

Then they met, Logan became ill, and the rest of their time together incorporated enough twists and turns to snag more than a little of Mick's attention. She was hooked and determined to find out more.

While she waited, Mick ticked off the memos Georgette had made for her. Her personal assistant had provided Mick with a small leatherbound notebook. Stamped on the front was Mick's name in gold lettering. Inside resembled a Filofax planner. Mick chuckled. For a vacation? Georgette was an excellent employee, but she was anal as hell.

One note read: *Electronically sign the forms for new overseas acquisition. Damn. Eleven signatures?* She signed them all while waiting for Logan. Next note: *Read and vet the notes Georgette had made at the Zoom meeting Mick had missed during her flight.* Check and check.

Where the hell was Logan? Mick glanced toward the restrooms, frustrated. Well, that's what she got for taking a working vacation. She'd agreed to meet Donavan and his significant other, who had helped design the new video game she was to see. Don had always been a creative genius, but Mick hadn't seen him in a while. She'd been too caught up with growing her company to take lunch with them in DC, and the guys could never arrange to meet her on their turf in New York. When the holidays approached, it seemed like a good idea to unwind, have a bit of fun, and discuss business over Christmas turkey and dressing. Mick hadn't confided in Georgette, but she was secretly pleased at the invitation. She and Don had been great friends in college. Time had chipped away at their schedules, but Mick was curious to see the video game. If she invested in it, this would be her first venture into the gaming industry.

"I should have assigned Georgette to this one," Mick muttered.

"Who is Georgette?"

Mick glanced across the table. She hadn't heard Logan slip into her seat. "Ah, Georgette is my assistant. My secretary. My all-around go-to person." Mick closed the notebook of lists and numbers. "Sorry. I became embroiled in business, as usual. Everything okay with you?"

"Yeah. Sure. I'm self-conscious, but that's my constant state of things. Ready to order?"

❖

They spent a good two hours unwinding, getting to know one another's little peccadilloes, the sort of things one only tells strangers.

"So you've never investigated your heterochromia?" asked Mick.

"My what?"

Mick touched the corners of her own eyes. "That's what it's called when your eyes are two different colors."

"Nope." Logan shook her head. "And as far as anyone knows, I'm the only one in the family who has this condition."

Mick laughed. "Studies show that it may be hereditary, but I'll take your word for it. At least you know your family. I don't think I met any of my relatives."

Logan sat flabbergasted. "You're kidding."

"No. Prior to age ten or so, I have no clue. I was too busy working and hustling to care." Mick shrugged. "And honestly, I don't want to talk about me. You're far more interesting."

"Ha." Logan laughed. "Now who is pulling whose leg?"

Surely, Mick knew full well how beautiful and exciting she was. Mick was glamorous, intelligent, obviously well-read if she knew about whatever she called Logan's eye colors.

Suddenly, Logan's self-consciousness overtook her curiosity about her dinner companion. This was a treat, having a meal across the table in a fancy hotel with such an engaging woman. It was way better than the family reunion she'd been dreading to some degree. Maybe she'd just call them and say she'd been kidnapped by a hot woman and wouldn't be home this year after all.

Chapter Two

Mick folded her arms across her chest and leaned back in her chair. It was a power move she'd perfected early on, one that held an air of superiority. She was aware of it, but this time it wasn't deliberate and wasn't meant to intimidate. She was intrigued by her younger companion. So open, so honest. Vulnerable, whether Logan knew it or not. Mick couldn't help studying her.

Life on the streets wasn't something Mick wanted to remember. She'd overcome the loneliness, the fear, and the insecurities she'd experienced all those years ago. If she was confident now, that confidence had come at a price. It was born out of taking risks and falling on her face, then dusting herself off and trying again. This charming creature before her lacked the edginess most of Mick's acquaintances and business associates wore like armor.

"Tell me more about yourself." Mick leaned forward, eager to learn more. "What were you like in school? When did you first know you were gay?"

Logan's lips parted, and her eyes grew wider. "I was nothing special. No, really. I was just your average kid." She smiled. "If I knew I was gay, I did nothing about it until I moved to DC. My community was friendly but terminally straight. Few people had gaydar, but I didn't want to chance being different, standing out. So I waited until I'd graduated high school."

"How about your folks?"

"Oh, they're fine with my brother being gay. They weren't at first. I'd hear them discussing him when they didn't know I eavesdropped. But with me?" Logan shook her head. "Mom is always trying to hook me up with an eligible boy. A nice boy. That's why I wanted a fake fiancé to accompany me. I figured if they could see I'm happy and that I can snag my own dates, maybe they'd stop hounding me about settling down." Logan looked away.

"Go on."

Logan sighed. "My sister is the mama's girl. You know? She and Mom share many of the same interests and hobbies. They talk every day."

"And you're more of a daddy's girl?"

"Yeah. And...I don't want to disappoint him."

Mick couldn't help interrupting. "You're still the same person. You're still daddy's girl. So what's the problem? How could you possibly be a disappointment?"

"Good question." Logan gave a small laugh. "I suppose if I knew the answer to that I'd have come out to the folks years ago."

Mick didn't want to piss off her new friend, but even though she grew up without siblings, she sensed something important in Logan's family that hadn't been addressed. "Let me ask you another question. When did you know your brother was gay?"

"Oh, I've always known that." Logan laughed again, this time loudly. "Anyone who knows him can tell you that my brother is gay. He tries not to be obvious, but he can't help it."

"He tries to be butch?"

"Well, you'd never catch him suiting up for football, but he watches the game with Dad on TV, even though you can tell he's not paying attention."

"And you?"

"Hell, I was the one passing the ball with Dad before I was in kindergarten. He taught me how to play softball. I was on the high school team while my sister took home economics and went to craft shows with Mom."

"And your brother?"

"He was an artist, a gamer nerd. He enjoyed skateboarding and video games."

Mick asked the question that needed a voice. "Did you become daddy's girl because your brother was gay and didn't have that much in common with him? To fill the space, so to speak?"

Tears shimmered in Logan's eyes, and she shook her head. "I don't think so. I think I've just always felt closer to Dad."

Mick found the family dynamics Logan described fascinating. "And there's nothing wrong with that." She clasped Logan's hands. "I'm sorry for asking such a stupid question. I've never had a sister or a brother. It was a lame thing to ask."

Logan withdrew her hands but smiled. "No offense taken."

When they'd finished their meal and noticed the line dissipating, they went for their luggage, only to find it gone. Even good-natured Mick swore, not that Logan blamed her. She was the one who'd have to wear those pants until she could shop, wash, or retrieve her clothing.

Logan had used up all of her patience, depleted her repertoire of conversation, exhausted her excuses and apologies, and now all she wanted was a bath, clean sheets, and a remote place to bawl.

The look in Mick's dark eyes told her that she wasn't alone.

The cherry on the cake of her day was when management at the hotel informed them that there was only one room available.

Mick cut Logan a quick inquisitive look. "Mind if I handle this?"

"By all means. I'm too exhausted to think."

Mick's manicured hands clenched and unclenched at her sides. "How many beds?"

"Oh, there are two." The clerk adjusted her necktie and beamed as if she'd just given them great news.

In an even voice, Mick asked politely if the hotel had any pajamas they might wear, given that they had lost their luggage.

When the flustered clerk seemed doubtful and asked if there was anything else she might offer, Mick said, "Just the one pair of pajamas, just the one room, one bottle of champagne, and one monstrous basket of fruit and flowers to compensate us for misplacing our luggage."

"Well, technically, you weren't registered at the time your luggage, uh, disappeared, so the hotel isn't liable for loss or damage."

The heat from Mick's already tense body was palpable, and the clerk held up her hands. "Let me see what I can do."

"We'll wait right here. Don't forget the champagne."

She nodded solemnly, and Logan digested Mick's words.

"What are we celebrating?" She tugged on Mick's jacket sleeve.

"The fact that by tomorrow the snow and ice will have cleared somewhat, and we won't have to spend another night in this madness." Mick glanced at her slacks. "I need to have my pants sent out for cleaning, so I need those pajama bottoms for the night in case I have to answer the door. Truth is, I sleep in the nude, but I'll make an exception tonight. I figured you'd prefer sleeping in the top."

Logan swallowed hard. "Well, maybe the craziness will be over for you tomorrow, but I still have my family to face, and the word madness doesn't come close to describing what's in store for me."

While they waited, Mick made small talk. "Mind if I ask why your phone doesn't work?"

Shitshitshitshitshit. She still hadn't phoned her parents. "I'm technology-challenged. I never learned the ins and outs of smartphones. And I'm…scatterbrained. I don't think of checking things like power packs, batteries, cords. The result is that I have an ancient cell phone with no wonderful features, and I don't use it much anyway."

"How did you keep in contact with loved ones during the pandemic?" asked Mick.

"Email and Skype." Logan shrugged.

"Ah." Mick seemed to accept Logan's lack of sophistication.

"Do you mind if I smoke? I'm getting a headache." She fidgeted, fingers trembling, and searched inside her purse for tissues, aspirin, cigarettes, and a lighter.

"Yes."

"Pardon me?"

"Yes, I mind if you smoke. It's bad for you, and the nicotine won't keep your head from pounding."

Indignantly, Logan took a step back, offended. "That's my prerogative, isn't it?"

"Not when I'm about to share a room with you, it isn't. Smoke sticks to your clothes, your body, everything."

"Well, I'm absolutely, positively certain that I want to smoke."

The clerk helping them coughed lightly. "This is a non-smoking hotel, ma'am, but there are chairs outside on the south side of the hotel, a small garden area where no one will bother you."

"It's freezing outside!" Logan protested.

"All the more reason not to light up," Mick commented.

The clerk shrugged. "As you said, it's your choice. That's the best we can do for you."

"*Fine!*" Logan turned to leave, and she heard the clerk telling Mick that it'd be a few minutes before she could locate the pajamas she'd requested.

Logan stormed toward the patio area the clerk had described. Mick caught up to her and touched her arm. "Not so fast. I'll go with you."

"I thought you disapproved."

"I do." She wrinkled her nose. "But it'll be a bit before we can get into the room, collect our goodies from management, and settle in, so I may as well join you." She lowered her face to meet Logan's squarely. "Unless you object to polluting the air in my presence."

"It'd be my pleasure." She'd quit smoking months earlier, but the strain of losing her job, the anxiety of facing her family and having them know she was in financial straits, the gut-wrenching feeling that she was a loser, and her fear that she'd never find another job during the holidays, all served her craving for nicotine, and she was damned if she'd be denied the last pack she'd left in her purse before she quit smoking. She'd kept it there just in case.

Mick seemed reticent but obliging, and even opened the door for her and helped her get seated in the icy metal frame chair. She seemed bemused as Logan struggled to light her cigarette with the wind whipping about them. Mick cupped her hands around Logan's in order to help shield her.

"Been smoking long?" Mick teased her.

"Haven't in a while. Used to."

"Why pick it up again?"

"You haven't met my family." She took a long drag and choked, which made Mick chuckle.

"Logan...I've heard that name before."

"Really? I haven't met any other women with the same name. Where'd you hear it?"

"It'll come to me." Mick seemed intent on her face. "What's so bad about your relatives?"

"What isn't?" She shook her head. "I shouldn't say that. They're really nice people—they're just...weird." When Mick smiled, Logan shook her head again. "No, I mean bizarre, worse than anything you can imagine and wonderful at the same time. Like I told you, I have a brother and a sister. What I didn't say is that my sister's a homophobe. Our parents are Ozzie and Harriet on crack. Mom's color blind and Dad's half-deaf, so I guess they make a great odd couple, neither one minding the other's faults."

She hadn't talked about them in so long, and it felt good to let it all out, to spill her guts as to their fractured foibles. "Have you ever found yourself staring at something disastrous and then slapped yourself for finding a kind of compelling beauty about the whole thing?"

Mick looked bemused. "No."

"Well, I have. I was brought up to admire the unusual, to find beauty in things that others think define the word catastrophic... like holiday dinners." Logan groaned. "God, my mom is a good cook, and I love my family, but having a meal with them makes me wish I was anywhere but home. They fight and bicker and pick at one another. They bitch at me, and now I have to tell them that I've just lost my job." She took several drags off her cigarette and pondered her own words. "Well, I don't have to tell them, but they know me too well—they'll know something's wrong, and then somebody, probably my brother or sister, will smart off, and I'll spill the beans and out myself. Then there's the fake fiancé thing." She groaned again.

"I can't believe you were going to lie to them about being engaged."

"Just to get them off my back. They're so concerned about my love life, and I had Marcus, who was also my boss until he had to close his bookstore. Anyway he was supposed to go with me and pose as my fiancé, but he's backed out on me. I just don't want to deal with it."

Mick clearly bit back a grin, but her eyes twinkled as she spoke. "So don't tell them."

"It's not that simple. I've already told my brother that I'm engaged!" She wrung her hands. "We spoke on the phone last week, and I told him that I was in love and that things were going well for me, and I couldn't be happier—all of which was a lie."

Logan paused to take a deep drag of her cigarette. As she exhaled and watched the plume of smoke rise into the sky, she also noticed large snowflakes falling.

Mick tilted her head, caught a snowflake on her tongue, and turned back to grin at Logan.

The sight reminded Logan of a scene in a holiday movie. At that moment, the classy businesswoman became a regular person. Giddy and delightful, and beautiful. Logan liked what she saw. If she grinned again, she'd attack her. Maul her. Throw her on the pavement and hump her brains out.

"Why would you do that?" Mick straightened her back and leaned forward.

"Huh?" For a moment Logan thought she'd voiced her desire for Mick aloud.

"Why? Won't he tell your parents?"

"I was counting on it! I didn't want him to know that I was afraid the bookstore was closing or that I had no one to spend the holidays with unless I went home. Admitting failure, when everything is going so well for him—he's bringing a couple of guests home for the holidays, by the way, to show off, most likely—and when my sister, the perfect princess, is most likely making money hand over fist and bouncing back from her divorce looking like Martha-Freakin'-Stewart?" Her eyes filled with tears. "They're like those tiny little fish that have sharp teeth, and you can survive if you're alone with one of them, but when they all get together and swarm around you, they're lethal."

"Piranha."

"Excuse me?"

"That's the fish."

Logan swiped at her eyes. "Right. And when they're all there, and one of them smells blood, they just go after you. Everybody has an opinion, and I'll get no peace until I'm back in DC."

Mick sat back in her chair. "Surely, it can't be as bad as all that."

"No, it's worse. My dad worries about whether or not I have money, Mom worries that I'm not eating right, and my brother hounds me about not having a love life. Doreen?" Logan snorted. "She hasn't been laid since God was a corporal, and she's so nasty-nice that it's no wonder her husband left her. She's a control freak, and everything is all about image to her. She's embarrassed by our family."

"And you're not?"

Logan was offended. "Hell no! Haven't you been listening? It has nothing to do with that. With me, it's...look, I'm the baby of the family and I graduated college, but my brother has all of this talent, and I don't. I'm happy as hell for him. Now that he has his degrees, he's following his dream. He's an architect, he's in a relationship, and he has this wonderful ability to invent things. Doreen's smart and beautiful, and she's a nurse. But I have nothing to show for the past ten years other than a degree in liberal arts."

"And you don't want to be thought of as the family screwup."

"Exactly!" She breathed a little easier, knowing that somebody finally understood the pressure she was under in being the perfect child, the family scholar, the one with the most emotional investment from her family.

Then she realized how she'd monopolized their conversation. "I'm sorry. Seems I say that a lot to you, but I am. You've been so patient with me, and I haven't even asked you about your family. I assume that's where you're headed, considering it's Christmas?"

"I haven't met them yet."

She blinked. "You mean not in a long while?"

"Never. I grew up in foster care, ran away when I was fifteen. I got my GED while working three jobs."

"Wow. That's dedication." Logan thought back to how easy her childhood had been compared to Mick's. Here she was bitching about how hard it would be to hang out with her family when Mick didn't even have one. What an ass she must look like.

Mick nodded. "I had no choice. Then my best friend from college invited me home for the holidays. I'm supposed to meet him and his family tomorrow." Mick shrugged. "In a way, I feel like they're my family. I've heard so much about them." A faint pink tinged her cheeks. "To be honest, I've forgotten their names, but I've heard tons of stories."

Logan smiled. "Sounds like you two are close."

"We are. Were. We haven't seen one another for a while, but I still consider him one of my best friends." Mick frowned. "When we Zoomed last week, he said he's looking for investors for a new project he has developed, so this trip is for business as well as pleasure."

Her holiday was planned around someone who was probably just using her for her bank account? Logan didn't know what to say other than that she was sorry if she'd made Mick uncomfortable.

Mick reassured her. "Not at all. Having a big family like yours sounds like a dream to someone like me, though. Maybe you need to give them, and yourself, a break."

Logan considered Mick's words while she finished her cigarette. Mick was correct. At least she had a family, dysfunctional as they were. Who were the people Mick was staying with? "What exactly do you remember about this family you're meeting tomorrow?"

"It isn't so much what he said but the look on his face when he spoke of them, a loving mother and father. Said he grew up in a boring small town where everyone knew everybody else's business."

"And this made you envious?" Logan looked at Mick suspiciously. "I grew up in a place like that. It wasn't so great."

"Not to you, but to the person without family unity, without many friends, without so much as a Christmas tree in December?" Mick shrugged.

Logan leaned over and touched her arm. "I'm sorry."

"No, it's okay." Mick seemed to think for a moment. "There might have been a brother? I'm not sure. I just know that my friend was ready to leave home for some reason." She grew silent.

"What?"

"Nothing. I mean, he was a little strange, and there was something personal that bugged him about the small town…I dunno. Forget it." She scratched her chin thoughtfully. "I am a bit worried. I mean, he and I haven't kept in touch, and now he wants me to meet his family."

Logan laughed. "Maybe he wants to set you up with one of his siblings."

Mick smirked. "Hardly."

Logan chuckled. "Well, my brother is bringing someone home with him this week, and I was told to be on my best behavior. Don't know who the guy is, but evidently he's someone important." She took a last drag on her cigarette. "I'm freezing. Bet you are, too." She wanted to get back to the warmth of the hotel. "Let's check on the room and see if they've found our luggage. I can't wait to brush my teeth again."

"What is it with you and your teeth?" Mick asked.

"It's a trick to help keep me from smoking. I don't want a cigarette when my mouth tastes like mint."

The clerk was ready for them, sans luggage. She handed Mick two key cards, and when she in turn handed one to Logan, Logan realized her predicament. She was spending the night with a stranger. Her father had worked for the airline for forty years, and her mother could wrangle secrets from the IRS and the FBI— they would find her. What if her family phoned her? What if they checked up on her the following day? Whose name was on the register?

They would check on her—she knew they would. Her dad would have a difficult time restraining her mother, from dragging him out in the weather to drive the few hundred miles from Kansas City to Chicago to pick her up so that she wouldn't be alone.

Mick turned to her. "I can think of worse things than being stranded with you." She smiled, and the sincerity with which she spoke warmed Logan. Maybe the best thing for them both would be to get laid, a distraction from holiday woes and luggage anxiety.

Her mind raced, and she felt heat flow into her cheeks at her outrageously naughty thoughts. The echoing darkness in Mick's gaze made Logan wonder if Mick was as eager as she was to dispense with niceties, caution, and common sense.

One night. What would it hurt?

Mick observed Logan on the other side of the bench. Logan seemed fragile yet strong, with hidden facets that begged to be discovered. What was it about Logan that tugged on Mick's protective instincts?

She's probably only in her mid-twenties. Not that your thirties are all that more mature. Yet Logan's lack of guile made Mick nervous. She hadn't been with anyone so innocent in years. The knowledge made Mick feel older than her thirty-five years.

She swallowed a lump in her throat. She never felt sorry for herself, not really. Now and then she'd experience a twinge of longing for things that had never been, experiences she'd missed. She'd been so busy surviving in her teens and trying to make her mark on the DC business world in her twenties that she'd neglected esoteric things like feelings, longings, dreams. Those, she'd surmised at the time, were for suckers who thought they could actually make a difference on anyone's life but their own.

Now, however, her insides seemed to melt every time Logan looked at her, reminding her that there were other roads Mick hadn't taken. She wanted to follow Logan, just to see where their mutual paths led.

"Are you just going to sit out here freezing your ass off?" Logan asked.

"Looks like it. Why?"

Logan took a drag and blew out the smoke. "I was wondering if you were trying to hand me a passive-aggressive guilt trip, hoping I'd feel sorry for you and cut my time out here short."

At that, Mick laughed. "Do I seem like that type?"

"Not really."

"Then that means you must be one of those smokers with a conscience, someone who occasionally does think about the other people you're with and want them to be comfortable." Mick bent her head to catch whatever Logan mumbled. "What was that?"

Logan sat up straighter, her voice clearer. "I said thank you for accompanying me. I…uh…I get nervous in new situations."

Mick nodded. She didn't really understand, because she rarely felt uneasy, even in the dark at an unfamiliar place. She saw Logan shiver and moved next to her. "Go ahead and light another one. You can't possibly have enjoyed that first one, because you've inhaled so quickly. I don't want you getting out of bed in a couple of hours because you didn't get your fix."

"Really?"

Mick held her hands around Logan's once again to block the wind. "I never picked up the habit. It must be awful."

"It is." Logan smiled ruefully. "I haven't smoked lately."

"Why do it?"

"It started out as a social thing. I never thought I'd become addicted. Foolish, I know."

"Have you ever tried quitting?"

"A few times. It never lasted. This time feels different."

Mick cocked her head and looked at her. "Why is that?"

"I never wanted to until now. I'd put them down then pick them up at the first sign of trouble. I don't handle stress well."

Mick took a sharp breath. "And you figured Christmastime wasn't stressful enough, so you're trying to quit now?"

Logan laughed. "I brought a good book to read. Nobody else in my family smokes other than my dad, who loves his cigars. I don't own a car, so I'll be stranded at home with miles of snow between me and the closest pack of cigarettes."

"Hmm. Makes sense." Devious little minx, setting herself up to succeed or fail with little wiggle room. Something told Mick that failure for Logan wouldn't be reaching for a cigarette so much as it would be disappointing her family. If she'd learned anything about Logan over the few hours she'd known her, it was that Logan loved her family, despite the bitching and fretting over the upcoming days she'd spend in their company.

"Penny for your thoughts," Logan said softly.

Mick shook her head, feeling herself moving from shallow waters to the deeper end of the pool. When was the last time anyone else had asked her for her real thoughts, as opposed to just a business opinion? Usually, they waited for her to unload it on them without their asking. Probably without their caring. But there was something about Logan, who seemed genuine and sweet, not to mention she was sexy as all hell, that made Mick want to open up. But that wasn't who she was, and she shook away the strange desire and deflected, as she always did when things got too personal.

"What's the title of your book, Logan?"

"It's called *The Wonderful Word Wizard.*" Logan smiled. "It's a new study on L. Frank Baum, the man who wrote…"

"*The Wizard of Oz.* I know who he was. Catchy title. I'll look for it."

Logan's smile widened. "You'll have to wait. It hasn't gone to print yet. I'm reading the ARC for it."

"Arc?"

"Advanced review copy. I worked in a bookstore. One of the perks was being asked to read books before they were on the market. A friend wrote this one, and she knows Baum's most famous book has been my favorite for decades."

Charming. Logan was a modern-day Dorothy, following her heart along an invisible yellow brick road, discovering what made the wizard tick, and Mick wanted to join her, to discover more about what lay ahead. For the first time since leaving DC, she wanted to cancel her plans to spend Christmas with Donavan. She was more interested in playing Scarecrow to Logan's Dorothy.

CHAPTER THREE

L ogan's thoughts skipped ahead into a beautiful daydream. Mick would suggest they have breakfast in bed. They'd kiss the following morning and go their separate ways. Why the hell not? Hadn't she put in her dues with being the good girl, the respectful daughter, the attentive sister, the faithful employee? Why shouldn't she have one wild fling before she was too old to enjoy being naughty? Not like Mick was a sports car she'd purchased during a bout of insanity, but a test drive shouldn't hurt.

What if Mick didn't feel the same, though? Logan choked back her doubts. She'd thrown up on her. So what? It was minor compared to other crap she'd heard that couples did to one another. Not that they were a couple, obviously. So maybe that didn't count.

They rode the elevator in silence, avoiding one another's gaze. Logan held the pajamas, which gave her something to do. Logan was so tired she could barely stand, while Mick seemed as lithe and fluid as a damned cat.

With the ding of the elevator door, she followed Mick a short distance down the hallway. Logan stood back as Mick stuck the key card in the appropriate slot then opened the door for her to pass first. A deep breath told her that Mick wore no cologne.

Logan scoffed at her thoughts. *Just go to bed, dummy. You're brain dead.* She opened her mouth to tell Mick that she was weary, when she felt both of her hands pinned against the door. Mick's long, lean frame against hers, left no doubt that her mind, and other body parts, were actively working.

"What about the smoke?" Logan's whispered words were meant as a smart retort, but they sounded like a plea to her own ears.

Mick frowned. "Pardon me?"

"Wet ashtray—my breath, inside of my mouth—aren't you leery of...?"

"You brushed your teeth twice, combed your hair, and washed your face. That's about as clean as you can get without stepping into the shower, right?"

Mick shattered her with a delicious kiss, one that tasted her, devoured her, and gave Logan an appetizer of the feast to come. She released her hands and Logan dropped the pajamas and wound her arms about Mick's neck, drawing even closer into the vortex of need she'd created.

"Well, it was just *one* cigarette," Mick whispered against her lips.

"But I have a whole pack, minus one."

"No smoking in bed, young lady. You won't have time, anyway."

Logan giggled, her mind racing with naughty thoughts of how Mick might keep her occupied.

Mick's tense muscles flexed, released, reached, and relaxed as she held Logan. Lord, she felt good, her tiny, compact body the precise panacea Mick needed, Logan's vivacious, while troubled, spirit a beacon for Mick's wandering soul.

She grinned in satisfaction when she felt Logan melt into her embrace. Mick's secretary, Georgette, had once told her that she was so laid-back she was almost comatose, and here she was with the most high-strung, uptight, individual she'd ever met. Logan had thrown up on her, tried her patience, and made her simultaneously want to protect her and run away as fast as she could. Mick had never liked surprises, primarily because most of them hadn't been pleasant, yet Logan made her eagerly anticipate what she'd say or do next. Everything about Logan, from her name to her eyes—one blue, one green—were unusual and appealing.

Mick frowned. Where had she heard the name Logan before? She was certain she'd never had anyone working for her at Finnegan Enterprises who answered to that.

Her mind splintered, and she lost her train of thought as Logan deepened the kiss she'd begun, her small hands gliding restlessly over Mick's breasts and shoulders, her tongue touching hers with precisely the perfect pressure, a warm, welcoming insistence that made Mick's heart race and her body heat up.

Involuntarily, Mick's hands reached to cup Logan's hips, and the sensation of feeling her sweet, warm center pressing against her groin was almost more than Mick could bear. She had to have her, and to hell with good intentions of giving her the shower first, of pouring champagne, offering her a bite of fruit, seducing her. Mick was the one being seduced, and she rather liked it. "Sweetheart, if you keep kissing me like that, I'll explode before we make it to the bed."

Logan's response was to grip Mick's shoulders.

Did she just purr? Mick chuckled and barely had time to blink before Logan once again pressed her lips against hers. No. *That was definitely a feral growl.*

Logan lifted her head and stared up at Mick. "So get on the bed."

Oh, thank you, God! Mick sent up a silent prayer that Logan wasn't bashful when it came to exploring another woman's body. She followed Logan to the bed. Logan held Mick's hips with just the right amount of pressure. She leaned into her body, and before Mick knew what had happened, Logan's tongue and lips tantalized and tasted the hot crevice between her thighs.

Mick threaded her fingers through Logan's hair. For someone who'd spent hours on a plane and as many hours sobering up after her mile-high drunk, Logan felt clean and fresh. Probably just her personality. She'd certainly never met anyone so frank and forthright.

Logan moaned as she positioned herself between Mick's legs and tasted, sucking and licking as if Mick's flesh was a delicacy and she couldn't wait.

With each intensive lick, it was all Mick could do to withhold the waves of need pumping blood through her body. She let go of Logan's hair and pressed her palms against the wall to brace herself, and she struggled to keep from bucking as the crescendo urged her into a frenzied groan of release. She held off as long as possible, but it was no use.

She felt more than heard Logan's hum of delight when she came, the soft sound buzzing against her thigh. Her hands clenched the air, scratching for something solid to hang on to, to keep her knees from buckling. "God, Logan!"

Logan stared up at her, grinning impishly. "Satisfied?"

"More than that. Come here." Mick extended her hand, which Logan took. "I think it's time I reciprocated."

Her heart raced with anticipation, but something didn't feel right. Logan was adorable, sexy, fun, and exciting, but she also seemed vulnerable and sweet.

"Oh, shit!" Mick suddenly remembered where she'd heard Logan's name. She stumbled, falling on top of Logan. Logan's immediate response was to groan in protest. Mick struggled to right herself, feeling as if she'd been about to screw her little sister. She'd thought of Donavan Brady as a brother, ever since they'd met their first year of college. "Oh, God!" Mick shrank from her.

Logan blinked owlishly, obviously hurt and worried. "What did I do? Are you okay? I mean, I didn't hurt you or anything, did I?"

"What? No! I…I just got dizzy."

Logan sprang from the bed and was on her knees beside Mick before she could formulate another sentence. Logan touched Mick's forehead. "Do you have a fever? Have you been sick? It's the food. You had one too many shrimp."

"No, no."

"Maybe you're allergic to shellfish."

"Logan, stop. I'm okay. You're right, I need to lie down a few minutes." *Holy Mary.* Mick called on every deity she could think of and all but crossed herself. Don would murder her. He'd confided that he thought his little sister was a closet case and was worried that Logan wouldn't have the nerve to live her life on her terms. She closed her eyes and groaned. *Damn.* Logan Brady made love like a sex kitten, but she was a baby dyke compared to her, and Mick was no babysitter. She avoided inexperienced sex partners and business partners like they were the plague. She'd built her business reputation on backing only the best game masters and engineers, and those individuals had made her rich beyond her wildest dreams. She'd also developed a standing in the DC gay community as a no-nonsense player who couldn't be tied down.

She went to the bathroom and busied herself changing into the pajama bottoms and bagging her clothes. *Shitshitshit.* She looked about for something to tie around her breasts since she'd promised the pajama top to Logan. Settling on a towel, she decided she could always remove it once the lights were out.

When she'd finished, she rang for room service to pick up her dirty clothes. Then she paced, wondering what to do about the woman whose feelings she'd obviously hurt, and probably the one person on earth she shouldn't have gone anywhere near.

What the hell just happened? Logan stared at the closed door. Maybe she was more fatigued than she thought. Had she done something wrong? Logan couldn't cover her disappointment at the feeling of abject rejection she'd felt when Mick pulled away and promptly locked herself in the bathroom.

Logan entered the bathroom right as Mick left it, clearly making an effort to keep from touching her in any way. Her reflection in the bathroom mirror offered no clues. Still the same witch-weird eyes, disheveled auburn hair that needed a trim, and pale skin dotted with freckles. *Fresh.* That's what her father had always said about her looks. Not beautiful in the classic sense, but girl-next-door peaches and cream, as he'd been fond of saying. Well, now, the fruit looked like it had been on the vine too long.

Great. Logan splashed cold water on her face and sat on the side of the tub while drying her face. Would this nightmare ever end?

"You okay in there?" Mick's voice filtered through the bathroom door and walls.

"Just peachy." Logan swallowed hard after answering. *I'm broke, jobless, with bad breath, dry skin, and no clean clothes. Of course, that's not attractive.* But why had Mick kissed her? Why had she let her go down on her? And why did it hurt so much to be unwanted by a stranger? Rack up another mistake to the thousands she'd made in her life.

"Logan?" Mick's voice held concern.

This only served to make Logan defensive. "Forget it, okay?"

"I can't." Mick tapped on the door again and tried the knob.

Logan was incensed. Mick had pushed her away. What right did she have to worry now? "A little privacy, please?"

Mick came in anyway. She was bare-chested, dressed only in the pajama bottoms, and she shook her head as she entered. "You're not using the toilet, and you're on the tub, not in it. I'm sorry, but I need to talk to you."

"Hey!" Logan brushed aside the apology by lifting her arms as if protesting. "I wouldn't want me either, really."

"No." Mick rushed to lift her from the tub and into her arms. "That's not what this is about."

Logan pushed against her. *Not pity—Lord, please, not that!* "Let me go."

"You don't understand." Mick clutched her tightly and held her head with one hand. "I know you."

Startled, Logan pushed again, this time freeing herself. "Well, not in the Biblical sense. You pretty much nixed that before it happened."

"No, I mean that I really know who you are. I was one of Donavan's college buddies—I was on that plane today because Don invited me to spend the holidays with your family."

Logan blinked. "Donavan? My family?" She groaned, sounding more like a pirate than a frustrated female. "I just went down on the friend my brother wanted me to impress this week?"

Mick gave a small chuckle. "Well, if it makes you feel any better, I was duly impressed."

Logan socked her on the arm. "Now we have to spend time together, and my brother will know about this." Just the thought of him teasing her, tormenting her, was enough to take the wind out of her already shaky sails. Then she got pissed. "To top it all off, I'm without luggage, and now I have no clean panties. I have to wear a clean pair to bed—there's no way I can wear the same ones, since you got me all hot and bothered." Her hands trembled. "I need a cigarette."

"Well, you can't go alone, and I've already put on the pajamas and have set out my clothes for the cleaners."

"Sucks to be you. Wear a coat if you're determined to go with me."

Sophisticated women threw themselves at Mick blatantly and regularly. Most were definitely less interesting, not as charming, intriguing, or sexy as Logan. There was something about Don's little sister that made Mick want to alternately screw her brains out and keep an arm about her with a Velcro leash attached, just so she could keep pace with Logan and make sure she stayed out of trouble. It was odd to feel so protective of someone she'd met less than twelve hours ago.

Mick wished she'd paid more attention to family tales Donavan had shared during college. Color-blind mother, half-deaf father, uptight older sister, and adorably naive and incorrigible younger sibling? Surely, she'd heard the stories. How could she have missed the clues at the airport when Logan basically described the same setup? Maybe families were just that interchangeable.

"You're broke, and I'm not, so an early breakfast is on me." Mick eyed Logan's slender frame then ushered them out of the room and into the hall leading toward the elevators.

"I warn you that I can eat like a horse." Logan looked at Mick closely. "You sure you want to go out dressed only in hotel jammies?"

"Doesn't bother me. Neither do women with appetites. Picky eaters make my ass itch." She punched the button for the lobby. She wished Logan wouldn't stand so far away, almost as if she hated her. "Look, nothing really happened."

Logan glared at her. "Thanks for the compliment."

"You know what I mean. I didn't touch you."

Logan snorted. "You aren't the one who needs to brush their teeth again and gargle with Gatorade."

"Say, what?" Mick couldn't believe her ears. "Nobody forced you to go down on me."

"You probably knew who I was the entire time and just wanted to see how far you could push Don's sister to be nice to you."

"It wouldn't have taken all that much to get you to sleep with me if that's all I'd wanted," Mick reminded her. "You fell into my arms at the airport, and you haven't exactly been standoffish since then."

Logan sputtered then collected herself. "I did not fall into your arms. I threw up! And the reason I've been so damned polite is because I have no money and no place else to stay. Sex with you was just a bonus to make me feel a little better." She clapped her hand over her mouth and flushed, her eyes widening at the admission.

Mick knew she was tired, frustrated, and angry, and she wished there was something she could do. She reached to pull Logan into her arms, but Logan shrank from her and pounded the sides of her own thighs with her hands.

"And what about my damned underwear?" Logan gave a small, anxious sob.

Mick caught Logan's arms and fell against the hallway wall, taking Logan with her. "I'll buy you some new panties."

Then the elevator dinged, the doors opened, and Mick heard an exaggerated gasp from whoever was standing inside.

Mick cocked one eye open and stared at Logan's big brother, who did not look amused.

CHAPTER FOUR

Sputtering, Donavan exited the elevator and dropped the piece of luggage he'd held. He nudged the slender blond man standing next to him. "My sister, and our bank roller!"

Upon hearing that, Logan unclenched her fists and pulled her hands to her chest. She turned to face them. "Don?" She looked at the other man and blinked. "Who are you?"

He, too, set aside his luggage then extended his hand. "I'm Paul. You must be Logan." He looked at Mick expectantly.

Don assessed the situation rather quickly. "Did she hurt you?" he asked Logan.

"No, I didn't hurt her. I'm a lesbian, not a lumberjack."

"Then why is she crying?"

Mick grasped Logan's hands and pulled her away from the elevator. Then all of them stood back, sizing one another up. Mick shook hands with Paul and introduced herself.

"What are you doing here?" Logan asked.

"Pop used to work for the airline, remember? He heard about planes being stranded and sent us on a detour shortly after your plane took off. Mom called when she found out you were at this hotel, but we couldn't find your name on their register. Instead, we found hers, and I figured I could come get Mick and maybe find you in the process." He pointed to Mick then back at Logan. "I tried calling several times on the way to Kansas, but you never answer your damned phone."

She flushed. "I need to charge it and probably need to replace the battery."

Donavan wasn't pacified. "Ever hear of just picking up a phone that works? You knew I was driving from New York yesterday. We could have met midway." He waved his hands expressively. "Well, I guess we did." Then he turned his attention to Mick. "How is it that you two...? Hello, by the way. And what's this about my sister's panties?"

"Wait," said Mick. "It's too treacherous for airplanes, but you two came in this weather? How?"

"Mom and Dad made us take defensive driving in all kinds of weather," said Donavan. "I have a car with awesome tires, and four-wheel drive. I'm the best driver you'll ever know. Now back to my sister, if you don't mind."

Mick noticed the horror in Logan's eyes. She knew she'd ask herself later what prompted her to do it, but she hugged Logan protectively, practically feeling the energy she'd felt earlier rapidly dissipating and leaving Logan jelly-legged. "Lover's quarrel between Logan and Marcus, but no blood was shed. Then I was surprised to find Logan on the plane."

"Off the plane." Logan shook her head. "I puked on her shoes."

"Wait," said Don. "Why didn't you take your company jet?"

Mick shrugged. "It's getting cosmetic work done. If I'd waited, it would have taken till Christmas Eve. I wanted the chance to talk to you."

"Private jet?" Logan asked, obviously bemused.

Paul looked bewildered. "Who is Marcus?"

"My sister's fake fiancé I told you about." Donavan pursed his lips. "You didn't really think you'd pull that one off, did you?"

Logan slumped, and Mick caught her, bolstering her, all but keeping Logan standing in front of her. Mick wrapped her arms around Logan's waist, talking over her shoulder to Don and Paul as Donavan's questions and comments bombarded them.

"I didn't know you two had met! So why do you two look as if you've just gotten out of bed, Logan? Why did you throw up on her?"

Mick continued, since Logan couldn't seem to form words. "We both live in DC and were bound to connect at some point. It took a few hours before I figured out who she was. When you'd phoned and asked if I'd be interested in financing the new computer game, her first name didn't register with me. I'd heard it before, and we'd met before today. Logan just doesn't remember."

"And here we are," Donavan finished, but his expression held disbelief. "Nah. You're pulling my leg. You never met before you got on the plane. But my sister is a closet case, so the two of you aren't a couple, no matter how it looks at the moment."

Logan gasped and sank against Mick a little more. "Say what?"

"How do you explain the clinch?" Paul asked, smiling.

Donavan nodded sagely. "I'm still working on that one. They were practically body to body when the elevator door opened. Why would a closet case and an in-your-face lesbian be discussing Logan's panties?"

"I am not a closet case, so please stop saying that." Logan's voice held a ring of anger.

"Not anymore, she's not." Mick laced her fingers with Logan's and tugged, feeling weirdly protective. "Sorry, sweetheart, they'd find out later anyway." She grinned at Logan teasingly, hoping to get her to relax and find the humor in the situation.

"You two should get your stories straight before we go home. Mom and Dad aren't dummies, and Doreen is smarter than all of us. They'll figure things out, so you might as well be honest." Donavan blinked and really looked them over, seeming to register the odd pajama combinations, then shook his head. "Wait. No, you're not joking, are you? You two got it on? I don't believe it."

"And why not?" demanded Logan.

Donavan looked incredulous. "Because Michaela is never with the same woman for more than a week. Do you know what they call her in DC's LGBTQ circles? The rich bitch." He touched Logan's arm. "And you, dear sister, wouldn't stand a chance with her. So whatever you think you have going with Mick, you don't. This was a one-time thing."

"Rich bitch?" Donavan's words angered Mick. More than that, it pushed a button. She hated when people thought they knew anything about her. And Donavan should have known better. "Why does having money and several girlfriends make me a bitch?"

"Your money isn't the emphasis," Donavan said. "They think you're a bitch because you never ask your conquests out again."

Mick kept her eyes on Logan but aimed her words at Don. "Does this look like a temporary fling to you?" Mick drew Logan closer. Then she planted the biggest, most passionate kiss she could muster on her. The kiss affected Mick more than she thought it would. She pulled back reluctantly. Her lips tingled and Logan's lips parted, seemingly involuntarily.

"Well, I never." Donavan sounded confused.

Mick caressed Logan's cheek tenderly. "Logan, how about we let them carry their luggage into the room and chill then join us in the restaurant?"

Logan nodded a slow response, still looking flustered and more than a little confused. "Uh-huh."

"The restaurant is closed," Paul said.

"Yeah," Donavan said but seemed to issue the word as a challenge. "And there are no rooms. We have to crash with you tonight, unless you want to drive back to Kansas in the dark." He smirked then added, "Because this man is tired and needs a bed."

Mick shook her head, pulled out a plastic card, and handed it to Donavan. "Here's the room key." She pointed toward their door. "And there's the room. You two settle in and we'll wait here. Then we'll find an all-night diner. I'm sure the cabbies in this town know of somewhere we could go at this hour."

Donavan surveyed Mick's attire. "You want to go out dressed like that?"

"Not really." Mick pulled her coat tighter around her. "But I have nothing else to wear until my clothes get cleaned."

Paul seemed oblivious to everyone else's moods and chimed in cheerfully. "I have clothes you can wear."

"Good. Nice meeting you, Paul. I'll take you up on that offer. Don?"

"Let's all go back into your room and get ready." Donavan's voice still held skepticism. "I haven't eaten this late at night since college, but I'm famished."

"Okay." Mick reluctantly agreed, but Donavan's remarks stung. It was true that she rarely went out on a second date with the same woman. Yes, she was rich, and if she wanted to remain so, she didn't have time to indulge in relationships that she knew would go nowhere. As for being a bitch, she supposed that was how others might see her. But until she met Logan, she hadn't met anyone worth both her time and interest. It might have only been a few hours, but Mick knew people, and she had no doubts she wanted to get to know Logan better.

Mick held Donavan aside. "Did you invite me as your friend or as an investor? Because you've crossed the line. I'm tempted to get on the next plane back to DC after your remarks."

He looked uncomfortable as hell. "I am sorry. I was out of line. My worry for my little sister pushed what little good judgment I had aside." He studied her face. "Truth is, I've missed you. I called your office a couple of times, but Georgette told me you weren't even in the city."

"So you didn't leave a message? I'd have called you back."

He flushed. "I don't run in the same circles as you do. I was afraid you wouldn't want to see me after so many years."

Before she could stop herself, Mick slugged him on the arm. "You asshole. You're still my little bro from college where we had spaghetti dinners on top of my bed because of your cat's fleas."

He grinned. "She's since crossed the Rainbow Bridge to be with other felines who couldn't get rid of their fleas."

"I'm sorry to hear that." And she was. They'd made quite a deal out of Don's cat who didn't like lesbians.

"In answer to your question, Michaela, I invited you first because you're my friend and I wanted to see you again. The business stuff is secondary."

Relief washed over her. "Good. In that case, I'm glad to be here and to have the chance to see your game."

His expression darkened. "And my sister?"

"That's none of your business. But I do like her. I hope you'll let this play out."

Don nodded. "Just please don't hurt her."

"I don't plan on it." She sucked in a deep breath. "And now that I'm aware of how others see me, I'll be more careful. No more fuck and flee."

Mick pointed toward the patio where Logan had smoked before. "I know the drill. Nicotine and a nervous breakdown before food." She and Logan had told the boys they'd meet them in the hotel lobby, giving Don and Paul the chance to unwind and refresh and giving Logan time for a smoke. Mick opened the door for her, and the blast of cold air hit them full force.

"Freakin' Chicago." Logan shuddered and reached for her smokes. She lit one, with Mick's hands cupping hers to shelter her from the wind. Then she inhaled deeply, almost choking. "Jeez," she said quietly. Then she took a deep breath and wailed out of frustration. What should have been a nice Christmas among friends and family suddenly loomed darkly over them. Logan knew that the shadow was largely in her mind, conjured out of her insecurities. Maybe what she felt was no more than nervousness because of her plan to come out to her parents. Don knew. Doreen was a question mark. But revealing the complexities of her relationships with her parents to Mick had opened all manner of what-ifs.

Mick took Logan by the shoulders and parked her on a cold bench, huddled next to her, and wrapped her arm about her shoulders. "It'll be okay."

Logan felt giddy, like she was losing her mind and didn't give a damn. "What a nightmare. I should have stayed in DC."

"And spent Christmas alone?"

"At least I'd still have my panties."

"You're such a fucking worrywart." Mick chuckled. "And you'd have missed the opportunity to hang out with me."

Logan stuck out her tongue. "Now is not the time to be a comedian."

"No, I'm quite a catch. Weren't you paying attention when your brother called me a rich bitch?"

Logan tried for a poker face but couldn't help her irritation. "I'm impressed. Really."

Mick sighed. "Sarcasm doesn't become you."

"Yes, it does. Just ask my sister. She thinks my sense of style is lacking, but she swears that the sarcasm makes up for it and makes me attractive." She inhaled and shivered against the wind.

"Look," Mick said. "I'm no good at anything other than making money. Ask me how many close friends I have or when I last took a vacation. I'd hoped by accepting Don's invitation, that just being around a family, might give me a semblance of normalcy that I've somehow neglected to find until now."

At that, Logan burst into laughter. "You are in for one rude awakening. This *vacation*, as you call it, will have you running back to DC within the first few hours after we get to Kansas."

Mick shrugged. "I've already reunited with one in-law, met an outlaw like me, Paul, someone not within the warmth of the family circle yet, and I've managed to keep from strangling you, so I think I've done pretty well so far."

Logan flexed her legs and rolled her neck, trying to pop it. "Just wait." Then she snorted indelicately. "Rich, my ass."

"Why is that so hard to believe? You heard your brother refer to me as his banker, right?"

"Yeah, but Donavan has been known to stretch the truth at times."

Mick flicked Logan's shoulder with her middle finger, popping her soundly, despite her coat. "Your sister is right. Keep the sarcasm, it's growing on me." She took the half-smoked cigarette from Logan and tossed it to the ground then ground it with one foot. "Let's go before they come looking for us."

"Hey, I wasn't finished with that. Bit high-handed of you, isn't it?"

❖

Well, you've always wanted a woman who wasn't after your money. Mick hid a smile as she, Logan, Donavan, and Paul sat across from one another at the all-night restaurant. Donavan knew she was well-off, but even he didn't realize just how much Mick was worth. While everyone else in college was drinking beer and chasing their next sexual conquest, Mick had been studying and working hard, determined to make something of herself.

Sure, there wasn't a family at home, a dad to pat her on the back and say *well done*, and there was no mother waiting with open arms with a hug. But Mick had motivated herself.

She grimaced. What bugged her was that she'd lost sight of more important things, like someone to share her values, not just her bed. Trouble was, once she'd acquired her fortune, she was never sure if companions were with her for her money, introductions to the influential business people she knew, or for the straightforward person she'd always been.

Listening to the animated banter between Donavan and Logan, she couldn't help but envy them. Even though they were squabbling and ribbing one another, they had that sibling rivalry, the camaraderie, and the love that had always seemed to elude her.

"So tell me again how you two met?" Donavan prompted her for the fourth time since they'd begun their meal.

Mick could tell that Logan was more than a little uncomfortable by the question. She'd already told him, but Donavan wasn't satisfied.

"Starbucks," said Mick, beginning a new string of little white lies to lighten the mood she felt coming over Logan.

Donavan waved his hands. "Don't tell me Starbucks. Which one? Where?"

"The National Mall, the shop around Constitution Avenue and Seventh," Mick cut in.

"Oh, yeah? What's her favorite drink?" Donavan had a smug look on his face.

Mick clutched for a moment then remembered something Logan had said just before they'd entered the hotel restaurant hours earlier. "She likes mocha Frappuccinos." She looked at Logan and smiled. The surprise in her eyes tickled Mick, and the grateful answering smile made her melt. She had no clue what a Frappuccino tasted like. She'd have to rectify that.

Donavan seemed nonplussed. "You met at the Mall? What's her favorite museum?"

"Donavan!" Paul chastised him.

Mick searched the few previous conversations she'd had with Logan. "National History Museum."

"Hmm. That's everybody's favorite," Donavan said.

Paul shook his head and stabbed the air with his fork mid-bite. "Not mine. I like the National Gallery of Art." He swallowed, took a drink, and stared at Donavan. "Why the inquisition?"

Mick reached under the table and squeezed Logan's hand to reassure her. The pressure cooker grip Logan returned told Mick that Logan was more than a little nervous. Was it because Logan had already lied about having a fiancé, and now she was building upon a new set of misinformation? Too many lies did tend to trip one up.

"Keep trying, Don," said Logan. "She'll always be a step ahead of you."

Mick drew Logan's hand onto her lap and bumped her thigh against hers intimately. "Yeah, Don, I'd have thought you'd be glad that your old college buddy and your sister had met."

"It's the mating, not the meeting, that has me worried." Donavan looked at them both shrewdly. "Logan is an adult, but she's still my baby sister. Logan, I love you. I love Mick. Let me be your big brother. You have slept together, I assume?"

"That's none of your business," Mick responded, winking at Logan, who immediately choked on whatever bite she'd taken. Mick thumped her gently on the back then continued jabbing at Donavan. "Would you have preferred the fake fiancé to me?"

Then Logan choked for real, and it took the remainders of two glasses of water and Paul fanning her face to calm her.

"You would have never pulled off the fiancé. Why not just come out?" Donavan asked.

Logan crossed her arms and glared at him. "Right, it's worked so good for you."

It appeared the two siblings were headed toward a heated argument. It sounded like this topic had been rehashed over and over.

Paul intervened, keeping Donavan occupied for the next few seconds, and Mick restrained herself from rolling her eyes when Logan's swung to meet hers.

Donavan was posturing. He wanted Logan to know that he had her best interests at heart. Mick stood and fished out her wallet. "I've got this, kids."

"But I'm not finished!" Donavan indicated the food still on his plate.

Mick didn't think Don had been finished grilling them, either. "Yeah, but we are, and your sister is crashing pretty hard, if you haven't noticed. I'm taking her back to the hotel, and we're going to bed. Stay and finish your meals." Mick slipped money onto the table and waved to Paul. "You two don't stay out too late. It'd be a shame if you overslept tomorrow morning."

"Yes, big sis." Donavan gave Mick a saccharine smile.

Mick helped Logan out of her seat, and conscious of the two pair of eyes trained on them as they turned to leave, she tilted Logan's chin and dropped a light kiss on her lips. "Think we fooled them?" Mick asked softly, easing Logan's coat onto her shoulders.

"Paul, maybe. Don, not for a second." Logan smiled weakly and waved at their waitress as they exited the eatery. Once they were outside, she slid on the slick pavement and almost landed in a heap at Mick's feet.

Mick caught her as she slipped on the ice, arms flailing. Mick pinned her against the brick wall. "Steady?"

"I haven't been on an even keel since we met." Logan wet her lips and blinked against the stinging wind. "I feel as if I've entered a fun house, and I'm not sure if it's supposed to scare me or thrill me."

Mick leaned in for another kiss. "Maybe both." This time, she kissed Logan long and hard, bracing her from the wind with her shoulders, cupping her face with her hands. Logan's body shook against hers, and her face was already cold and damp with falling snow. "Logan." Her name tasted sweet on Mick's lips, and she couldn't repress the urge to take another kiss, to feel Logan's tongue touching hers, her cheek against her chin.

"Oh!" Logan withdrew. "You don't have to do this. Nobody's watching now."

Mick frowned. "Do you really think any of this is for your brother's benefit? Maybe I want to pick up where we left off in our room."

Logan took a deep breath and swelled indignantly. "This whole night since we left the elevator, I've wondered if you were putting on a show for him or if you were really that interested in me."

"If you weren't so tired, you'd see that Don and I are having fun verbally sparring with one another. He knows about Marcus and that you have no fake fiancé. So does Paul. We're just having fun at your expense."

The look of confusion on Logan's face changed to one of amazement. "Pulling the answers to my favorite drink and museum out of your ass was a pretty neat trick."

"You told me you liked Fraps," Mick reminded her. "Just before we went into the restaurant last night."

"Oh. Yeah." She nodded. "Still…the museum."

"As Donavan said, it's usually everybody's favorite." She sighed, unsure how to answer the other questions. Was she just putting on a show? Logan was cute and sexy, so it was easy to see how that attraction was real. But anything beyond that wasn't her style, it was true. "C'mon, let's go. You're shivering."

When Logan hesitated, Mick bent toward her. "Either head for the hotel or be prepared to be ravished on a public street in the middle of a snowstorm. Up to you."

Logan grinned, and it was all Mick could do to keep from following through with her promise.

❖

By the time they got back, Logan was too tired to be shy as they prepared for bed. She spent little time in the bathroom, donned the oversized sleep shirt, and crawled between the sheets of the bed she'd share with Mick, while Mick took care of her own business. Logan was acutely conscious of Mick's body when she crawled into bed beside her, and although Mick didn't touch her and said a polite good night, Logan was, nonetheless, totally aware of her lean, hard body mere inches from her.

Mick turned out the bedside light, and for a moment, the only things Logan heard were the slight sounds of sheets rustling.

"Thank you," she said quietly. "I've been nothing but a pill since we first met, and all you've been is kind."

Mick rolled over and drew Logan against her body so that they spooned. With one of Mick's arms beneath her head and the other resting on her abdomen, Logan felt safe and oddly secure. Was this what she'd been missing? She'd worked long hours, going home to an empty house that didn't boast so much as a cat to greet her. It'd been months since she'd dated, much less become involved with anyone.

"Maybe I needed someone like you to be kind to," Mick replied. "I've been so wrapped up in my work and little else that it's been a long time since I really gave a damn about who I was with, if that makes sense." She chuckled in the dark. "In other words, I'm not normally kind—usually I'm oblivious to what's going on around me."

Logan almost bent to kiss Mick's arm, she was so glad for her frank honesty. "Are you saying that I'm hard to ignore?"

"Extremely so." Mick squeezed her gently.

Logan sighed. "Tomorrow will be rough, I'll warn you now. The day after that, even worse."

"Oh, I doubt it."

"No, listen to me. Hang on to whatever considerate feelings you have right now, because it's gonna be a bumpy ride once we wake up and have to face the family. Don and Doreen are always at one another's throats. Mom and Dad will drive you crazy with their idiosyncrasies, and I'll most likely smoke like a fiend."

"Interesting."

"What?" Logan turned, even though she couldn't see Mick in the darkened room.

"You haven't had a cigarette for hours." Mick chuckled. "You also haven't brushed your teeth. Remember your tacky comment in the elevator about after sex you needed to gargle?"

Logan shushed her by clapping both hands over Mick's mouth. "Now that's just rude." She felt Mick smile beneath her palms.

Both of Mick's hands closed over hers then traveled upward to her elbows. Mick held her firmly in place. "I'm sorry. No offense intended. So brush your teeth if you wish, then come back to bed, please."

"Why?"

"I want to talk then go to sleep."

Logan sighed. "You are the talkin'-est chick I've ever met."

Mick cracked up. "And you definitely win the Midwestern accent of the year award with that one." She sat up in bed, hauling Logan with her.

Logan grudgingly followed Mick's lead and snuggled beneath her arm. "I can't possibly face my family with you close to me twenty-four-seven."

"Why not? What's wrong with me?" Mick drew her close before chucking her chin. "I'm not so bad."

"Oh, no!" she reassured Mick. "It's not you, it's me. It's them! It'll be a madhouse, and you'll be subjected to a million questions once they find out we've spent the night together and we're not at least engaged." Her eyes got wide. "You can't tell any of them that I went down on you. Do you understand?"

Mick seemed horrified that she'd think such a thing. "As if I would?"

She shook her head. "They'll know. My mother has this built-in mom radar, and right now bells are going off like *ding-ding-ding-ding-ding* in her head. She knows something's not right, and I'm betting she's trying to reach me as we speak."

Mick gestured toward the telephone. "Call her, in that case. Put her mind at rest, and ease your guilty conscience. Not that you have anything to feel bad about, and besides, we're both adults."

"God, no, not at this late hour. I'm sure Don has already called, anyway." Sighing, Logan snuggled deeper into the confines of Mick's arm and hugged her body as if she was an old friend or a favorite large teddy bear. "Thank you for being honest. I felt rotten, and I couldn't figure out what I'd done that turned you off."

"You didn't turn me off." Mick slid lower until they were face-to-face. "Know what's wrong with you?"

She shook her head and swallowed. Hard. "What's that?"

Mick kissed her softly, and the electrical shock that zipped through Logan tickled her lower extremities.

"Nothing, sweetheart. Absolutely nothing."

Either I'm tired, or we're both punch drunk stupid. "And I just called you honest. Don't charm me, not tonight. I can handle honesty a lot better than I can a good lie."

"I'm telling the truth." Mick kissed her again, this time much harder and longer. When she finally lifted her lips, she pushed Logan none too gently onto her back, muttering. "That feel like a lie to you?"

"Nooo." She frowned. "I dunno." Confusion mixed with fatigue was never a good combination. "Look, can we just forget about all of this? Within four or five days we'll part company and not have to worry about any of it." The attraction to Mick was meant to be a fling. Mick was gorgeous and mysterious, and now that they would spend the holiday together staying uninterested would be nearly impossible. Logan would give it her best try. "You can go back to your hordes of women, and I can go back to my cat-less apartment."

"I thought you said you were a terrible liar." Mick kissed her again. "It's late, so go to sleep."

Logan thought about that before she drifted into sleep later. The muscled body behind hers seemed to relax, and soon she heard deep breathing. She was glad that Mick had managed to fall asleep, because something told her that neither of them would have peace or rest once they awakened. They'd known one another only a few hours, and already they were embroiled in a lie or two.

She nearly bolted upright. *Aw, shit.* She'd confided in Donavan that she was engaged. He remembered and knew it was bullshit, but had he told their parents?

She stifled a groan and covered her face with the blanket just as she heard the door to their room release. Two shadowy figures stood against the hotel hall's lighting, and Paul and Donavan entered and closed the door behind them.

Her brother walked straight to her side of the bed she shared with Mick and knelt. "I know you're not asleep, because you're not snoring."

Logan resisted a smartass repartee and pulled the covers down from her face. She blinked against the light from the bathroom as Paul flipped on the switch. "So?"

"So, I told you to be nice to the girl. You didn't have to sleep with her!" He turned toward Paul. "Turn that fucking light off. Use the one in the bathroom."

Logan swore under her breath. "I was shit-faced during the first few hours after I met her. I had no idea who she was!"

"Bullshit. I left a message on your cell phone describing Mick."

"Well, I didn't get it, or if I did, I didn't listen to it, because my battery needs replacing."

"Whatever. I just wanted you to know that I'm on to you, that I know this so-called relationship is a farce, just like the one with Marcus." He paused. "You're a pain in my ass, but you're still my baby sister."

"And she's your friend, or have you forgotten?" Logan couldn't believe he was asking if she was pimping herself out for his business. In truth, she'd pretty much forgotten his project until this mess with Mick.

"That's the part that puzzles me." Donavan pulled her out of bed and into the bathroom. He shut the door, leaving Paul in the dark.

Logan chuckled. "Okay, now I see what you're implying. But if Mick is as wealthy as you say, she doesn't need your little game to make her more money, so she's not coming on to me in order to get her hands on your project. Maybe she genuinely cares for me. That ever cross your mind?"

"Seriously? No. I love you, but you're not Mick's type. So pretending you two are a couple or that you're suddenly smitten with one another doesn't feel true."

"And why not?"

"Because frankly, sister dear, you aren't nerdy enough. Never have been, never will be. You don't know a *bite* from a *byte* and have trouble just turning on a computer. Mick is the kind of woman who gets turned on just looking at specs for a camera or a video game."

"I may be smarter than you think," she shot back, stung. She already felt like she wasn't good enough for just about anything in life. Not being good enough for the woman she'd just had sex with sucked.

"She probably counts prime numbers in her sleep. You're well-read, but you're not on par with her."

"Pretending to have a fiancé was a mistake, pretending to be a couple was one too." She sighed deeply. "I get it. Point made."

Donavan had his I-told-you-so expression as he crossed his arms. "And you're ten years younger than me."

That was low, and now she was angry. It was a jibe he'd used often when they were growing up, just to get under her skin, as brothers were wont to do. "I am not a mistake. Bite me!" she whispered loudly.

"You're not my species, thank you." He opened the door and pushed her toward her bed.

Logan crawled into bed fuming, unable to fall asleep as she listened to Don and Paul make preparations for bed.

Screw him. She rolled onto her back and stared at the ceiling, wishing she knew Mick's prime numbers to count herself to sleep.

CHAPTER FIVE

Mick glanced sideways at Logan. They'd been traveling westward for hours, and Logan had slept most of the journey, often dipping over to rest her head on Mick's shoulder in the back seat of Donavan's beat-up Dodge. Mick inhaled the subtle scent of her hair and thought back to the conversation she'd overheard when Logan and her brother had thought Mick was asleep.

Logan didn't seem the type who slept with someone just to elicit information from them or to prime them for a financial fleecing. Mick had been around long enough to know when somebody was greasing her, and Logan didn't have the mindset, even if she did have the sexual savoir faire to accomplish the task. Not to mention she hadn't asked a single question about what Mick did for a living.

One thing Donavan had been correct about was that Logan snored when she was truly asleep. She didn't sound like a lumberjack, but she had a definite nasal thing going on. Mick snorted as Logan took a long, shuddering, dreamlike breath.

"She had asthma as a kid." Donavan's voice broke into her thoughts.

Mick met his eyes in the rearview mirror. "Was it bad?"

Donavan shook his head. "Not really. Sometimes. There's a park about three blocks from our house in Overland Park, and the folks always knew when she'd sneak out of the house, because

Logan would wind up with a case of the sniffles. She loved the pond, but she was allergic to the honeysuckle in the spring, the freshly mowed grass in the summer, and then she'd catch a cold during winter if she stayed too long."

"I'll bet she was a cute little girl," Mick mused as she looked down at her, angelic looking even when heavy breathing.

"She was adorable. Smaller than most kids her age, but sharp as a tack. Big blue and green eyes. Made you want to keep her under your arm in case she got lost or hurt."

"And did she?" Mick asked.

"All the freakin' time." Donavan smiled and glanced back at Logan. "She'd take off because she got bored, and the folks would send me looking for her. Pain in the ass, that's what she was. They should've named her Pita. Pop called her Squirt, because she was so small. Still is."

Paul looked up from the road map he'd been reading and gave Donavan a once-over. "And what did he call you and Doreen?"

"Doreen was Kitten. I was Buddy or Buddy Boy. Pop always thought I'd be the one he'd teach to play catch or the son who'd become a KU star athlete. Little did he know, I'd only hang out at football games with him so that I could admire the tight ends or the quarterbacks." Donavan chuckled.

"Was it difficult on you," Mick asked. "Growing up gay?"

"In Kansas? We had our underground at the time." Donavan shrugged. "Oh, well, that's what the East Coast is for, misplaced or misguided Midwesterners."

Mick considered her words, not wanting to seem too intrusive. "So why did Logan wind up in DC?"

"She wanted to go to Georgetown University, and once she graduated, a friend of hers opened a bookstore and hired Logan to manage it for him. He's her roommate." He narrowed his eyes and said shrewdly, "Surely, you've met him, if you and my sister are so tight. I think his name is Marcus."

She simply rolled her eyes at him, knowing full well he hadn't bought into the charade, and Logan had confirmed it to him in their non-private bathroom talk the night before. Mick wondered why Logan had felt the need to have a fake fiancé, especially when her brother was out. Had he bugged his little sister, as had the others, every Christmas about being single? What had made it so hard for Logan to be herself when it sounded like her family really loved her?

Before Donavan could pester Mick with more innuendo or questions, Paul, thankfully, told him to concentrate on the road. "Isn't our turn coming up?" he asked, looking at the map.

"So it is." Donavan flipped the turn signal. "Say good-bye to Interstate Thirty-five, boys and girls, and somebody tell my snoring sister to wake up. I can smell my mom's pecan pancakes from here."

Mick looked at her fitness watch. "At ten at night?"

Donavan nodded. "The trip without bad roads should have taken us only eight hours, not eleven, and if I know my mother, she's doing what she's done for years when she's stressed. She's baking pies and making pancakes. Pop is ready to barf from the smell of rising dough, and Doreen is making her fifth or sixth call to check on us since we left Chicago."

"Why?" Paul asked. "I didn't think the two of you even liked each other."

Donavan pointed to a supermarket and cackled. "When's the last time you saw one of those back East?" He turned the steering wheel until the car made a forty-five-degree turn and then responded to Paul's question. "For your information, Doreen and I are extremely close, she just doesn't know it. And I'd prefer that you didn't tell her. I rather like Doreen thinking that I'm the snobbish, self-righteous, not to mention embarrassingly gay brother who doesn't give a shit."

Mick checked out the landscape as they drove past various business and residential areas. She was pleased to know that Overland Park had familiar coffee shops and pharmacies whose names she recognized, but the generally one-story strip malls were what drew her attention. There was something comforting about seeing so many non-chain restaurants and boutique clothiers.

"We'll swing through old downtown," Donavan said conversationally. "I know that the folks are anxious to see us, but it's on the way." He turned onto Santa Fe and pointed out various sites. "There's our farmers market and the old clock tower. Saturdays during spring, summer, and fall, you'll see people sitting outside at the bistro tables, listening to live bands or walking their dogs. Across the street is where my sisters and I studied tae kwon do."

"You took martial arts?" Paul said. "I'm impressed."

"Don't be. None of us ever got past the yellow belt." Donavan turned again and maneuvered the Dodge onto Metcalf. "We're almost there." He took a deep breath. "I don't know why, but it's good to be home."

Home to Mick was anyplace she happened to have a roof over her head. She never once recalled the feeling Don expressed in that sigh.

He sounded wistful, and Mick wondered what he was thinking. Was he anticipating homemade baked pies and pecan pancakes, or was he contemplating the events Logan seemed to dread? Either way, Mick was certain that before she made it back to DC, she'd receive an education in family dynamics that she'd not forget.

Logan awakened with Mick rubbing her shoulders and urging her to sit up. She wiped drool from her cheek and shoulder. *Great. How sexy.* All she could think of as she groggily focused on familiar neighborhood surroundings was that she needed to find a bathroom and that she wished they'd awakened her in time to put on some makeup or at least brush her hair. One thing was assured. Regardless of her attraction to Mick, there was no way she could find her appealing. Donavan was right, she was way out of Logan's league.

She looked in front of Donavan's vehicle and saw Doreen's smart new sedan and winced. Great, the whole fam-damily at once.

The front door to her parents' two-story bungalow opened, and her mother burst onto the covered front porch, waving frantically, grinning and looking a mixture of relieved, stressed, aggravated, and ecstatic.

If she cries, I'm done for. Logan smiled weakly and waved back. "Hi, Mom!"

"Have courage." Mick's velvety voice whispered as she passed to retrieve their basket of fruit and crackers from the trunk. Since their luggage hadn't been found, the hotel had piled two bottles of wine—one red, one white—and innumerable individually wrapped crackers and cheeses into the basket, alongside various fruits.

Logan heard Donavan snort, as he, too, went toward the back of his car. "Oh, shut up!" she muttered.

She plastered a smile on her face and headed toward the snow-covered plastic bunny rabbits, whirly-gig windmills, and pink flamingos in the flowerbeds near the house, trying not to giggle at the sight of one bird with an icicle dripping from its beak, looking forevermore like an enormous booger. Yet another flamingo had fallen facedown in the plastic tulips with his butt in the air.

Before she made it up the front steps, both of her parents were holding out their arms to welcome her. She let them envelop her and inhaled deeply, recognizing the unmistakable scent of his cigar, mixed with Old Spice. Her mother would have chastised him had she known he'd been in the basement smoking.

"It's about time," her father said gruffly. "Your mother has gone through two bags of flour and a canister of sugar since noon. You'd think you were bringing home an army." He eyed Mick curiously.

"Where's Doreen?" Logan asked, hugging her mother.

"Upstairs puking—she has some sort of bug," her mom said, rolling her eyes a little. "It's probably the flu that's going around. She needs to go to the doctor. She's only had the damn thing for two solid weeks, but you know your sister. Stubborn as her father. Haven't I been trying to get him to have that mole on his back examined since last August?"

"What about her?" Her father protested with a nod toward her mom. "It's the dead of winter, and she's still wearing those sandals with socks that don't match."

Her mom released Logan and glanced at her Birkenstock-clad feet, one of which bore a bright orange sock and the other a hot pink one. She gave a wry snarl. "It's my bunions giving me fits. White socks get dirty too easily." She extended her hand to Mick as she set down the hotel gift basket. "Hi, I'm Cora."

"Mick." The four of them who'd stepped from Donavan's Dodge chorused the reply.

"She's with Donavan," said Logan, hoping to forego the farce she'd already begun with Donavan.

Her mom blinked. "Your brother brought home a girlfriend? Welcome!" She turned to Paul. "So you're Donavan's friend from college, the one with the genius IQ?"

Donavan shot Logan a glare. "Mom, this is my friend Paul. We live together."

Right, Donavan was out? Not so much. He couldn't even introduce Paul as his significant other. Logan returned her brother's glare.

Her mom's eyebrows lifted. "Where's your friend from college?"

Mick held up her hand and waved. "That would be me."

Her mom looked confused, and her dad just glanced between the four of them, looking thoughtful. "Well, as long as you're all here, we can figure the rest of this out inside where it's warmer." Then she walked back into the house, motioning for everyone to follow her as introductions continued on the porch.

"Logan, you look thin. Come have some Dutch apple pie." Her mom led the way toward the kitchen, and Logan looked around. Things hadn't changed much since she'd been home the previous summer.

"I'm not hungry, Mom, but I do need to use the restroom."

"Well, the toilet hasn't moved. You know your way around." She picked up a bowl with a wooden spoon and stirred frantically, nodding in the direction of the half bath just off the kitchen.

Logan took in the disarray of dirty dishes lining the kitchen island and the row of pies lined up on the counter nearest the sink.

Chocolate, pecan, apple, and what looked like peach. She peeled off her coat and hung it on the back of a chair then dashed for the lavatory before her mom could start cutting into the desserts.

Good God. She stared at the bathroom's latest décor, ladybugs and sunflowers, which looked completely out of place considering the season. A Santa hand towel hung from the towel bar and creamy vanilla snowflake guest soaps spilled from a cherry red soap dish. Logan listened as the others made their way into the kitchen and made small talk, and she wondered how long she could get by with just sitting in the tiny room to collect herself.

When she finally walked out, her parents were in the middle of a heated discussion over his cigar smoking. Her mother, who always punctuated her speech by using her hands, waved the wooden spoon she held and inadvertently flung a large wad of dough across the room.

Donavan burst into laughter and pointed as Doreen walked down the stairs, landing on the bottom step just in time to receive goop in her face.

Logan's mind seemed to capture everything in slow motion. Her sister was, as usual, dressed conservatively, with every hair in place, no wrinkles in her slacks or button-down dress shirt, the sweater draped and the sleeves tied in cover girl perfection at her breasts. Within a split-second, the facade collapsed, and Doreen looked mortified, totally undignified, and pissed off to the max. And ill.

"Oh, shit, honey, I'm sorry!" Her mom slammed the bowl back onto the counter and dusted off flour-encased hands on her apron.

Everyone stared, drop-jawed, as Doreen's eyes grew rounder and her face greener. Motioning for Logan to move, Doreen buzzed past her into the bathroom and began making the most disgusting sounds.

Logan trotted behind her, closed the door, and held Doreen's hair from her face as she threw up violently. "Damn, Doreen."

"Oooh!" Doreen knelt on both knees and continued groaning.

Sounds from the other side of the door blurred as Logan concentrated on the less than auspicious reunion with her sister. Doreen looked tired, not just sick, and she'd lost weight.

"How long have you had this flu?" Logan asked sympathetically.

Doreen shook her head. Logan, for lack of anything better to do, continued holding Doreen's hair and attempting to sound reassuring.

"That's okay. I'll take you to the doctor tomorrow if you like. I'll have to drive your car, of course." Logan reached above as far as she could stretch, her fingers grasping for clean washcloths. She found one, then pushed it under the sink, turned on the tap, and soaked it.

Doreen shook her head again, more emphatically, this time waving her hands.

Logan took a deep breath and tried once more to be Doreen's support system. She squeezed the wet rag with one hand. "Mom's right. You are stubborn, just like Pop. I won't nag, though. Just promise you'll take something for this, even if it's an over-the-counter medication."

Doreen sat back and accepted the wet washcloth. Her eyes had dark circles beneath them. "It's not the flu. I'm pregnant."

Logan dropped Doreen's hair and leaned heavily against the door. "You're kidding, right?"

Doreen winced. "I wish."

"But…" Logan searched for words.

"Yeah, I know. I'm not married."

"Does Shithead know?"

"Shithead isn't the father, dork." Doreen wiped her lips then her forehead, and tears streamed down her face. "You tell anyone, and I'll kill you, I swear to God, Logan."

"Okay, I won't." Logan didn't know whether she should hug her, comfort her, or just sit back and wait for the explosion she was sure to come. "So if Keith isn't the father…?"

Doreen bit her lips then cleared her throat. "Uh-uh. Not yet. I can't keep it a secret for long, considering I'm a couple of months along, but you'll all find out in time. I'm not ready to talk about it yet. I have no idea why I blurted that out."

"It's okay." This time Logan leaned forward and hugged Doreen, who seemed surprised by the gesture.

She tentatively touched Logan's back. Then she leaned into Logan and sobbed. "Why now? Just when I was getting my life back?"

They jumped as the door behind Logan reverberated with sound.

"Hey! Everything okay in there?" Her mom banged on the door again, and her voice sounded concerned.

"We're fine, Mom!" Logan called. Looking at Doreen, she whispered. "I won't say anything, but don't leave me hanging like this. I gotta know more."

Doreen nodded and dried her eyes. "Say your hellos, catch up on gossip, have your pie. I'm staying here tonight, so we'll talk later I promise." She punched Logan. "And what's this shit Donavan tells me about you being engaged? Since when?"

Logan sighed. So he had told the family. Excellent. "Tomorrow. I'll tell you all about it tomorrow, if you'll promise to just go along with me on this."

"So it's not true?"

"No, but I'm not going into detail while sitting next to a toilet of vomit." Logan wrinkled her nose.

Doreen reached for the handle and flushed. "Helluva way to begin a holiday."

"Tell me about it." Logan recalled how she'd done the same when meeting Mick. She pulled herself from the floor, already exhausted by the family drama and she hadn't even had any pie.

"So who's the blond?" Doreen asked, smoothing her clothing and hair.

"Paul. He's with Don." Logan quirked an eyebrow.

"You mean like his best friend or his...?" Doreen shrugged and kept her shoulders lifted, almost as if hopeful of a different answer.

"What do you think? Isn't your ass cold by now? Get off the floor."

Doreen's shoulders fell and she looked crestfallen. "Shit. Donavan's going gay on us at Christmas?"

"Come on, Doreen, it's not like he just decided his sexual orientation yesterday." Logan extended her hand and hauled Doreen to her feet. "Jeez Louise."

"Oh, don't sound so politically correct, Logan. Just because I live in the middle of nowhere doesn't mean I'm ass-backward in my thinking. I was just hoping he'd use more discretion than to bring his lover home to meet the folks."

Exasperated, Logan sighed. "And why shouldn't he? We did."

"That's different!"

"No, it's not!" Logan launched into a familiar family squabble with her. She and Doreen had known and discussed their brother's sexual proclivities for years, but neither had broached the subject with their parents. If Donavan wanted to remain in the closet, it was his prerogative. His as well as hers. But it was true he'd brought Paul home to meet the parents, and she'd back him all the way. Even if he couldn't bring himself to say it.

"Are you two coming out of there or not?" Her mom pounded on the door again.

Logan reached for the doorknob and felt Doreen's hand on her arm. They locked eyes for a moment, and Logan nodded, understanding. Doreen gave her a weak smile of gratitude, and the two of them took deep breaths.

Once more into the breach.

CHAPTER SIX

Their parents were still bickering, this time about sleeping arrangements.

"Donavan and Paul can sleep in the basement," her mom insisted.

Logan eyed her mother's hands. This time they were spoon and dough-free. She whacked a rolling pin against the dough on the table and began flattening it in earnest.

"But that's my office," said her dad.

"Bullshit. It's where you smoke those nasty cigars, and you know what your doctor said about that!

"Home sweet home," Logan said. She sent an apologetic look to Mick.

"Donavan's twin bed isn't big enough for the both of 'em."

Her dad looked confused. "You think they'll mind that? They're still gay, aren't they?" He shrugged.

"Chrrrrrrist, Ben! Lower your voice. Let's not get into that right now, besides, the Christmas presents are in there, no one's going in that room."

Logan and Doreen exchanged horrified looks then had to turn away, hiding their faces. Logan peered upward and found Mick staring at her with a blank expression, but she could tell from Mick's glittering eyes that she, too, was having a difficult time keeping a straight face. Her brother might not have come out, but clearly, their parents thought that Paul wasn't just a friend.

Her mom reached across the cooking island and poked her dad with the rolling pin. "Does it really bother you that your son and his lover will be doing God knows what?"

Her dad pointed to Mick and gave her a quick harrumph. "Nah. If I'd worry about anyone making hanky-panky this week, it'd be her! No offense, young lady, but I'm not sure how you fit into all of this. If you're Donavan's girlfriend and Paul is his boyfriend…? No offense, but what the hell, you know?"

"Understood, sir." Mick still maintained a disinterested posture and neutral appearance. "You'll find no hanky or panky here." Evidently, she was going to leave any explanations to the people who wanted to give them.

Did Mick mean that there would be no sex? Damn. Logan felt her face flame, and the urge for nicotine stung her hard. "I need some fresh air," she announced, reaching for her coat.

"If you're gonna smoke while you're here, you might as well use the basement like your father," her mom said, not bothering to look up from her task. "It's too damned cold for you to go outside in this weather."

Logan grabbed her coat anyway, and snagged Mick's sleeve, tugging. "You coming?"

"You want me to?" The question sounded innocent enough, but Logan knew she was about to laugh.

She rolled her eyes and pointed toward the back, cuing Mick with her eyes like she was some sort of dominatrix. "Get your coat."

Mick gave a small, obliging nod and did as asked.

The backyard was as frozen as the front. The only place that indicated anyone had been outside was the patio where the grill stood. Her dad had no doubt swept snow and ice from it.

Logan lit her cigarette then pointed to the chef's footprints. "Daddy grills all year, doesn't matter the weather. He grills pork chops to go with Mom's massive Christmas breakfasts of scrambled eggs, fried potatoes and onions, and French toast casserole. He'll also get tired of leftover turkey by the third day, if not before, and he'll grill bratwurst with bell peppers and onions."

Mick chuckled. "If that's the case, we should invest in a covering for him this year. You know, some sort of awning or tent to keep him out of the cold as much as possible."

"That's one of the things I admire most about you." Logan sat on one of the three swings her father had constructed of wooden boards and metal chain. "Instead of trying to change someone, you think of solutions to help them. Like with Donavan. You don't even know what this computer game is, do you? Yet you're willing to invest in the project to help get his idea in stores?"

Mick shrugged then sat in the swing next to Logan. "I like helping." She seemed to choose her words carefully. "For instance, do you think your father will change or will he continue to grill, no matter the weather?"

"He'd grill if he was on one of those wheely-walker things."

"Then he needs support. It's not like he's a crack addict." Mick studied Logan. "And what about you? What interests you?"

Logan stared into the snow before them. "I loved working at the Book Boutique, but they had to close. The virus pretty well shut down the small businesses in that area, and some of them will never be able to reopen."

"Then choose a new location. If you want to stay in DC, look for an area that can support independent bookstores. Don't give in to the negative belief system that says things will never get better. Make them better."

Easy for you to say. Logan tamped down on the urge to speak. Mick had probably never been broke in her life.

"What other traditions does your family have at Christmas?" asked Mick.

Several things came to mind. "We take a tour of the neighborhoods to view the Christmas lights everyone puts up. There's a big display a church puts on. A radio station plays their music choices while the church lights on the lawn dance to the music. It's quite spectacular."

"Sounds interesting. I've never toured a residential area like that."

Logan nodded. "There are the festivals within festivals. The Greek Orthodox church has a supper with Greek food. Various churches have pageants, and some of their choirs are unbelievably good."

"How about your family?" asked Mick. "If I'm to spend Christmas with them, I'd like to know what to expect, what I can contribute, that sort of thing. I asked Don when I accepted his invitation, but he just told me to bring my hat and my ass and leave my hat at home."

"Sounds like him. I think sometimes he just pops off with whatever comes to mind." Logan thought a moment. "Mom and the lady next door, Mrs. Grassle, swap fruitcakes. We usually toss Mrs. Grassle's cake into the trash, because hers are soggy. We wait to open presents until Christmas Day. Like I said, we have a fancy Christmas breakfast, then we open gifts. Lunch is a big deal, our main meal for the day. That afternoon we watch movies here or go to the theater to watch them. Dinner consists of leftovers or Dad's grilled meats and veggies. That's about it."

The back door opened, and her mom ventured outside, wearing a puffy, down-filled coat and her open-toed sandals. "I told you to smoke in the basement." She perched on the free swing seat. "Remember when your dad set these up for you kids? You were only five. Doreen thought she was too big, but the three of you would get out here and swing so high I thought that you'd fall out and bust your heads open."

Logan looked at her mother's bare legs and wondered why she came outside. Surely it wasn't just to grouch about her smoking. *Breathe. Just breathe.* "Mom, aren't you freezing?"

"I'm going back inside. I came out to tell you girls that the boys have carried that one pair of pajamas to your bedroom, Logan. I figured you girls might want to stay up giggling and talking girl-talk. I guess the boys will sleep in the basement." She paused.

"But do you mind telling me why you girls only have one pair of pajamas between you? Where's your luggage?"

Logan shrugged. "Who knows, Mom? We arrived with it at the hotel. We sat down to eat, and when we got up, our luggage was gone."

Her mom seemed to ponder this a moment. "So you're wearing the same underwear you wore yesterday? Eeeew, Logan."

Logan choked on her cigarette so badly she had to snuff what was left in the snow. Mick clapped her on the back.

God bless her mom. She spoke whatever flitted through her mind, whether it was appropriate to voice it or not. It didn't appear she'd go back into the house until they did, so Logan stood and headed for the back door. She heard the snow crunch behind her as Mick and her mom kept pace.

Logan's stomach knotted at the thought of spending the night in her childhood bedroom with Mick. Bedrooms were personal. The secrets they revealed weren't meant to be shared. The old-fashioned metal headboard where she'd laced her fingers through the scrolling frame, the faded floral wallpaper where she'd counted dozens upon dozens of tiny rosebuds. Plus the myriad of built-in bookshelves that housed Logan's girlish reading material...well, she wasn't ready to invite anyone into that part of her life. What if Mick made fun of her? Worse, what if Mick was indifferent, not realizing how important that one room had been and how many adventures it had offered? There'd been flights as Logan had pretended she was stewardess Vicki Barr, and dangerous medical assignments she'd undertaken as nurse Cherry Ames. Logan had read all of her mother's old books and had treasured them. The Trixie Belden mysteries. Nancy Drew. Donna Parker.

She felt someone nudge her. "What?"

Her mother stared into Logan's eyes. "I said it's good to have you home and asked how long you can stay this time?"

Logan didn't know what to say. Now didn't seem the appropriate time to tell her mother that she'd been let go from her job. "Can we talk about this after Christmas?"

"Sure." She sounded okay, but Logan knew her mother, just like her mom knew her children. She likely already knew that her youngest child was distressed.

Logan wrapped her arms about her mom's neck and shoulders, having to tiptoe to do so. "I love you, Mom. I'm okay, but I need your advice on a few things."

She felt her mom nod.

"Never feel that you can't talk to me." She released her then held Logan's face in her hands. "And thank you."

"For what?"

"For letting me know I'm still invited into your circle. I miss our talks. You used to tell me everything, unlike your brother and your sister, who tell me nothing. Do you know what's up with Doreen? Why she's so gloomy? What's making her so sick?"

Shit. You knew that was coming. Logan chastised herself for getting tongue-tied. There was no way Doreen could keep her pregnancy a secret much longer. But if her ex-husband wasn't the father, who was?

"Lo?" a voice called from above the stairs.

Logan looked up to find Doreen motioning for her to climb up and used it to escape her mom's question. She ascended, followed by Mick. Doreen looked exasperated. "I'd hoped we could talk. Privately."

Mick took a deep breath and nodded, looking flustered. "Of course. I'll go find Don and Paul."

Logan watched Mick go back downstairs. It was nice that she wanted to spend time with her and not just with Don. Then she turned and looked down the hallway, but Doreen was gone. Logan walked the few steps to Doreen's old room and found her sister sobbing quietly on the bed.

"What did Mom say?" Doreen turned swollen eyes toward her. "She knows, doesn't she? You didn't tell Don, did you? Oh my God, what am I going to do about this baby?"

It had never occurred to Logan that Doreen would have an abortion or that she might give up the baby once it was born.

Logan had no clue how to comfort Doreen other than to sit beside her and wrap her arm around her shaking shoulders.

"Why don't you tell the baby's father, Doreen? At least you'd have someone to commiserate with. I mean, you must trust him at least a little if you slept with him."

Doreen groaned. "You're right. But I can't. You've got to help me get through this holiday. I'll do something about the situation afterward, I promise."

"Well, Christmas Eve is coming, so you need to think fast."

"I know!" Doreen's tears flowed even more freely.

Logan had an idea. "Mick is new to town. She mentioned something about doing some Christmas shopping, and that doesn't give us much time. Stores will probably close early on Christmas Eve. Do you want to go with us? It'd get you out of the house."

"You've been on the road for so long. Aren't you tired?"

"I slept all eleven hours. Mick slept part of the way, and Don and Paul took turns driving while the other one snoozed."

Doreen glumly nodded. "Okay. Thanks. We can take my car."

Logan chuckled. "We'll have to. I don't have one, and I don't want to shop with Don."

"What's up with him anyway?" asked Doreen. "Is he with Paul, or is he with Mick? That's a helluva name for a female."

"Her name is Michaela. Mick is her nickname."

"Oh."

"And no, they don't have a threesome going, which is what Mom and Dad think. She's here to work on some business thing with him. How about we go to Walmart right after supper?" Logan fidgeted. "I hate to sound like Rainman, but I'm not wearing any underwear."

"What!"

"Mick and I left Chicago without our luggage, some sort of hotel snafu."

Doreen sat back with a horrified expression. "You're not wearing any underwear?"

Logan laughed. Her family members all knew her predilection for clean undies at all times. Whenever they'd all taken trips together, someone always asked Logan if she had plenty of panties.

Logan laughed then headed toward the door. "Yeah, and I haven't told anyone else in the family, but I lost my job."

Doreen placed her hand on Logan's shoulder to stop her from leaving. Then she opened her arms to give Logan a hug. "You need some money?"

"You know me so well." Logan walked into her big sisters embrace. She squeezed her back. "Thanks, sis."

The warmth coming from her sister made Logan wish she had stayed in touch more. Was it her imagination or Doreen's condition? Now that they were adults, Doreen seemed softer. Maybe it was good that she'd come home.

CHAPTER SEVEN

Mick returned from talking with the guys in the basement late that night. As she snuck into Logan's room a cute little snore greeted her. Logan must be asleep. She slid into the bed and tried to cuddle with her.

"No," came Logan's groggy response.

Mick scooted closer to the outside edge and pulled on the blanket.

Logan yanked the covers and turned to the wall.

Damn, was Logan asleep, or did she really just snub her? Either way, Mick had to sleep too. She reached down and pulled the bedspread up to her neck, then took in the room.

She'd seen tons of houses like this one in her profession and had begun her company by flipping them. The Bradys average three-bedroom two-bath was nothing fancy. They had stretched it to the max, making Don a small room out of the den upstairs, the dining room turned into one downstairs. The crowded table in the eat-in kitchen was cozy, the perfect family gathering spot. Cora had apologized for the lack of room, yet looked happy to have each and every person there. It would have been the perfect place to grow up. As Mick's memories went back to her childhood, she considered something. If she'd given any of the foster families a chance instead of running away, would she have found a family like the Bradys? She fell asleep and tossed and turned, dreaming of cold nights huddled in an alley or abandoned building.

The next day Mick discovered everyone had slept in. No one batted an eye that it was after ten in the morning when Mick showed her face, since none of them had been up long either. She'd been a little disappointed to find Logan gone, as she'd been hoping to see what she looked like when she first woke up. It was an oddly romantic notion for someone who usually didn't stay the night at all.

Cora took a well-deserved break and ordered pizza for lunch. After all the pizza and a whole pecan pie was devoured the four "kids" as Logan's mom called them washed and dried what few dishes there were then branched off to do their own thing.

Ben parked in front of his big-screen television set in the living room, the boys headed for the basement to play video games, and Cora made popcorn and joined Ben.

Mick was used to doing things alone. Families seemed to do things in groups. It felt nice to be included. Usually she kept to herself, but she decided to make the best of the situation and see how the other half lived.

Logan, Doreen, and Mick piled into Doreen's car and headed toward the Oak Park Mall.

"A sports place." Mick pointed toward Academy Sports. "Okay if we stop here first?"

Doreen and Logan looked at one another. "Sure."

Doreen might not have known why, but Logan clearly had an idea. "A gazebo is an expensive gift to buy someone you don't know well," she murmured quietly to Mick.

"You two go ahead. I'll stay in the car," said Doreen. "Not like you'll be gone long, right?"

"Right." Mick got out first and waited for Logan. Then she grabbed Logan's hand and strode toward the door. "I know what you're thinking, but this is like buying a burger for me. No big deal."

Logan didn't seem pleased and looked back to the car.

Mick knew exactly what she wanted to get and before long the purchases had been made. The manager even agreed to drop off the large, steel, canopy gazebo.

"You're sure you can put this together?" he asked.

"We can do it." Mick extended her hand for him to shake.

"Okay," he said. "We'll deliver it Christmas Eve after we close for the holidays. It'll be around noon."

"Think your dad will like it?" Mick asked on the way back to Doreen's car.

"He'll love it." Logan still acted as if she couldn't believe Mick had done that.

The rest of their shopping was leisurely, despite the frantic air that permeated the mall. Doreen, of course, had finished her shopping, so she didn't buy anything. Mick wondered why she was even there. Logan hadn't spent much, since she'd shopped in DC for all but stocking stuffers. With Ben's airlines experience, he seemed to think their luggage would be found before Christmas. Maybe he had some magical powers. Mick's experience was once a bag was lost, it showed up just in time to leave again or not at all.

She didn't want them to spend money on her. She had everything she needed, or could get it herself. "Don't feel like you need to pick up anything for me," Mick told them. "And I heard Don say that he'd purchased something for Paul, so he won't be without a gift."

Logan locked eyes with her. "Don't tell me what I can and can't do. If I get you anything at all, it'll be inexpensive but personal. It's not about money."

"Good. Then I don't want you to say anything else about what I bought your dad."

Logan wasn't angry, but Mick knew there wasn't much Logan could contribute to the pile of presents under the tree that year. Logan had said her mother would at least be making Christmas stockings with names on them. She decided to buy a card game for Donavan. Something with the word Humanity. Ah, there it was.

"I've heard that's hysterical fun." Logan peered over her shoulder.

"It is," Mick said. "That game will leave you gasping for air. We'll have to play it while we're all home."

"Now to get something for Donavan's and Paul's stocking. Any suggestions?"

"Let me think about it." Mick led her to another spot in the same store and pointed to yet another card game. "How about this one for Paul? Let me get these."

They headed for the counter and waited to pay for the purchases. "How do you think your sister is faring out there?" Mick looked out the glass to see Doreen wandering about, peering aimlessly into display windows.

Logan shrugged. "Okay, I guess." She got closer to Mick and whispered. "She told me something, and I promised I wouldn't tell."

"Then don't."

Logan looked disappointed.

Doreen had been quiet today. Did she suspect Mick's feelings for her baby sister? Logan had said she was homophobic. Or maybe she was jealous that Mick was monopolizing Logan's time.

"But I'm dying to tell someone, and I can't tell Donavan. He'd blab."

"Still, if she trusted you with a secret, don't. tell." Mick heard her harsh tone, and immediately changed it. "Really, I don't need to know." Mick considered all she had shared with Logan. She'd been easy to talk to. Would Logan keep her confidences? Mick didn't like the feeling of doubt that put her on edge.

Logan sighed. "You're right. I'm sorry. I'm worried about her, but there's no need. Doreen can't do anything about her situation, and I can't help. C'mon. Let's wrap this up. I want to get Mom some sort of spa gift."

Mick smiled. "Now you're talking my language. I know the perfect place."

Mick paid and took the bag holding the games. "Grab your sister. Maybe she'll know where the store is in the mall."

❖

Within a couple more hours, the three of them had purchased gourmet popcorn at Topsy's, coffee at Starbucks, and foot scrubs for both Doreen and Logan's mom, right under Doreen's non-observant nose. They left, but as an afterthought, Logan went back inside and chose two more gifts. She was running low on funds, but it was important that her mother and sister take care of themselves. She bought spa socks that were microwaveable. Then on her way toward the entry she turned back and bought another pair for Mick.

"Sorry. Forgot something." She rejoined the others. "Do we need to stop anyplace else?"

Mick eyed the large bag holding the gifts. "I thought you were darned near broke."

Logan swallowed hard and shook her head. "Why would you think that?" She cut Mick a sharp look, to which she discreetly mouthed *sorry*. Mick didn't know she'd told Doreen about her lack of income, and Logan didn't want Mick to tell anyone else. It didn't matter because Doreen didn't seem to be paying attention, thankfully.

Screw it. It was Christmas, a time of secrets. She took a deep breath. And maybe it was a time of new beginnings. This was the season of love, compassion, selflessness. Her mother's troubled feet, her sister's pregnancy—those took precedence. Didn't they? And she had enough money to survive on for the next two months. Maybe three if she was frugal. If the coronavirus pandemic had taught her anything, it was that life was short and that there were no guarantees.

Another thought worked its way from the back burner to the front of her mind. Although it wasn't preferable, she did have other options than staying in DC. Her parents would love it if she moved back home. They were getting older and could use her help around the house. Doreen would probably need help with the baby. Besides there were still a few brick and mortar bookstores in the metro. There were several community colleges and universities if she needed to go back to school. Possibilities were endless.

Why wasn't she excited?

❖

Their second evening passed quickly. Logan hunted through her bureau drawers and found oversized Kansas City Royals baseball tees for her and Mick to wear to bed. She remembered Mick saying that she slept in the nude, but Logan wasn't ready for that. Mick would wear the T-shirt and get over it.

Mick seemed to look around the room, trying not to stare at the souvenirs and what-nots that collectively made up the memories of Logan's girlish childhood. Logan couldn't help wondering how her bedroom compared to Mick's back home. Somehow, she couldn't imagine Mick Finnegan surrounding herself with photos of friends or posters of teen crush rock stars. She imagined a minimalistic room with expensive furniture, sheets whose thread count was one thousand or more, satin pillows, and a crystal chandelier.

They were already in Logan's double bed and ready to turn out the lamp when someone knocked at the door. A tentative voice whispered loudly, "Lo?

"Come in, Doreen."

This was nothing new. They'd often talked long hours into the night when they should have been asleep. This time was different, though. Would Doreen stay with Mick in the room? In the bed?

Doreen entered and closed the door behind her. "I'm sorry," she said. "I couldn't sleep."

Logan instinctively opened her arms, and her sister practically fell into them. The bed gave a bit with her weight as Doreen crawled onto the bed beside Logan.

"I am so, so sorry." Doreen's fists unclenched, and she dabbed her eyes and blew her nose with one of the tissues she'd been clutching. "You haven't told anyone, have you?"

Logan shook her head. "No." She nudged Doreen. "But you're about to." She cocked her head toward Mick.

"Oh, what the hell." Doreen sobbed then confessed. "I'm pregnant, Mick. And nobody knows but Logan and now you. I'm not married, I'm divorced. The baby isn't his, anyway. I don't know what I'm going to do. In a couple of months, it'll be obvious."

Logan and Mick commiserated with Doreen, but there wasn't much to do other than let her cry and bemoan her circumstances.

"I've always wanted a baby," Doreen said. "But not like this, not as a single mother. And what about the folks? How can I tell Mom and Dad?"

Logan felt helpless. She sympathized with Doreen's position. Pregnant and single at Christmas.

"And then there's Donavan." Doreen said through sobs. "He'll make a huge deal of this, and I can't help myself. I'll be pissed off then get Mom and Dad upset."

"I think Don will surprise you," said Logan, squeezing Doreen's shoulders. "He will absolutely love being an uncle."

"A gay uncle." Doreen sobbed. "Just what I need. He'll probably show up at the hospital wearing blue or pink—or both—and sporting a T-shirt that says World's Best Gay Uncle."

"What's wrong with that?" asked Mick, obviously unable to remain quiet any longer.

"Well...well..." Doreen sputtered. "That just isn't done here. Overland Park isn't exactly conservative, but nobody is in your face with their homosexuality. What would people think?"

Logan felt Mick's body tense. She begged Mick silently not to confess her sexuality now, in Logan's childhood bedroom, with her homophobic sister beside them in bed. She wasn't ashamed or anything, she just couldn't deal with Doreen's questions right now.

But Mick didn't say anything. She rolled over with her back to Logan, who felt they'd dodged the proverbial bullet. This wasn't the time for a discussion about sexual politics.

"Doreen?" Logan turned her attention back to her. "What about your job? Will you be able to stay on while you're pregnant?"

Doreen took a huge breath and let it out in a whoosh. "Damn it, Logan. I'm pregnant, not addled. Don't worry about me. The hospital has a great insurance plan, and as a nurse practitioner, I can still administer shots and dispense advice."

Logan couldn't help pushing her luck. "Doreen, you have to tell Mom and Dad."

"I will."

"Now," Logan insisted.

Doreen shook her head. "When I'm ready."

Logan lifted her head, picked up the pillow, and whacked Doreen as soundly as possible. "If you don't tell our parents that you're about to give birth, I will!"

For once that night, Doreen appeared speechless, if only for a moment. When she finally found her voice, it cracked with emotion. "Lo, that news isn't yours to share. Besides, you'll break their hearts."

"No, I won't. Mom and Dad will be overjoyed. You're about to give birth to their first grandchild." Logan backed off. Doreen was right. The news was Doreen's to share, not Logan's.

Hope flitted across Doreen's face. "Do you really think so?"

"No." Logan's snark returned. "I'm blowing smoke up your ass. Of course they're going to be excited. Now go back to bed, will you?" She hugged her close. "I think you're underestimating them. Our mom and dad are terrific."

Logan appreciated that she'd finally remembered how lucky she was to have them all.

Mick rolled over the moment Doreen closed the door. "I'm not trying to cause a fight, but remember when you told me in so many words that your family was dysfunctional? Well, they're not. You are." She knew she treaded on dangerous ground but couldn't keep from adding fuel to the fire she'd started. "If any of them are homophobic, it's because of you and your insecurities. We train people how to treat us. If I've learned anything in business, it's that."

"What are you talking about?"

"You're not authentic. You aren't yourself when you're around the people who love you the most. Then you become uncomfortable when they don't hand you want you want—validation."

Logan threw off the covers and rose. "You've been here forty-eight hours and think you know them?"

"You've been with them twenty-five years, and yeah, I think I know them better than you."

She tossed the covers aside and sat on the edge of the bed. "You haven't given them the chance to know you. You're so busy being what you think they want, acting as you think they'd have you behave, that you've lost sight of both them and yourself."

"That's a load of crap."

"Is it? Stop pacing and look at me, please. I understand how you might not want to come out in public, but I don't see the point of an adult hiding who they are when they're with family."

"Probably because you've never had a family."

Mick's jaw clenched. "That was low."

Logan immediately came to the bed and knelt. "Oh, God, I am so sorry. I'm not normally so nasty." She took Mick's hands. "Please forgive me, Mick. Please."

Mick was torn. Put up walls so she wouldn't feel Logan's pain, or take a chance, comfort her? Logan's shame and remorse were obvious. She reached out and let her hands hover over Logan's shoulders.

Then Logan clasped her arms about Mick's waist and laid her head in her lap. "You're right. I'm not honest with them. I intended to tell the folks and Doreen this week. I haven't found the right moment."

Mick hugged her. "And it's not my place to tell you when to do so. I'm sorry for bringing it up. I'm not used to this."

Logan raised her tear-stained face. "What? Waiting on a baby dyke to grow up?" She laughed.

"You could say that." Mick wanted to make light of the situation, but she was tired, and the past few minutes had given her pause. She wasn't accustomed to handling others' emotions. Hell, she rarely allowed herself the luxury of feeling her own. Emotions were messy. Inconvenient as hell.

One thing was certain. Those damned Norman Rockwell paintings only captured innocence, not the pain of awakening.

Chapter Eight

Mick inhaled deeply. The smell of fresh coffee and flapjacks blanketed the downstairs the next morning.

"Ben!" Cora called from the kitchen table where she sat drinking her morning brew and constructing a last-minute grocery list. "Ben!"

He yelled back from the basement, "What?"

She pushed the pen and paper across the table to Logan. "Go ask your father what he needs from the store. It'll be closed early day after tomorrow, and I'm betting he doesn't have everything he wants for those brats he cooks every Christmas."

Logan rose to leave, and Mick rose, too. Maybe she'd go see what the boys were up to.

"No, you stay." Cora patted Mick's arm. "I want to have a chat."

Mick felt a twinge of panic. What could Logan's mother possibly want with her?

Cora motioned for Mick to follow her upstairs. There was one closed door between Logan's room and her parents' bedroom. Cora opened it and motioned for Mick to have a seat near a square piece of furniture that looked like a crafts table. The twin bed under the window was covered with boxes and bags. This must be Donavan's old room. Cora went to a closet, opened it, and pulled out five quilts, one after the other, and stacked them on the square table.

"I work all year on things to give my kids for Christmas. I want your opinion on one of these for Logan." She pulled a colorful quilt from the pile and unfolded it.

"How pretty!" Mick was genuinely impressed and more than a little relieved that they weren't about to have some serious conversation.

"Do you think so?" Cora placed one corner of it before Mick. "Does she still like the color purple? I should have asked her this past summer, but things moved so fast I just didn't."

Mick traced the bright yellow flowers, puffy umbrellas, and purple blocking with her fingertips. "This is great—it looks like a scene from a greeting card."

Cora beamed. "Thank you. I made the pattern myself. Logan loves daisies and spring showers in April. She also loves those little purple things. They're really weeds, but she'd gather them and put them into her Easter baskets. So you think this will work for her?"

"Absolutely."

Cora folded the quilt, placed it on the bottom of the stack, then pulled out another. "I thought I'd give this one to Donavan." She unfolded it. Various sized boys' T-shirts filled the blue borders. "He's outgrown these, needless to say." She pointed to a couple obviously made for a small child. "But I couldn't throw them away. They're too old to give to charity."

Mick couldn't keep from touching Cora's hand to reassure her. "I can't imagine anything better to give your son. What great memories. And what a thoughtful gift."

Any trepidation Mick might have felt before being alone with Cora vanished. For the first time in years, she felt she was truly home. She'd never had anyone make anything for her. Certainly not a quilt, something so personal that took several weeks or months to complete. Cora and Ben's children probably had no idea how blessed they'd been to grow up in such a family. All Mick had was money.

"What's that, dear?" Cora asked.

Had she spoken? Mick didn't know, so she voiced what she'd been thinking. She cleared her throat to cover the shakiness that filtered her voice. "What I mean is, I don't make anything other than money." She laughed nervously. "I don't even know how to make a mixed drink. I can't cook a meal. I don't sew. I admire you and your family so much."

Cora did the most unexpected thing. She hugged her. Mick's eyes filled with tears.

"Don't feel bad," said Cora. "Logan can't cook or sew. She never felt the need because there was always someone to do it for her—me, her grandmothers, her sister. That's why I worry about her so much. She's so thin, I know she's not eating well. Her coat has a hole in it. She only wears pullover tops. I don't think the child knows how to sew on a button."

"Have you tried teaching her how to sew?" asked Mick.

"Heavens, no. She had a toy machine when she was small, but she preferred books." Cora's face took on a dreamy look. "There's a culinary school here. I've hoped for years that Logan would join me in taking a class or two, something we'd both enjoy."

"What sort of class?" Mick asked. Not only was she getting to know Cora, but she was gaining some nice insight on Logan, too.

"Italian cooking. We all love lasagna but none of us make it. There's a class that teaches that plus other Italian dishes. Tiramisu. Mexican food, same thing. Salsas and sauces." Cora grabbed the quilts and started piling them back into the closet.

"Here, let me help." Mick held them while Cora placed them carefully back on the shelf.

When they were done, Cora grabbed one of Mick's hands. "You're not Don's girlfriend, are you?"

Mick's throat went dry. How they could mistake her for Don's girlfriend was truly beyond her. And the conversation she'd overheard between Logan and Doreen made it clear that everyone knew Don was gay, they just hadn't come to terms with it yet. "No, just a friend."

"I see." Cora lifted her chin higher with every word. "So Paul is his...?"

"You should ask Don," said Mick, hoping Cora would leave it at that.

Cora's chin lowered. "Right."

She didn't sound convinced, but it seemed that was as far as Cora's curiosity extended. She released Mick's hand and headed toward the stairs. "I hear another cup of coffee calling my name. If Ben has added his list of items to what was already on that slip of paper, it might be time for you kids to go to the store."

"Tell the others that I'll be down in a few minutes." Mick waved good-bye as Cora descended the stairs. Then she walked toward the upstairs bathroom.

It seemed that she and the others had been going ninety miles per hour with their hair on fire ever since Chicago. If she didn't fit in with this bunch of Midwesterners, nobody seemed to notice. They were like the Addams family on crack. Odd, sweet, quirky, amiable, and a bit terrifying in their abilities to overlook the obvious. What Mick didn't understand was how they could recognize and even accept Donavan's gayness, but they seemed to hold a double standard for their youngest child. Or did they? Mick meant what she'd said the night before, that Logan trained them how to treat her. Maybe the problem was that none of them talked about it openly.

"Ridiculous." Mick stared at her reflection in the bathroom mirror. Ben and Cora seemed to love all their kids. Why in pluperfect heaven or hell should their children feel compelled to hide?

Mick sat on the edge of the tub and propped her elbows on either knee, then held her face in her hands. Did she feel uncomfortable in the Brady home? Hell no. Was she disgruntled with Logan? Not really. She'd only known Logan a couple of days or so. If she'd met her in DC, would she have sped up the process of knowing her? Probably not. But she'd have lured her back to her apartment and spent more time with her in bed. Alone.

Mick growled. She was no better than Logan when it came to not being authentic. Not if she hid how interested she was in her. Not if she held back when what she really wanted was to kiss Logan senseless.

She stood and flexed. Why was it that she was reticent to come on stronger? Same reason Logan was reluctant to be herself. Maybe she'd been too rough on Logan. Logan wasn't ashamed of being gay. She would come out in her own time and in her own way, and it seemed that maybe Mick had forgotten what it was like to be young and worried about other people's reactions.

It was time to go shopping and see what Logan was like when her family wasn't around.

Sure enough, Logan, Donavan, and Paul sat at the kitchen table, coffee mugs in hand, waiting for them. Logan held a brown mug out to Mick. "Here, this one's for you."

Mick saw the mug she had used the day before. Already her coffee was prepared how she liked her women, sweet. Wow, Logan knew how she took her coffee? It made her feel as if she belonged. She had her own designated mug. "Thank you," she said.

"Dad added his items to the list," Logan said. "He also gave me twenty dollars."

"I'll add to that. I have a fifty," said Cora. "That should give you plenty with money left over for wherever you go for lunch." She paused, looking pensive. "You aren't coming back here for that, are you?"

Logan blinked. "No. We haven't discussed it, but sure, I mean we can eat while we're out."

Cora seemed relieved. "Oh, good. Not that we don't have plenty of food, but I need to make the fruitcakes this afternoon. Half a dozen, I think, what with Ben's friend Artie, the neighbors on either side of us, one for us, and one for each of you kids to take back when you leave."

Donavan grinned and looked at the others. "Every year, Mom bakes a shitload—sorry, Mom—a truckload of fruitcakes. No matter what you've heard about how disgusting fruitcakes are, you haven't sunk your teeth into one of Mom's. They're scrumptious!"

"They beat the heck out of Mrs. Grassle's cakes," muttered Logan. "That's our next-door neighbor to the north." She pointed to empathize.

Cora shushed her. "She uses canned fruit and doesn't drain the syrup they're packed in. That's why her cakes are so...moist." She scrunched her face when she uttered the final word.

Donavan laughed. "I thought women hated that word. And her cakes are more than that. They're water-logged."

"Well, don't tell her," said Cora.

"Do we dump them in the trash as usual?" Donavan asked, blinking in mock innocence.

Cora went to her purse on the counter near the toaster, fished out a bill and handed it to Logan. "You kids have fun."

Mick finished her coffee and took her empty cup to the sink. She quickly followed the gang out the door to start her day with a spring in her step.

Chapter Nine

With only three days before Christmas, Logan wasn't surprised by the number of people on the Plaza. They had a difficult time finding parking. The snow fell in soft flakes, but the temperature had warmed enough that she didn't think it would stick on the streets.

"This is beautiful," Mick said as they crossed the street down from the four-story bookstore's parking garage. "I'd heard of this area before but had never visited Kansas City long enough to visit the Plaza. Do you think we can stay for a while?"

Logan grinned. "As long as we get Mom and Dad's groceries before we go home, I don't see why not."

Logan watched Mick's expression as a horse-drawn carriage passed and lined up on a side street. "Looks like they're getting ready for the tourists eager to fulfill their Christmas dreams." She smiled at Mick. "I've always wanted to do that and I'm a local."

"Yeah, I feel the same way about the ones in Central Park," Mick answered. "Maybe it's a seasonal thing to do, huh?"

"Maybe. I've secretly wanted to ride in the Cinderella carriage."

"Why secretly?" Mick asked, bemused.

Logan's heart fluttered. "Because I'm a romantic at heart?"

Mick laughed. "You do realize that Cinderella was a heterosexual."

"I disagree. Our dear Ella exists because of a heterosexual writer."

"Hey, you two coming?" Don asked. He held a store door open. Paul had already disappeared inside.

"I think we're going to start with coffee," Mick answered for them both.

Logan had to admit that Mick's easy, take-charge attitude made her a little swoony.

"The Starbucks is down there on the right." Don pointed across Forty-Seventh Street Parkway. "We'll meet you there. Paul loves this place." He waved then hurried inside.

They headed to Starbucks, and once they got their drinks Mick began furiously scrolling on her phone. "Oh, they have some great shops here!"

Great. Mick sounded as if the brands she called out referred to regular chains and not to stores that required a down payment for a jacket. Perhaps to her they were. Happy with cheaper fare, Logan responded, "Personally, Hello Kitty is more my level of retail at the moment."

Mick patted her hand. "Can't you just window shop, then? I do need to get some things. We'll stop by Hello Kitty, I promise."

Why did she feel as if she was being patronized, that if she was good, she'd get rewarded? Did she resent Mick's money, or her own lack of it? The chasm of difference in income made her acutely aware if they were in DC they would never have met. It wasn't that they traveled in different circles, it was as if they lived in two different universes. Sophisticated, stylish Mick was her complete opposite.

"Back to what we were talking about earlier," Mick said. "Cinderella. Who wrote it?"

"No one knows." Logan shrugged. "The myth has existed for centuries. The Brothers Grimm wrote the version you and I know. One married, the other didn't, so…" She shrugged. "Times were different back then. What if one of the writers knew she was gay, but wrote it heterosexual for the masses? Ella the original could've swung either way, couldn't she?"

"I did read a version in a gay fairy-tale book once," Mick admitted. "Kind of kinky."

The guys came in, placed their orders, and joined them at the tall table nearest to the door.

"What have the two of you been discussing?" asked Donavan.

"Whether or not Cinderella was a dyke." Logan sipped her drink as nonchalantly as if she'd just asked someone to pass the napkins. Given that she hadn't officially come out, it felt daring to say something like that out loud.

"Don wants to go to a shop on the next block," Paul said, barely acknowledging her daring word choice.

"Don't blame me. You want to, too!" Don said, rolling his eyes at Logan.

"You're so cute," Mick said. "Like an old married couple."

This time it was Paul who choked on his coffee.

Don actually blushed. "We could get some of our list at the cheese store." His attempt at changing the conversation worked. That was a fun place.

Logan was glad to see her brother happy. She tried to help redirect the uncomfortable subject. "We can get some wine, too. Maybe some of the fixings for mom's cheese balls. After lunch we should get to the errands and head home."

"Dang, girl, you're already planning our getaway? We just got here," Mick said.

"Maybe we should split up?" Logan suggested. She didn't think window shopping in designer stores would do anything but remind her of how broke she was, and how much she enjoyed Mick's company, something she'd lose when Christmas was over. "How about if I go with Paul and you go with Don to do his thing?"

"Yes!" Paul shouted. "I love that idea."

"Okay then." Mick looked at Logan with a question in her eyes, but then turned away and smiled at Paul. "Maybe there's trouble in paradise?"

"Nothing like that," Paul said. "But I would like your opinion about my gift to Don."

That was the most words at one time Logan had heard Paul say. She felt honored he had asked. "It's settled then. Let's meet at Hello Kitty in two hours?"

"Ugh, sis. Hello Kitty?" Donavan groaned. "What are you, ten?"

"I am still a little girl at heart." She smiled and hoped it hid her embarrassment. Mick must think she was the most uncultured, uninteresting person on the planet. Mick could go look at Armani while Logan checked out the stuffed animal shop.

They went their separate ways. Paul seemed to know exactly where he was going. Logan followed willingly until he stopped outside of a jewelry shop.

"Your parents know that Don is gay, right?"

"Yes, considering what Mom said yesterday, I think so. Why?"

"Can you keep a secret?" Paul asked.

Of course, she'd been keeping her own, not very successfully, for a long time. She nodded.

"I'm asking him to marry me," Paul said. He marched inside with a huge grin on his face.

Logan sighed. *I've heard so many confessions this year that I feel like a priest.* This was one secret-filled Christmas she'd never forget.

Two hours and a dash through Hello Kitty later, the group contemplated where to go for lunch as they sat in the car.

Logan was hungry but didn't want to be the only voice in the matter. Indecision always frustrated her. "Where to? Someone decide."

"I'd love a burger, nothing fancy," Paul said.

"Not a drive-through, please?" Mick added.

What's wrong with fast food? Once again, Logan was reminded of the different worlds they lived in, right down to their food choices.

"Is it after three?" Don asked.

Logan said, "Yes. Why?"

"I know the perfect place." Don started the car and pulled out of the lot.

When Logan saw the iconic fountain with its four heroic horsemen, she relaxed. Don turned onto Mill Creek Parkway headed north. It didn't matter where they ate as long as it was burgers and not Plaza food so she could afford it. But then the golden arches in the distance made Logan think Don hadn't heard Mick's request. He passed the chain and then turned at Valentine Road. The uptown theater had a new marquee and face-lift since Logan had been home. Where were they going?

The sign in the window said *Hamburger Mary's,* with another beneath that read *Eat, Drink, and Be...Mary.* The cute décor and character said Mary's was popular. Logan had never been there.

"I didn't know you had one of these in KC," Mick said with enthusiasm.

"I didn't know there were any others," Don replied. "I wanted a place where we could be ourselves for a while."

"Huh?" Paul sounded perplexed. Logan knew she was.

"You'll see. Come on, gang." Don ushered them inside.

When the door closed, the scents of grease, charcoal, and flowers were as confusing as Don's eagerness. The interior resembled a bar more than a restaurant, complete with a stage.

Mick smiled and looked genuinely glad to be there. "You'll love it." She quickly hooked her arm at Logan's elbow as if it was the most natural thing ever.

The beautiful glamazon who greeted them surprised Logan even more.

She watched as her brother motioned for Paul and gently placed his hand at the small of his back and guided him to the booth their hostess selected for them. When she smiled and motioned to their seats with all the gusto of her best Hollywood starlet impression, Logan grinned.

The bright purple walls, complete with cartoonish drawings of the outlandish Mary, seemed to welcome all. Logan sat beside Mick at a small table. The place was packed. The last time Logan had visited home, the only place LGBTQ people were open was at the bars. Everything seemed up to date in KC, except her.

"Darlings, welcome to Mary's!" A deep baritone voice came from the hostess. "Someone will be with you in a moment."

Logan didn't realize she had dropped her jaw until Mick lifted her chin with her index finger to close it. "It's okay, hon. We can be comfortable here."

Don giggled as he stretched his arm out behind Paul's shoulder. "I told you about this place, remember?"

Paul nodded like he recalled the conversation. "This drag restaurant is a burger joint?"

"One and the same. But they don't play bingo until evening."

"Bingo?" Logan asked.

"For charity," Don answered.

As if that explained anything, Logan had never heard of the place. She studied the other patrons. Parents with two kids in booster chairs ate burgers and fries. A male couple passed a tall leg-shaped drink back and forth that reminded Logan of the lamp in the movie "A Christmas Story."

"They have a great Sunday brunch at the one in Vegas," Mick added.

A waitress stopped to take their order. "First time at Mary's? I'm Betty. Let me know if you have any questions."

"We may need a few more minutes," Mick said.

"Sure." She hurried to another table.

"Kansas City has changed since the last time I was home," Logan said.

Mick continued to peruse the menu. "I like the Mary's in West Hollywood."

Logan couldn't help staring. "First Las Vegas, now Hollywood. You must travel a lot."

"I do," Mick said. "And I know every kitschy bar and grill between the East and West Coast."

"Since RuPaul came out in all her glory, the world's different," Paul said. "Our community isn't as separated."

Donavan added, "Why do you think I moved away? In New York, I can be myself, and not walk on pins and needles around Mom and Dad. They love us but still...I don't think they want to talk about it. It's hard to compartmentalize my life."

"You always said you felt uncomfortable at home," Mick said. "I get it now."

Logan guessed that was true, but she hadn't been openly gay when she lived here. Regardless of her brother's status, she'd chosen to hide hers. The world had changed, and she was acting like it hadn't. In DC she was out, so what was keeping her from being herself at home? She thought about what Mick had said, about not being authentic. Somehow, she'd managed to internalize the idea that being gay would disappoint her parents, but deep down, she was pretty sure that wasn't true. She forced herself to relax a little. "Just order for me. I need to find the rest room." Logan stood and motioned to Don. "First, do you have a minute?"

Don accompanied her to the hallway near the restrooms. "What's up, sis?"

"I'm happy for you and Paul, really I am. You can call me a closet case if you want, but I'll do this my own way, in my own time. Okay?"

"Mick is soooo out of your league." Don grinned like he'd won a prize trophy.

Hurt by his comment, Logan shook her head. "It's still new. Who knows what will become of our relationship."

"Right..." Don's voice lowered. "Mick will break your heart. I've seen it before."

The door to the restroom opened.

"I thought I recognized that voice. Logan, how have you been?" Misty Parker, Logan's personal nightmare from high school, stood awaiting a response.

The head cheerleader, captain of the volleyball team, overachiever, and perfect ten looked as if she hadn't changed one iota. Long blond hair, hourglass figure. "I'd love to meet this Mick. He sounds like a dreamboat."

"Misty Parker." Don droned out her name. "Why? You don't have time to steal this love interest. We're only home for the holidays."

"Ouch, Donny." Misty added the sickeningly sweet expression that had always gotten her everything she wanted. "I'm curious to see who finally chose our little Logan."

Little Logan? How dare she? Misty had a way of making anyone feel as if they were back in middle school and the last one chosen for dodgeball. Did some people ever grow up?

Logan glanced back at the table. There sat Paul, the blond, good-looking barista who had stolen her brother's heart. His GQ model-like features were exactly what Logan needed. Determined to put Misty in her place once and for all, Logan marched over and took Paul by the hand.

"Honey, I want to introduce you to Misty, from high school."

Satisfied by the wide-eyed, open-mouthed veneer of shock on Misty's face, Logan grinned.

Paul said, "Ah... Hi, Misty."

"Hi, Mick," crooned Misty, looking him over.

The real Mick's nostrils flared as she ignored Logan and ducked her eyes behind her menu.

"Why in the world are you at Hamburger Mary's?" Logan asked. She sat down next to Paul and petted his arm as if they were lovers.

"I had to take care of details for my bachelorette party next week. The manager here helped us book Missy-B's and wanted me to drop by."

"A party at Missy-B's? How quaint." Logan wasn't used to going to either place, Mary's or Missy's, but she'd heard of them plenty.

She swallowed hard, feeling guilty at the way the other three at her table seemed to ignore the whole situation. It was her problem, but she'd dragged them into it. The cool kids always made fun of her at school. She might never get another chance to put one over on Misty. She'd been a thorn in her psyche for nearly a decade.

"You should pop in before you go. That is, if you're staying through New Year's."

"We'll see, I have a full schedule this visit."

Their waitress returned with a loaded tray. "Hope you all are hungry!"

"We are!" Paul pulled a plate toward him. "Nice to meet you, Misty."

Logan moved their glasses to make room for their meals. She dismissed Misty with a flippant, "Good luck with your wedding."

Misty left and Don frowned at Logan. "Oh, no, you didn't."

"Yes, she did." Paul moved the dishes around, frowning. "She certainly did."

"What?" Logan asked. "I just wanted her to think I was with someone hot. I'll probably never see her again. When else will I ever get a chance to put her in her place?"

Mick shook her head again, the hurt clear in her eyes. "Logan, that was so not cool."

Don sighed. "If you aren't ready to be who you are, that's fine, but lying hurts us all, kiddo."

"You can't involve the rest of us in your deception," Mick explained. "No matter your reason. That's dismissive of us, of our struggles. It's beneath you."

Logan looked at the meal in front of her, her appetite no longer there. In her heart she knew the three of them were right. Maybe she was stuck in another generation, socially. Suddenly, Logan felt as if she'd disappointed the whole world. Perhaps she had.

CHAPTER TEN

Cora met the gang at the door with a smile. "Did you kids have a good time?"

They'd only been gone a few hours. They each entered with arms full of bags from their trip to town. Mick sniffed the air. She'd never smelled a fruitcake, but that had to be the scent coming from the kitchen. The flour on the front of Cora's apron confirmed that she'd indeed been busy while the four of them were out of the house.

Doreen descended the stairs. "I hope you brought wrapping paper and tape."

"We did." Donavan held up a bag. "Hey, can we set all of these presents on your bed until we get them wrapped?"

"Sure." Doreen waved her arm. "But I warn you, I'll go to sleep early tonight."

Mick's phone buzzed. "I need to take this. Excuse me." She put her groceries on the counter. Thank God she'd set a reminder on her calendar on the way home.

"I'm sure you have more important stuff to do than put away things. Logan can help me. Take care of your business, hon." Cora shooed her away and motioned to the stairs.

Mick quickly made her escape and her way upstairs to Logan's bedroom. She wanted to be alone to gather both her thoughts and feelings. In the last forty-eight hours, they'd become a tumbled mess.

Had she read the signs wrong? At the hotel in Chicago, Logan seemed more than eager to jump into bed. It was fine if she didn't want a relationship, but why had she snubbed any advances since they were here? The nagging feeling didn't sit well.

With an opportunity to look closer at Logan's childhood, Mick traced the princess-dressed child in the photo wedged in the frame of Logan's mirror. Cora had undoubtedly made the rainbow cake with sprinkles. Ben was dressed as a clown and stood behind Logan to help her blow out the candles.

Logan, Doreen, and Don were lucky kids. The multitudes of foster homes Mick had bounced through had rarely celebrated birthdays.

Mick sat at the cute wicker vanity and checked her phone. No messages, no emails, nothing. She had given her staff two weeks off for the holidays. Work was the furthest thing they'd think of. The touch of her real-life sank in. Her life was all work and little play, making Mick a dull girl indeed. It was time she demanded more from the life she'd built.

She grabbed a photo album from the shelf and flipped through the pages. Was she falling in love with the Brady family, or was it Logan who'd begun to tug at the edges of her heart? They were all a hot mess, every single one of them. They were also loving and giving. Maybe that's what attracted her to them.

She'd never understood people who were still stuck in the closet. Especially these days and times. It wasn't like it had been ten or more years ago when gays had to be careful. People were more open-minded now. Maybe Logan was one of those bi-curious types and only wanted to try her wings. Either way, they needed to talk. Mick wasn't in the rescuing business, and Logan hadn't asked for help, other than at the airport.

As if thinking of her would make her appear, Mick smiled as Logan came in, even though her feelings were still messy. There was just something about her that Mick wanted to lean toward instead of away from.

"Hey, are you okay?" asked Logan.

"Yeah, but I'm not sure about you. I can't believe you set us up like that to cover your sexuality. Rude, Logan, just rude." She hadn't meant to berate her right away, but the deeper feelings needed to stay stuffed away until she could sort through them later.

Logan looked properly chagrined. "I'm sorry, but Misty was head cheerleader and all-around pain in my ass in high school. I guess she still pushes my buttons and makes me self-conscious. I froze and then acted stupidly. I'm sorry."

Mick pointed to the trophies in the bookshelf and then picked up the tiara from the vanity. "Looks to me like you did okay. What's this?"

"My crown from the year I was homecoming queen."

Mick's early teenage years without friends, cliques, or people to support her were sad memories. She couldn't fathom having the title of homecoming queen. "Yeah, you did fine. At least you finished high school."

Logan seemed to have only heard the first part of the conversation. Her jaw set tightly. "You might think that, but the tiara is the one good thing from that night. Misty stole my date and made the rest of my final year hell."

Mick couldn't imagine holding on to a grudge from when she was a teenager. "How long ago was that? It's your choice to live in the past or grow from it and embrace your future."

Logan looked truly remorseful. "You're right. Don made it look so easy. Nobody talked about it or made him feel bad."

"Maybe Don didn't need to come out. That's why it seemed easy; he was already living as who he was."

Logan gave her a quick hug. "I really do like you." She looked so sweet, so vulnerable, so unsure of herself.

Mick wished the embrace lasted longer. Logan was opening up to her. It had to be difficult to face fears of the past and those she presumed were in her future. Maybe Mick could find a way to help. "Were you bullied in school or something?"

"Never." Logan shook her head. "I've always been my own worst enemy. I've always been frightened of what I might find if I looked deeply into a mirror, so to speak."

"It's not up to me, but if we were going to become an us…I'm just saying, I refuse to be locked in a closet."

"Easy for you to say. You don't have anyone pushing you to succeed. You already have."

"I don't have anyone. Period." With all her money, Mick still didn't feel successful. "And what does being successful have to do with being closeted? You can be both, Logan."

Logan went to the door and made sure it locked. When she returned and put her warm arms around Mick, she melted into them.

"You can have anything you want," Logan whispered in her ear.

Mick took Logan's hand and tugged her to the edge of the bed, not caring that the conversation had been waylaid. "You have no idea." Her voice caught in her throat. "Money can't buy the blessings you have."

Logan moved closer and let Mick cry on her shoulder.

Uncomfortable opening up to anyone, Mick considered if all her wants were met. It was easier to concentrate on the woman who held her than dwell on her past. She took a deep breath and inhaled the scent at the nape of Logan's neck. It would be easy to nibble on the earlobe inches away. Easier still, Mick could transform the comfort offered into something more physical. Within minutes, they could tangle horizontally on the bed and she could push away the loneliness that seemed to be engulfing her lately.

Happy that Logan reacted to her advances with a sense of urgency, Mick forgot about everything else. Her wants morphed into a sexual need. She stretched to take off the T-shirt and watched as Logan unbuttoned her blouse. Mick kissed a trail from her collarbone to her belly button and made her way to the snap of the jeans.

Logan sat up. Her eyes grew wide. "Did you hear that?"

"What?"

A rapid knock on the door answered everything.

"Girls?" Cora yelled from the other side. "Dinner is almost ready. Why is the door locked?"

Logan choked on a giggle, but instead of covering her own mouth she placed a palm over Mick's lips. Mick bit her gently.

"We'll be down in a minute, Mom," Logan yelled.

Mick couldn't help wondering what would have happened if Logan hadn't locked the door. Would Cora have entered uninvited? Did mothers do that sort of thing? Mick had no idea. Then again, if the past few days had shown her anything, it was that the Brady family had few boundaries. They were semi-respectful of one another, yet their spirits continually bumped and shoved against each other, jockeying for position at the dinner table, in the car, during conversation, or even in a mall. And they made room for each other, even if the other person had to work their way into whatever the situation. They had each other's back.

As they redressed, Mick knew what she had to do. "Logan, you'll know when it's the right time to come out. I won't pressure you."

Logan paused at the door and looked at her with concern. "Are we becoming an us?"

"Could be on our way. Let's take it a day at a time, okay?" Mick tried for a reassuring smile. *God help me.*

Mick followed Logan to the kitchen. The countertops were layered with Cora's fruitcakes from her afternoon baking spree. The four-burner stovetop held dishes of meatloaf, mashed potatoes, gravy, green beans, and corn. A wicker bowl next to the stove held homemade rolls. Mick glanced toward the living room where Ben, Paul, and Donavan had set up TV trays. It seemed the menfolk were watching a game of some sort. She hadn't watched a good game in a while. Maybe she could join them.

Cora motioned toward the food. "Grab a plate. Looks like we girls will eat here at the table."

Logan started to do as directed then thought better of it. "Mom, Mick and I need to talk. Do you mind if we take our food upstairs?"

Cora hesitated before replying. "Go ahead. I'll pull up a chair in the living room with the boys."

Mick reached for Cora's arm. "No, please, Mrs. Brady. We'll eat down here." She turned to Logan. "What the hell, Logan? She's gone to a lot of trouble, and she's your family."

"You're family, too." Logan lifted her chin stubbornly. It was a ludicrous statement, given that Mick had been with the family for only a few days, and she'd known Logan for about that long. But the sentiment was sweet, however misguided.

Her mom moved between them and held out both arms as though to stop an impending argument. "Somebody needs to explain what's going on." She looked directly at Logan. "You first."

Logan reached for one of Mick's hands. It felt clammy. Logan's eyes closed momentarily, and her lips parted. When the beautiful eyes opened, fierce determination stared back at her.

Mick resisted the urge to run. When she squeezed Logan's hand, she hoped Logan felt all the support she had to give.

Logan nodded once and took in a deep breath as if gathering her courage. "Mom—"

A loud outburst from the men in the living room interrupted them.

Paul rushed in and grabbed a dish towel off the oven door handle and dashed back out.

"Hold that thought," Cora said as she took the roll of paper towels from the counter and followed.

"I'm gay," Logan mumbled to her retreating back.

Mick sighed inwardly. She wasn't sure how she felt about Logan's not coming out, especially since it wasn't clear what was happening between them yet. What the hell. Maybe this was what family holidays were all about, even if it wasn't your family.

Logan didn't know whether to be relieved or thankful as she followed her mother to the living room. Her dad stood beside his recliner, his eyes glued on the TV. "See that, son?"

"Yeah, Dad," Donavan replied without emotion, looking at his phone.

Her dad pointed at the screen jumping in place with excitement. "Never count out those Chiefs no matter the score."

Her mom wiped at the front of his pants. Paul, on his knees beside her, mopped at a dark brown glob on the carpet.

"What happened?" Mick came in with a full plate.

"Touchdown Kansas City!" Dad thundered back. "I may have dumped my food on accident."

"Great!" Mick emphasized her enthusiasm when she plopped on the love seat and balanced her plate on her lap. So, Mick was a football fan too. Another example to Logan of how little she knew her.

Donavan's eyes seemed fixed to his phone as he scrolled through messages between bites. Logan knew her brother hated sports and only sat there to please their father.

Paul, on the other hand, seemed upset. "Damn! Mr. Brady, you think they'll show the replay again? I missed it."

"Sure, they will," her dad said. "They'll no doubt replay that one over and over on every newscast tonight. And during the highlight show." He looked tickled to death to have someone as excited as he was about his Chiefs. Mick nodded in agreement as she ate.

Donavan had clearly had enough. "Dad." He drew out the name to get his attention. "We can't watch the highlight show. We have work to do."

"Oh, man." Paul sounded as if he'd received a punishment. "Can't we work tomorrow?"

Logan pondered how much time that work would take. She didn't have that much time to spend with Mick. She glanced in Mick's direction. Enthralled by the game, Mick stretched her neck to see the screen behind her mom. Mick's support offered only moments ago seemed totally forgotten. So much for eating together and having an intimate chat in her room.

"Ben, you need to change your pants," her mother said. "And lower the volume." She swiped the remote out of her dad's hand. With the game muted, the room plunged into silence. "The girls and I were having a serious talk in the other room when you so rudely interrupted."

"Sorry." Her dad sounded contrite, as if he'd been scolded.

"Let's continue our conversation." Cora took the towel from Paul and the discarded remnants of her dad's mess. "I'll bring you another plate, Ben."

"I don't deserve you," her dad replied. He turned the volume up and winked at Logan.

The banter between her folks was cute. Logan returned with her mother to the table in the kitchen, leaving Mick to watch the game.

Mom chuckled. "It's me who doesn't deserve him! Now, what were we talking about?"

Logan was certain that there would never be a perfect time to come clean with all that was jumbled in her life, but she had to say something. The secrets and anxiety of keeping them bore down on her. "You wanted to know what was up. I'll tell you." She pushed the food around on her plate. "I lost my job."

"I know."

If she hadn't just taken a bite, her mouth would have fallen open. *I'm going to kill my brother.* "How?"

Her mom put her fork down and patted Logan's hand. "We called the bookstore to see if anyone knew your flight plans. The recorded message said they were closing for good. There is no shame in this, Logan. A lot of small businesses didn't make it through the pandemic. It's not like it's your fault."

The hurt bottled up inside Logan broke to the surface. "We tried. Our staff went down to one other clerk and me. Then I took a pay cut. Online sales and orders increased, but not enough to pay salaries and overhead. As the manager, it feels like I failed."

"Aw, honey." Her mother stood and hugged her. "You're not alone. An awful lot of people feel the same way. You'll find something else."

When her mom's warmth encircled her, the tears Logan had held back finally came. "Don and Paul have something. Mick has everything, and even Doreen..." The sobs luckily kept her from saying anything else.

"We'll help, and you'll be okay." Her mother crooned and rubbed her back just like she'd done on homecoming night and other tear-filled times. "You'll find your path, I promise."

"You can't promise that."

After a heavy sigh, her mom added, "Oh, but I can. You may think I'm just your mom. But let me tell you..." She returned to her chair and pointed at Logan's plate. "Eat something, before it gets cold."

"Okay, so tell me." Logan took a bite and waited for the wisdom she was so hungry for.

"Stay-at-home moms get the shaft. We work harder than anyone at a real job. The only pay is appreciation, and that's sparse or nonexistent most times. Give me a second, dear." She filled a plate from the stove and delivered it to the living room.

While her mom was gone, Logan looked at the familiar setting. Subtle changes she neglected to notice were everywhere. A new arrangement of silk flowers perched on the island among the fruitcakes. People who made fun of fruitcakes had never tasted her mother's delicacy. The meatloaf she ate was heavenly. Logan's last effort at cooking had been a disaster. Her meat-lump as she called it had tasted like cardboard. *How does mom do it?*

"Thanks for dinner, Mom. It's wonderful," Logan said as her mom returned.

"Now, I didn't tell you that for you to appreciate me. It goes much deeper."

"But I do, we do, and no one says it enough." Logan mopped the last of her gravy with a biscuit.

"As I was saying," her mom began again. "Being a homemaker is *my* thing. And you've no idea how many times I've been asked what I do. Like it isn't enough. I am not freeloading off my husband. Because I don't get a paycheck my work doesn't count? The nerve of some people." She glanced toward the window.

"Anyone in particular?" Logan knew her mom and Mrs. Grassle tolerated each other and played nice most of the time.

"I won't go down that road right now. We all have challenges. That's what I'm saying. You are young. Life hasn't settled in for you yet, but when it does, you'll be as happy as we've been. Don't let your worry about other people's perceptions keep you from being who you are."

Doreen came downstairs to join them for dinner. "What did I miss?"

It was all Logan could do not to burst into a mixture of laughter and tears. One secret out, another behind a closed door. Slowly, the stinky onion that was her life unfurled. She couldn't wait until the whole mess was unraveled.

Chapter Eleven

O kay," Mick said once she and Logan had done the dinner dishes and joined the guys in the basement. "Hit me with it. What is this game about? What would make this *the* game for anyone to play?"

The four of them gathered at the table where the Brady family used to play cards and board games. Mick noted that Donavan had already set out a couple of large notebooks.

He tapped one. "We have all of our sketches and notes in this one. The written simulations and screenshots of them are in the other notebook."

"Did you finish any other degrees?" Mick asked.

"Besides architecture the year after you graduated?" He nodded. "Yes. I have a minor in art, and I'm taking online classes toward my MBA." He indicated Paul. "Paul's currently working as a barista because of the economy stuff, but his degree is in engineering, so between the two of us, we think we've come up with a solid game. It's named for you right now—*Finnegan's Treasure*."

Mick was taken aback. "Flattering. But why?"

Donavan excitedly dove into the topic. "The player, whether a male or female, is always the primary character. But the object they seek is another matter. The goal of the game is to build a character from scratch—ours is named Finn—and have them discover what makes them tick."

"How do you go from being a soul to a fully developed person?" Mick asked.

"You and I played games back in college. Think of the game *Spore*. Know how it begins with this microscopic organism, like an amoeba? And it grows? Same premise. We're all a compilation of our experiences over the years."

Paul leaned forward, hands clasped, eyes excited. "We are the results of everything, from those experiences to how we view ourselves. I think you'll like what we call the Forest of Distortion."

Donavan picked up where Paul left off. "The trees are mirrors, reflections of how we see ourselves."

Mick brightened. "Ah, I get it. How we see ourselves is often a distorted image taken from how someone else views us."

"Right! And it's up to us to decide which 'mirror' is real and which one isn't. The door you choose takes you down a certain path. Choose another, and it takes you down a different one. It creates a million options to see who you'd become based on different choices." Donavan sat back, a proud look on his face.

Logan, who had been quiet up till now, leaned forward. "How did the two of you come up with this?" She shook her head. "I mean, most video games are based on murder and mayhem, war…"

Donavan took Logan's hands in his. "You have to ask? You of all people?"

"What does that mean?" Logan asked.

"You've struggled with your identity your entire life, sis. You see yourself right now through lenses that aren't yours."

"Bull." Logan shook her head.

Donavan insisted. "When Misty is in front of you, you see yourself as she does, as someone not worthy of someone's attention. But you're not the only one with mirrors. I know Dad looks at me sometimes and sees me as quarterback Patrick Mahomes wearing the number fifteen Chiefs jersey." His eyes reflected sadness. "We have to get past people's visions of us if we're going to be able to choose another door and see where it leads."

Logan's eyes filled with tears. Mick didn't know which one of them to hug. Seemed Donavan had depths Mick hadn't realized, and she'd known him for years. As for Logan, she appeared more vulnerable than Mick had ever seen her.

"Gamer nerds read a lot," Paul said. "We can take anything and go deeper into it. It's not what appears on the surface that makes something interesting. It's going beyond and seeing how we can make it an interactive experience. That's where our true joy lies, and what's more fascinating than discovering what makes us tick as individuals?"

"Finding out what makes someone else tick." Mick wasn't sure if she'd thought the phrase or spoken it until Donavan's eyes locked with hers and he nodded slowly in agreement.

Logan squirmed. "Why do I suddenly feel as if I'm beneath a microscope?"

Silence echoed off the large room's walls for a few seconds. The ambiance was one of tentative anticipation, as if they all waited to reveal a secret.

Mick looked up from the notebooks. "Is there a way to interact IRL?" Seeing the puzzlement on Logan's face she explained. "IRL is short for in real life in gamer lingo."

"Oh, like the popular game the last few years where people got points if they were at the correct GPS locations."

"Exactly!" Paul told her. "I was thinking about that and, yes, we could do that. Say if the character went somewhere and did something. Not just be there, but actually interacted with the environment."

"Yeah, I really want this to be interactive for everyone, not just gamers." Donavan looked at Mick, his expression hopeful.

Logan seemed to be concentrating. "Players are forced to get out from in front of their screens? Cool." Her brow furrowed, forming a scowl on her face. "What if a player volunteered somewhere? Like a dog shelter or something?"

"Brilliant!" Mick shouted. "Touchdown, Logan Brady." She mimicked Ben's football comments from earlier. She stood and began pacing with excitement. "We could give avatars a level up when they go to coordinates of charitable organizations." Rubbing her hands together, Mick was on a roll. "And more if they repeated it weekly or monthly. Every city has food pantries, shelters, and publicity for those places is cherished. I've increased my net worth tenfold since the pandemic by giving opportunities to those forgotten." At Logan's look of confusion, she said, "I picked up businesses who had to shut down."

"As they help others they improve themselves in the game?" Donavan stroked his chin. "Very interesting. The doors they choose then lead them to places where they can have new experiences that help other people."

Logan understood the idea better now. "What about places that do rehab for the downtrodden?"

"Oh, this could be good." Donavan grinned from ear to ear.

"Alrighty!" Paul clapped his hands. "Anyone want to play a video game?"

❖

"Logan sure falls asleep quickly." Paul's voice seemed far away as Logan struggled to keep her eyes open.

"Always has." Donavan affectionately tousled Logan's hair. "Didn't matter where we were or what time it was, if Logan was sleepy, she found a place, curled up, and started snoring."

Whispers of darkness swirled in Logan's mind, seducing her into a deeper, more relaxed state. She felt light and floated seamlessly between realms of awareness. Dialogues from both worlds enticed her. One set held safety, the other danger. Torn between her need for comfort and her desire for adventure, Logan searched for reasons she couldn't have both. Suddenly, she felt pulled, torn, unable to reach either side.

"Wait! I can do this," she cried. "I need more time. It's not right—don't leave me. Don't make me choose yet."

Strong hands shook her. "Logan, wake up. You're having a nightmare."

"What?" Logan opened her eyes to see her brother standing over her, his hands on her arms.

Her head was in Mick's lap, and she stroked her hair, brushing it from her face where it had tumbled. "Wake up, sweetheart. You're safe."

Logan blinked sleepily. Somehow during her nap, they'd all migrated to the sofa, with Paul in her dad's lounger across from them.

Don chuckled. "Guess now that you're back in Kansas you may have felt like Dorothy did in the field of poppies, doped and abandoned."

Logan rose, stretched, and glanced down at Mick. It was nice to wake with her head on Mick's lap. She seemed soft and gentle and not at all what Logan considered a driven businesswoman. "Donavan never misses a chance to razz me about my obsession with *The Wizard of Oz*." She asked the time, mostly to take the focus off her. She blinked when told. "That late?"

"We've been playing this game for hours," Mick told her. "It's great!"

Still sleepy, Logan couldn't bother with the game. "The presents. We all dumped them on Doreen's bed."

Donavan laughed. "Believe it or not, Do came down and offered to wrap them for us. Mick and I found what you and I had purchased for her and pulled those out. They're in your room. That way she'll still be surprised when we open gifts on Christmas."

"Oh. Good. Thanks." Logan still couldn't believe she'd fallen asleep for so long. "Hey! That's the day after tomorrow!"

"Give the girl a cookie." Donavan shook his head. "Doreen said she felt better, well enough to do some baking." He indicated a tin of chocolate chip cookies and another stacked with lemon-raspberry bars.

"Wow." Logan had almost said *guess her morning sickness has passed.* She wondered briefly when Doreen would let the rest of the clan in on her secret. She took a bite of her cookie. These were almost as good as Mom's. She nibbled and studied the big screen over the fireplace with the game running on it.

Four separate squares revealed each player's world. All but one had beautiful settings. There were two displays of elaborate cityscapes and one in an exotic forest. The tiny stick figure in an empty room in the lower corner must have been hers. Logan picked up the game control she had abandoned for a nap. The figure bumped against a wall as she twisted and punched the buttons. Damn, was there a door?

Then the real doorbell upstairs sounded. The outside world had invaded. All action on the screen stopped. Donavan had paused the game.

He glanced at his watch. "Guess Santa came early. It's five in the freakin' morning!"

Rapid footsteps pounded above them. Shortly after, Doreen appeared and stopped halfway down the stairs. "Mick, it's for you."

"Okay," Mick said. She threw the game controller on the sofa and quickly followed Doreen. The guys shrugged and resumed their game while Logan tried but gave up. Whoever was at the door was taking their own sweet time. She could have spent that much longer with Mick.

"Don, who else knows Mick's here?" Logan asked.

"I have no idea." Donavan acted as if it was no big deal that someone had shown up at the house at five in the morning and returned to the game.

"Well, someone rang the doorbell." Logan had to find out and rushed up the stairs.

She heard the guys laughing as she reached the top step. They'd better be amused with something on the screen because she hadn't said anything funny.

Logan found the entryway vacant. A quick glance into the kitchen didn't give her any answers either. Muffled voices came from upstairs, so she headed that way.

"Good morning, baby girl." Her dad greeted her on his way down, yawning widely.

"Morning, Daddy. Is Mick up there?"

"I think she's talking to your sister."

"Okay, thanks." Logan moved past him.

Worry crept in. Mick wouldn't tell Doreen that Logan was gay, but if Mick confessed she was, what came next? But it wasn't fair to expect Mick to hide herself, either. Logan paused beside the slightly cracked open door to eavesdrop.

"Maybe you should talk to someone," Mick said.

"Ya think?" came Doreen's quick reply.

As they shared companionable laughter, Logan knocked softly, disliking the feeling of being left out. "Morning, sis. I hope I'm not interrupting." She pushed her way into the room. "Oh, there you are." She looked at Mick.

The room went silent. Whatever they had been talking and laughing about was done. The awkwardness was as it had always been when Logan entered her sister's domain. Logan shuffled her feet.

"And that's my cue," Mick said. She playfully placed a bright red bow on top of Doreen's head. "You two gals have fun. I know I will." She tweaked Logan's nose playfully as she returned to the hallway. "I'm going back to the game. Later." Mick hurried off to join the guys in the basement. Logan stood looking at Doreen, not knowing what to say. Mick's absence left her with even more questions.

"Don't just stand there. We have presents to wrap." Doreen yanked the bow from her hair and threw it at Logan.

"Wait, I thought you were done."

"I was until the airport delivered your luggage." She pointed to the purple suitcase beside the door.

"That's who was at the door?"

"Yes. Mick's stuff is in your room." Doreen searched for empty boxes and riffled around with a pile of paper sacks. "I have some still to finish, and we'll need another major wrap session since Mom and Dad snuck in this morning with more. Can you help?"

Logan sat on the bed and took in her surroundings. "Looks like the North Pole threw up in here." Wrapping paper, boxes, and bows covered every surface. "How can you move?"

Doreen shrugged. "I don't mind. It's better than when I got here."

Logan was confused. "Dang, Doreen, it's the best room in the house."

The pride of their mother, the guest room, had a spectacular view of the backyard and garden. Mom had beautiful classic wood trim and wainscoting installed and added a plush king-size bed. The room said welcome and gifted any visitor with a warm hug.

"This was my room for eighteen years. Do you see anything that even says I was here?" Doreen's face morphed into sadness.

"That was ten years ago. Surely, you don't think Mom should have kept it the same? You've been married and divorced since then."

The posters of rock groups and teen idols that Logan only got glimpses of because of the "Brats Not Allowed" sign posted on the door came to mind. She realized the forbidden room of her childhood still intimidated her.

But her big sister had softened. Logan instinctively opened her arms. Doreen rushed to her, bent down to rest her head on Logan's shoulder, and held on for dear life. The enveloping hug was smothering. As tears flowed, Logan considered it was hormones. She tried to comfort her.

"Do a dear," Logan crooned the old song they used to sing. It didn't work. "Tell me what's wrong."

"When I left, I didn't think I'd be back. I'm a failure. And now with a baby..." She spoke between sobs.

Logan patted Doreen's back. "You're going to be a terrific mom. If you let us, we'll all help. You are *not* a failure."

"Easy for you to say." Doreen pulled away and went back to the other side of the bed and ruffled through packages. "You can do no wrong. Did you know I envied you growing up?"

Logan was taken aback. "Why?"

"Because Don and I had rules to follow, expectations to meet. By the time you came around, you got to do anything you wanted. You were a free spirit and said exactly what you thought."

Was that how her sister saw her? Maybe Donavan was right after all. She was an adult now and should at least try to act like one. Though she didn't feel like a free spirit anymore, she liked how Doreen saw her. Logan cleared a place on the bed and patted the space beside her. "We have all day to wrap. Come talk to me, Do."

Doreen sat beside Logan. "I've been living in my husband's shadow, doing what he thought was right. I lost any sense of myself. I didn't even know him, and then when I did, I was trapped. Divorce feels like a failure."

"I wish I'd known what you were going through." Logan saw Doreen more clearly than she ever did before. Maybe she had misjudged her. It seemed Doreen was having a difficult time as she looked for her purpose as well. "You got out, Do. You can start over."

"It's hard being surrounded by all the memories," Doreen continued. "You got a degree. You moved away. And every time I talked to Mom, she'd chatter on about you and your life in DC or Donavan and his in New York City."

"But, Doreen, I was running away. You stayed. You're the strong one."

Doreen seemed to take that in with surprise.

Logan knew she could help and that this was the right time. "Do, the way Mom and Dad ignored Donavan's obvious gayness made me want to hide. I'm gay too." She expected some kind of reaction, disappointment or awe. Instead, it was Logan's turn to be surprised.

Doreen smiled. "You like Mick, don't you?"

This conversation should be about Doreen, not her, but her curiosity got the best of her. "What did Mick say?"

"Nothing, but I'm not stupid, so answer my question. You like her, huh?"

Logan felt the heat in her face. "Yes, but that's not the point. Do you know every time I talked to Mom, she sang *your* praises? How you volunteered at church, and how you worked double shifts at times at the hospital, and all about your help through the whole pandemic thing. I could never live up to that. And now, with the baby, she'll be overjoyed."

"It could be a good thing, I guess."

With a grandchild, a lot of the pressure on her would let up. Logan shook her head. "You don't get it. This child…" Logan placed her hand on her sister's stomach. "This baby is a new start for us all. The hope of the family will be a blessing."

Doreen placed her hand over Logan's. "Do you really think so?"

"I know so."

"Who is the father?"

Doreen shook her head. "You don't know him. We met when he moved to Kansas City and started physical therapy for a knee injury." Doreen chuckled. "Dad would like him. He's a former football player. That's how he hurt his knee."

"How far along are you?" Logan asked.

"Four months. Abe and I met last July, and…" She blushed and shrugged. "But I want this, Logan. I don't want to give them up for adoption, either."

"Them?"

Logan sucked in a deep breath and let it out in a whoosh. "Holy crap, Doreen. Twins?"

"I know." Doreen sighed.

Logan frowned. "Have you told the father?"

"No. I haven't found the right time. I was thinking of doing so right after Christmas."

"Football player, eh? He doesn't play for the Chiefs, does he?"

Doreen whacked her with a roll of wrapping paper. "I told you. He had a severe leg injury. He doesn't play for anyone now. He's a cop."

"You can't keep this from Mom and Dad much longer, Doreen."

"I plan on telling them after Christmas."

Doreen's door creaked open, and their mom entered. "Spill it."

"Mom!" Doreen and Logan shouted in unison.

"What? The door was already partially open. All I did was push it a little. Now, tell me what it is you're keeping from me. Don't make me wait till after the holidays. And don't tell me that you and shithead are getting back together."

CHAPTER TWELVE

Doreen gasped and leaned away from their mom as she entered the room. Logan stared, open-mouthed, at the two of them. Oh, dear. Was it Logan or Mick who hadn't secured the door?

"Mom," Logan began, "Doreen is right. This needs to wait."

She gave a huff and placed her hands on her hips. "That's not very nice of you to keep me waiting."

Doreen rose and hugged their mother. "Okay, but not right now. Can you give me a couple of hours or so?"

Their mom's lips curved into a smile. "Of course. I suppose I can wait until after we exchange fruitcakes with the neighbors. That's why I came up here, to enlist your help."

Happy to have some time before the inevitable drama, Logan sighed. "But, Mom, it's early."

"The earlier the better. Then we can settle down and concentrate on our holiday. I thought I'd have Ben and the boys take a cake to the Grassle family and have you girls take one to the Morrows on the other side of us."

"Thank you for not making me see those awful Grassles." Logan shook her head. "There's something off about them."

"Oh, Harry drinks a bit, but Helen is okay," said her mom.

"Well, Harry is still a jerk, and their son is a jerk in training."

"Come on. Let's get this over with." Her mom led the way out of the room.

Doreen's eyes closed momentarily, and she held Logan back. "That was close. Thanks for backing me."

Logan nodded. "Yeah, well, everyone else will probably take a nap. They've been up all night playing that godforsaken game. But you've got to tell your guy, soon as we get done with breakfast. Promise me."

"Okay, but I'm making waffles and helping clean up first. But you're right, I'll call him this morning."

They entered the kitchen, and something bugged Logan, but she couldn't put her finger on the problem. The kitchen was clean. All the pies and cakes looked amazing. She chuckled, though, when she saw the bottle of bourbon sitting between two of the fruitcakes. Had her mom had a bit to drink while she baked? Logan supposed it wouldn't be the first time, although she'd never witnessed her drink anything stronger than coffee.

The scent of bacon filled the air, and the guys and Mick came up from the basement, bleary-eyed. "Smells great in here," Donavan said.

"I think that's a permanent scent in this house," Mick said with a smile. "Morning, everyone."

"Morning, Mick, you're too sweet," her mom answered. Then she turned her head, "Ben, you and the boys grab your coats and take this fruitcake over to the Grassles." She turned to Logan and Doreen. "Where are your coats?"

"Sorry. I'll fetch them." Logan went back upstairs and got them. On her way back down the stairs, she heard her mother gasp.

"Oh, no. Ben, no, for God sakes, no!"

"What the hell?" Logan heard loud voices in the front yard. She peered over her mother's shoulder to glance out the window overlooking the strip of land where the Grassle property joined that of the Bradys.

"Get out there, quick, girls, before Ben and Donavan hit one of them."

Logan had no clue what had caused the ruckus, but she did as she was told. She opened the front door in time to hear Harry Grassle say he'd seen Donavan and Paul share a kiss.

"A fruitcake from a fruit, how appropriate" The derogatory name he called them was all it took to have her dad pop the old drunk on his oversized snout.

"Dad! Oh, my God!" Logan ran toward the two old codgers as they threw punches and tumbled into the snow.

"Kill him, Pop!" Young Cameron Grassle dove into the middle of the brawling men.

"You little son of a bitch!" Donavan pulled Cameron away and pummeled him in the face, causing him to cry out in pain.

"Donavan—no!" Logan didn't know what to do other than yell at him.

"Here!" shouted Cameron. "Take your stupid fruitcake back." He tossed it at the only targets who weren't fighting, Doreen and Logan.

The cake whacked Doreen in the forehead, causing her to slip on the icy ground. She fell and groaned.

"You little bastard—she's pregnant!" Logan clapped her hand over her mouth as soon as she'd said it.

"Wh-what?" Her dad raised his head. He had a choke hold on Harry and didn't release him, but he turned to face Doreen and Logan.

From the front porch, her mom shrieked, "What did you say?"

Donavan let go of Cameron. Shock crossed his face. Then unadulterated joy. "I'm going to be an uncle?" He doubled over laughing.

From her seat on the ground, Doreen groaned and flopped back into the snow. "I give up. Just shoot me. Now."

Logan ran to her. "Doreen, I am so, so sorry. It just slipped out."

Her mom joined them and held out her hands to Doreen. "Let's get you inside."

Doreen rose, then picked up the fruitcake that had caused her fall, and she threw it, returning a blow to Cameron's forehead. "How does it feel, asshole?"

"Son, did you just announce to the neighborhood that you're queer?" asked her dad, frowning.

"Oh geez, Dad." Logan couldn't help joining the conversation. "It's okay to be gay—and that's the politically correct term. But it's not okay to live like you are or say you are?"

"Well excuse me. I am new at this," her dad said in his own defense.

The Brady family's rainbow laundry was hanging out now, for anyone and everyone to view it. Sirens wailed in the distance and the sounds grew closer. Neighbors across the street came outside and stared. They looked more curious than angry, but Logan couldn't help wondering who of them had called the police.

Out of the corner of one eye, Logan saw Mick holding one of her mom's culinary masterpieces and walking toward their neighbors Mike and Karen, who were standing in their own yard.

Two black-and-whites pulled up, and four uniformed po- licemen walked up the driveways, two on the Grassles' and two on the Bradys'. Their guns were still holstered, but two of them carried metal batons. One officer thumped his against his palms, as if the action alone would diffuse any situation. All four looked as confused as the neighbors.

As the four police officers pulled members of both families aside to question them, another vehicle with flashing lights drove up and parked in front of the Brady property.

It wasn't until then that Logan noticed particulars about the first four responders. One was unusually tall, muscular, dark- skinned, and intent on talking to Doreen, who leaned against her for support.

"She's knocked up," the Grassle kid yelled with a cackle. "I hit her square in the face with a fruitcake, and then she returned the favor. I think the bitch broke my nose."

"Is that true?" the cop asked Doreen.

"Yep," she said. "I nailed the little creep right in the face."

"That's not what I mean." His dark eyes bored into Doreen's.

Logan studied him and located his badge. His uniform said A. Dixon. This had to be the mysterious Abe, the father of Doreen's twins.

Then she jerked her attention to what was going on with her father and Donavan. They were still bickering with Harry and

Cameron, and the Grassle menfolk were hurling insults and taunts, which didn't help a bit.

Eventually, the policemen had had enough and brought out the handcuffs when her dad and Grassle tried to take swings at one another again. Logan watched as first her dad and then her brother were told to stand still, turn around, and place their hands behind their backs.

"What about her?" Cameron Grassle bellowed as he was led toward the van, also in cuffs. "She hit me." He looked over his shoulder at Doreen.

Abe's handsome face showed a montage of emotions, from surprise to regret then finally determination. "Doreen, I have to place you under arrest. I'm sorry."

Doreen smiled up at him. "Abe, it's okay."

"You can't take her because she hit him with a fruitcake." Logan rushed to save her. "Please, don't do this. I'm the one who hit that little shit. Take me instead."

Before she knew what was happening, one of the other three in uniform stared at her sternly. "You were in on this? Turn around."

Her mom looked as if she'd collapse at any moment. To Logan's relief, she watched Mick go to her and wrap an arm around her mom's shoulders.

"I'll follow you, Donavan!" called Paul. "Don't worry, honey, I'll get you out."

Her dad was about to climb into the van but paused and shook his head. "I wish I could tell you to call our lawyer. There's no telling how long we'll be in jail."

Logan was put into the back of a patrol car.

So much for Doreen's waffles. Now she'd be lucky to get bread and water in the hoosegow. This had to be the worst Christmas vacation in the history of holidays.

Who in their right mind would choose to become a part of this crazy family? Any relationship she and Mick had would probably be over as soon as Mick got back to DC. Heck, if Mick didn't book a flight back today she'd be surprised.

CHAPTER THIRTEEN

Tears streamed down Cora's cheeks as she watched her family disappear in the distance.

Mick asked, "Why can't you call your lawyer, Mrs. Brady?"

Seemingly defeated, Cora turned to go back into the house. She paused in front of Mick. "Because we don't have one. I'm not sure what to do now. None of us has ever been arrested."

Mick thought quickly and checked her watch. Her personal attorney would be on vacation. She couldn't in good conscience disturb him. "Why don't you put on a fresh pot of coffee and let me see what I can come up with?" She followed Cora inside then went upstairs to fetch her laptop. Surely, there would be a listing for attorneys in the area.

She set the laptop on the kitchen table and called to Paul. "Hey? Do you have any idea which attorney is best in this area? I have no idea where to look in Kansas."

He sat beside her and pulled the laptop in front of him. He typed something then waited. "This woman, Ali Smith. She seems well known in the LGBTQ community here."

She could go to wherever the Brady bunch was being taken and bail them all out. But that might also embarrass them all to the point that they'd never want to see her again. Mick was pretty sure Donavan would get over it, but she wondered about Logan, Ben, and Doreen. The Brady clan was a proud bunch. Not destitute, but hardly wealthy. From what Mick had seen, Logan had held back telling her parents about her job situation primarily because of pride but also because she didn't want Ben and Cora to think she was back home expecting a handout.

Mick opened several windows on the computer. One window held jail information. Johnson County was big, and there was more than one place that might have housed inmates. She hung her head. Inmates. Jeez. That term made things sound so much worse. In another window, Mick pulled up the Johnson County Courthouse website and perused what they had to offer. Aha! A list of judges. She scanned the list. So many?

Enough, damnit. Start calling. Mick's first call was to the closest police precinct to verify directions where the family had been taken. She identified herself then explained the situation.

"Hang on a second." The clerk who answered set the phone aside for a moment then came back. "They've been taken to the courthouse in Olathe. Do you know where that is?"

"I can find it. Thank you!" Mick relayed the information to Cora and Paul.

Cora set three mugs on the kitchen table and filled them with steaming hot liquid. "I'll drive you. Beats sitting here worrying about all of them, but first I'm having my damn coffee. Those fools, out there throwing my fruitcake and insulting one another. They can wait."

Mick exchanged a glance with Paul. She hadn't thought Cora the type to swear, but the situation was frustrating, and she'd certainly earned her right to coffee. Besides, another fifteen or twenty minutes wouldn't matter. Even if it was Christmas Eve, the three Brady family members were probably only just now arriving at their destination and being booked.

A sickening heaviness settled into Mick's stomach. She wasn't sure why she'd fallen in love with the Brady family, but truth was that she had. All of them had snagged a piece of her heart. It would be easier to hop a plane back to DC and let Cora handle this on her own. But Mick couldn't turn her back on any of them. Ben and Cora were the parents she'd have chosen if she could, and she already thought of Donavan as a little brother.

The doorbell rang, jarring her thoughts.

"Who the hell?" Cora strode toward the front door and opened it.

Mick poked her head around the corner and saw the serviceman's uniform. "Oh, Mrs. Brady, that's for me." She went to stand beside Cora.

"There are several boxes," the man said. "Where do you want them?"

"In the garage, please." Mick turned to Cora. "Is that okay?"

"Well, it depends upon what's in there." Cora shrugged. "No live animals or explosives, right? Because this seems like that kind of day."

Mick patted her shoulder. "It's a present for Mr. Brady. Could you open the door for us?"

Cora muttered something under her breath and ambled toward the kitchen's exit to the garage. She opened the door then seemed to press something on the other side of the wall.

Mick heard the garage door lift and prayed the parts to the pergola or gazebo or whatever it was called were all there.

It took only a few minutes for the deliveryman to complete his mission. Even though she'd already paid in full for Ben's gift, Mick handed the man a twenty. "Merry Christmas and thank you."

He grinned and returned her good wishes before heading back to his truck.

Cora stepped into the frigid garage and looked at the box, reading the label. "I hope you're able to put that thing together."

"I'm sure Paul and I can handle it," Mick said, not as hopeful as she sounded. They were both far more comfortable with code than wrenches. "Couldn't we wait until everyone's home?"

Logan, Ben, and Doreen were in jail. Mick's few experiences with cops as a teen had shown her coldness with little hope of a good outcome. Once she was a grown-up, she'd made contacts in DC. But this wasn't DC. Mick felt out of her element. She also felt like more than a guest at the Bradys. Surprised to find the family had inched their way into her heart, she vowed to help them all. No one should be locked up during Christmas. And the thought of Logan being cold and hungry made her want to hit something. The need to protect her was overwhelming and strange, given how briefly they'd known one another, but there was no question that she wanted to ride to Logan's rescue. Right now, it didn't matter why. She'd analyze it later. Maybe.

Logan's heart pounded erratically. She watched Doreen squirm in the front seat. She'd wanted to sit next to her but hadn't planned on Abe being the guy to arrest them. He was questioning Doreen. The rest of the Bradys had been squeezed into the back seat.

"How long have you known?" Abe called from the cab and asked.

"A few days."

"And you didn't tell me? Did you even intend to?" His voice seemed to rise with each syllable.

Logan knew Doreen had to be ready to throw up from nervousness, but to her credit, Doreen faced forward unflinchingly. "Look, it's my body. Mine! And I haven't figured out what I'm going to do."

The vehicle swerved as Abe shouted. Then he righted the SUV. "What do you mean by that? Weren't you going to talk to me first?"

"Of course. But I had no idea when to tell you. I didn't know how you'd take it, for one thing. It's not like we've been sleeping together all that long." Doreen seemed to realize the two of them were speaking in front of her brother, sister, and dad. She turned to meet Logan's gaze. *Sorry*, she mouthed.

While Logan felt bad for her sister, Donavan seemed to be enjoying himself. He sat on one side of her and grinned like a maniac. "I'm going to be an uncle."

"Shut up, Donavan!" Her dad's voice was terse, as if it was all he could do to keep seated. He glanced at Logan. "Squirt, did you know about this?"

Before Logan could answer, Doreen interjected. "Logan saw me throwing up when she first came home, and when she asked me if I was sick, I told her I was going to have a baby."

He blinked before staring at Logan again. "So you did know and didn't tell me."

By now, Logan was ready to scream. Her neck stiffened as muscles tensed. With her wrists cuffed, all she could do was stomp her feet. "I've been home for like, four days. You can't be mad at me."

Don lightly kicked her. "Stop that."

Logan kicked back.

"You people cut it out," called Abe.

"Go to hell." It was out before Logan could stop herself.

Donavan giggled but winked at her. "Watch it, or you'll be sleeping on a hard cot tonight when Dad and I get to go home."

"And what makes you think you won't be spending Christmas in jail?" Logan asked.

"Because Do's baby daddy is a policeman." Donavan cocked his head toward the cab of the van. "A very large one. And I'm not the one giving the cops cause to fret over me." He leaned forward. "I'm also not the one who announced to the whole neighborhood that Doreen is pregnant."

Logan hadn't meant to blurt it out like that. But that twit of a neighbor kid was throwing a pound of cake at Doreen. Logan's brain seemed to come out of its snooze. "Who threw the first punch?" She looked at her father and brother.

Donavan shrugged. "I think I did. But Cameron threw the first fruitcake. That's sort of like throwing the first punch, right?"

Logan frowned. "I'm not sure, but we can lead with that once we go before the judge. Hey, what did Paul mean when he said he'd get you out of jail? He doesn't have money, does he?"

"Paul doesn't even have keys to my car," said Donavan. "I think that was just his way of telling me not to worry, that he'd do what he can."

Her dad leaned forward. "He called you honey, right there in front of God and everyone in the neighborhood."

For a second, Donavan looked stricken, but he didn't argue or make excuses. "Dad, I've been meaning to talk to you about us."

Her dad snorted. "Just like your sister's been meaning to tell me she's pregnant, I'm sure." He looked at Dorren. "Hey, when are you due?"

"In May." She paused. "There's more, Daddy."

His face seemed to drain of color. "More?"

"Daddy, I'm having twins."

Once again, the vehicle swerved, most likely as Abe absorbed Doreen's information. "Really?"

"Uh-huh." Doreen sat quietly.

Logan's dad looked at her accusingly. "And I suppose you knew this as well?"

Logan couldn't help feeling guilty. She shrugged and looked at Doreen.

"Daddy, I swore her to secrecy," said Doreen. "Besides, she's my best friend. I had to tell someone."

Warmth flooded Logan's body. Doreen's best friend? Half the time, she didn't think her sister even liked her.

A slow smile creased his face. "Twins. That's great, kitten." His voice softened with each syllable. "I can't wait until you share this with your mother. I think she'll be thrilled."

Doreen sobbed. "Not horrified because I'm not married?"

He shook his head, and his eyes filled with tears. "She'll be delighted, honey. Once the shock of it all wears off, she'll be crocheting baby blankets and booties, taking you shopping, buying you maternity clothes. You watch."

Logan relaxed a bit and leaned her head against her dad's shoulder. The holiday that had panicked the hell out of her a week ago suddenly morphed into something different from anything she had ever imagined. Gone were the gut-wrenching, fist-clenching fears. In their place was something she hadn't experienced in years...hope. Granted, she was handcuffed in the back of a police van on Christmas Eve, but still.

Thoughts of Mick flitted through her mind. How would Mick view all of this? Were the Bradys too much of a good thing for the lone wolf female? Would Mick adapt or turn her back, thinking the Bradys had too much domestic drama? She swelled with pride. Donavan had come out, despite whatever fears he might have had. Her dad obviously accepted Doreen's babies, whoever the father was and even if Doreen wasn't married.

One thing was certain. Logan had to come clean. She had to come out of the damn closet with her family. Now didn't seem the appropriate time, but then no time ever did.

Better yet, she needed to get honest with herself. She cared for Mick, and if she wanted this relationship to become one that was exciting, nurturing, and gratifying, she had to become...what was it Mick called it? Authentic.

CHAPTER FOURTEEN

Mick had lost her bearings ever since Cora backed the old Buick out of the driveway. They'd meandered through side streets instead of taking expressways. At some point, they passed a school for the deaf, crossed over railroad tracks, and wound up perusing Santa Fe Street.

Paul rode in the back seat and tapped Mick on the shoulder. He held up his cell phone. "This map says that the jail and the courthouse are side by side—my guess is that the courthouse is the smaller of the two buildings." He peered out one of his windows. "If you can call that small."

"Cora," Mick said, "go ahead and park near the jail—"

"Actually, it's called the detention center," Paul said from the back.

"Oh, dear." Cora took a deep breath. "Detention center. My children are inmates."

Paul cut Mick an apologetic look. "Sorry."

Mick picked up where she'd left off. "Cora, go ahead and park closer to where you and Paul need to go to check on Ben and the children. I'll walk to the courthouse and see if I can find someone there to help us."

"Nonsense." Cora plowed through the snow to the other side of the courthouse. "We'll drop you off first so you don't have to walk through this mess."

Resigned, Mick thanked her. She turned in her seat toward Paul. "You have my number?"

"Got it. Don't worry. We'll be okay. Just don't take too long, okay?"

Cora stopped the car. Mick climbed out and faced the brisk wind. Damn, it was cold. She shut the door, patted it as if to tell Cora to move on, and headed for one of the doors.

Locked.

Mick heard voices somewhere to her right. She rounded the corner of the building and saw what appeared to be a wedding taking place in a lovely gazebo on the courthouse yard. Sure enough, with frigid temperatures and snow billowing around them, someone stood before the couple, and she wore a long, dark robe. She had to be a judge.

Considering the date, Mick thought it better to wait for the ceremony to be over. Better to find one judge outside in the cold than to risk going in and find no one.

She leaned against the building to brace herself against the onslaught of wind. The judge seemed young and pretty. She wasn't sure how she'd approach the woman. A lot had happened since Logan had first thrown up on her shoes. Should she begin with the Brady men and neighbors shouting in their front yards? How would she describe the food fight without sounding like an idiot? Adults didn't do that sort of thing, did they? Certainly not with heavy, brick-hard fruitcakes.

She heard applause and cheering and looked up in time to see the couple kissing. Mick sucked in a deep breath of frosty air and shivered. This was it. What if she failed to get the judge's sympathies or advice? The strangest thought occurred to her. She wanted to escape, to run away. But why? She wasn't the type to be afraid of much, certainly not something like a legal scuffle. Mick had worked as a paralegal back in DC to help put herself through university classes. Not like this world was foreign to her. So why was she suddenly spooked?

"Are you waiting to see Judge Blankenship?" a female voice interrupted Mick's thoughts.

"What? Oh yes, yes. Thank you."

The woman motioned for Mick to join her. "She went to her chambers to hang up her robe. Otherwise, it might still be damp come next Monday morning when she needs it." She smiled. "Can you believe people marrying outside in this weather? But Blankenship's a friend. The couple had reserved the gazebo, and the husband is in the National Guard and on his way overseas."

The heavy door gave way as they entered the building. Inside, only a few lights lit the way through the paneled halls. Eerie shadows danced when they passed by on their way to the back of the long corridor that separated the foyer from the various courtrooms.

"What brings you out on a day like this?" asked the woman. She opened a door, and inside the room was bright sunshine, a deep mahogany desk and chair, several bookcases, and a coat tree. On the desk sat a nameplate—Ali Smith.

"So you're not the judge?" asked Mick.

"No, just a legal eagle doing a favor for a friend. She was nice enough to secure an office for me while I help her. But Judge Blankenship and I are close, so I may be able to help you."

"I-I-uh, I don't know where to begin." Mick cleared her throat and took off, starting with her visiting the Bradys and ending with the fruitcake war. By then Smith was sitting behind her desk, mouth slightly agape.

"Really? Fruitcake?"

"Yeah, and the whole thing sort of spiraled out of control when the kid—he must be about fifteen? Anyway, when he hit the pregnant girl with a cake her brother socked him on the jaw. And now they're all in the detention center next door." Mick took a breath. "I was hoping you could help get these good people home for Christmas."

Ali Smith interlocked her fingers, steepling them. She pursed her lips a moment before speaking. "Did you say this teenager called the pregnant girl's brother a fag?"

"Among other things."

"I see." Smith pushed herself away from her desk and stood. "Let's visit them all, shall we? And when we get there, let me do the talking."

❖

"I want my conjugal visit." Her dad gripped the metal bars of the jail cell. "And what about my phone call?"

"Dad, shush." Logan urged her father. The Bradys had all been lumped into the same two cells, men in one and women in another. The Grassle men had been detained in another. The women's cell was out of sight of the others—probably in case one of them wanted to pee—but she could hear every word said.

While her dad was probably half-serious, half-joking, Logan doubted the officers on duty on Christmas Eve would find him funny. They'd been in jail about two hours and already Doreen's back hurt and Logan's bladder felt as if it might burst. The men, it seemed, didn't have the same problem. Logan had heard the telltale sounds plus the urinal flushing. *Gross.*

Abe came into view. "Would you girls like something to drink?" he asked politely.

"A private bathroom would be nice." Logan hoped her expression looked pathetic enough to invite sympathy.

"Sure thing." He unlocked their cell. "You two come with me."

Instead of leading them back by the men's cells, he took them in the opposite direction and through two doors.

Thank you, thank you. Logan went into the small bathroom by herself. She heard Abe ask Doreen if she was okay, if there was anything she needed, and he apologized for having to arrest her and the rest of her family. That's all she heard, but it was enough to give her insight as to the sort of man Doreen had chosen.

And chosen was the correct term. When Logan emerged from the restroom, it was obvious that Abe and Doreen were in love, just by the look in their eyes.

When they went back to their cell, Logan heard a familiar voice. Instead of going inside her cell, she ran around the corner and gave her mother a hug.

"Mom!"

Her mom returned the hug, sobbing as she clutched Logan's hair.

One of the policemen moved to separate them, but Abe shook his head. "Leave them for now. Mrs. Brady, have you retained counsel for your family?"

"No, but help is on the way." Her mom looked confused. "That's all I know."

Mr. Grassle, in the cell across from her dad's, seemed to be coming out of his morning drunk. "Hey, I know you."

Her dad lurched for the bars and shook them. "Don't you talk to her. You're the reason we're all in here."

Before Mr. Grassle could say anything else, two more people entered the cell block. Mick and a small woman who looked to be in her thirties came in shaking off snow.

Logan had the urge to run to Mick and throw her arms around her. Instead, Mick kept her distance and watched the scene unfold from the end of the hallway, and Logan thought it might be weird to go running to her.

"Ali!" Abe seemed surprised.

She held up her hands. "First, I want to speak to the young man who called someone a fag."

Dead silence. She looked about until she spotted Cameron Grassle, hiding behind his father. "You. Come here."

Cameron reluctantly did as she asked and moved to the front of the cell. "Yeah?"

"The appropriate response is 'yes, ma'am,'" said Smith. "Someone should teach you better manners." She gave his father a scathing look before continuing. "Did you not know that it's against the law to discriminate against someone on the basis of sexual orientation? Well, it is, and it's called a hate crime, and it has consequences."

The kid's eyes grew wide.

Smith did what Logan's dad would have called *read him the riot act*, and before she was done, she had the boy in tears. His father looked on bleary-eyed.

Then she turned first to one father then the other. "If your neighbor agrees not to press charges, are you going to behave yourselves over Christmas? Because if you aren't, you'll sit here until next Monday." She narrowed her eyes. "And you really don't want to spoil everyone's holiday by having us think about this for the next few days when we should be relaxing and enjoying time with *our* families."

Logan didn't know how Ali had come to their rescue but was glad she did. She also was grateful Mick was still here.

Within a few short minutes, Ali had spoken with the officers, filled out the requisite paperwork, and the Christmas jailbirds were able to leave the detention center. There were too many of them to fit into her mom's car, so Logan and Mick told her that they were catching an Uber and going somewhere to get a bite to eat and talk.

"You deserve a break." Her mom hugged Mick tightly then kissed her on the cheek. "Thank you."

Mick had pulled strings to get them out? Logan did hug Mick then. She gave her a long squeeze and held on. In that moment she made a decision. Logan had made plenty of mistakes in the last year. She should have been a better daughter, sister, friend. Had losing her job and spending time with her family made her grow up emotionally? Perhaps time in a jail cell had been eye-opening. Denying her feelings was the real mistake, and she intended to fix it.

Logan would tell her family about her feelings for Mick tomorrow. *Merry Christmas.*

She turned to her mom and nodded. "We may be home late. Don't wait up."

Chapter Fifteen

O kay, alone at last." Mick said once she and Logan entered their cab.

"Where to?" the driver asked.

"The Fontaine," Mick answered. Then she turned her full attention to Logan.

Logan had heard of the fancy hotel on the Plaza but had never set foot in it. "I thought we were getting something to eat."

"The menu at the hotel bar is fantastic. I've been to Kansas City before on business and this is where I stayed."

"Oh." Logan entertained the idea of getting a room with Mick. The thought made her warm inside. "Okay, then."

"No offense, Logan, but I don't want to go back to the house. I've had enough family life. I want alone time with my girl."

Mick continued, looking a little uncertain. "Maybe we could book a room and have some private time."

"Right." Logan was glad they were on the same page. "Pick up where we left off in Chicago."

"I was thinking the exact same thing," Mick said.

Logan was suddenly nervous. She and Mick hadn't been sexually intimate in her childhood bedroom just steps away from her parents. Maybe Mick wasn't ready to be an *us*.

"To be honest, I'd have looked for something to keep us in Chicago if Donavan and Paul hadn't shown up."

Mick laughed. "Really? You were a basket case in Chicago, worried about what your family might be thinking and fretting over the loss of your damned panties. If I'd known you felt that way, I'd have bought you new underwear."

Logan was touched by everything Mick had done to help get her family released. "Did you already know that attorney, Ali Smith?"

"No, we met today. Though she did remind me of someone from my past."

"You haven't told me much about your past."

"You never asked. I'm an open book."

Logan chuckled. As a book nerd, Mick had made the perfect offer. "So, tell me more."

"What would you like to know?"

Logan started with something easy. "Who did the lawyer remind you of?"

"Ali Smith?"

"Yes." Logan watched Mick sigh heavily. She thought she wouldn't answer.

"Just a girl I cared about. Turned out she cared more about my money than she cared about me. It didn't last. But then that's the story of my life. People find out I have money and that's all they want."

Logan thought that sounded sad. "Not everyone is like that, Mick."

"Yeah. Well, that's been my experience."

The cab driver slowed down. He pulled to the front entrance of the fancy hotel and stopped. "You ladies have a nice day."

Mick got out and stood by the window. As she folded a bill into the cabbie's hand the man's enormous grin surprised Logan.

"Wow, merry Christmas and thanks!" The cabbie handed Mick a card. "You need anything while you're here, just ask for Jimmy."

Mick glanced at the card and placed it in her pocket. "We will. Merry Christmas, Jimmy."

"Happy New Year," Jimmy shouted as he honked. He gave a friendly wave and pulled away.

Mick took Logan's arm, and the two of them strolled into the lobby.

Logan was suddenly famished, her hunger raging for more than a bite to eat.

Mick walked with confidence up to the front desk. "Do you have any rooms available?"

"Ah, we are pretty booked. Let me check. We only have a couple of deluxe suites available tonight. How long is your stay? Miss…"

Mick handed her a gold card.

"Ah, yes, Ms. Finnegan, The presidential suite is all yours. Welcome back."

"Thank you. It's good to be back." Mick motioned Logan toward the elevator.

It was like being in some kind of movie, and she definitely didn't feel like she belonged in the presidential suite. Maybe other women found it impressive, but Logan found it daunting. "What about lunch?"

"You hungry or horny right about now? I can tell you which one I am." Mick looked down at her, her eyes dark with desire.

"Okay, but we aren't staying the night." Logan couldn't deny her own need as she looked into Mick's eyes. "I need to be home for Christmas morning."

"Of course." Mick pushed the top floor button. When the doors closed, she turned and stared at Logan. "Don't worry, Cora and Ben will have their little girl home for Christmas. But I want my present now." Mick slid her hand up Logan's shirt. The soft skin of her breasts like velvet against her palms. Mick had wanted to make love with Logan for the longest time. Chicago's hotel memory had haunted her dreams the last few nights.

Logan's breath hitched as Mick pinched her nipple.

"Are you going to deny me a present?" Mick began kissing her.

The elevator dinged.

"At least wait until we get into the room." Logan's voice shook with anticipation or raw attraction. Either way, she was finally the same girl Mick had met in Chicago, not the reticent half-in, half-out lesbian she'd become once she was among family. Logan bit Mick's bottom lip, pulled away, and ran playfully out the door.

Mick slid the card key into the double doors of the suite then pushed them open, inviting Logan into her world.

Logan's mouth dropped open in surprise. "You've stayed here before?"

She spun around the foyer of the large room. Mick could tell that Logan was impressed. Mick wanted to treat her like the princess she always wanted to be, the one who got to ride in the fancy carriage. This was a good start.

"Once or twice. I thought of getting an office mid-country and never found what I was looking for in Kansas City. This worked instead."

"Wow." Logan went from room to room, checking out the amenities. "There's a full terrace, a kitchen and everything."

"I know," Mick said. "And the bedrooms are to die for." She opened a door and the deep royal blue king-sized bed beckoned to her.

Logan followed her in. "This is a bit much for a lunch date."

"Oh, I plan to work up an appetite." Mick took off her shirt as she sat on the thick comforter. "I forgot how soft this was. Come join me."

Logan hesitated then came close and took Mick's hand. "I've never been anywhere this fancy."

"If you were mine, I'd pamper you till this was every day. You deserve it." Mick reached to help Logan remove her shirt. "You've been through a lot this week."

"It feels like we've known each other forever," Logan said. She returned a kiss and melted into Mick's arms. "How is that possible?"

"I intend to get to know you *a lot* better."

Logan reached for the blankets and pulled them back. She quickly discarded her jeans.

Mick removed her clothes and scrambled in beside Logan. She began the journey of exploration down Logan's slender neck. She nibbled Logan's earlobe and kissed gently at each freckle. Mick had wanted to do this since the first time she had seen Logan naked in Chicago. She could feel Logan tremble as she moved down her body. When she reached her panties, she laughed. "I remember how I stole these in Chicago."

"You can have them now," Logan whispered.

"Oh, thank you." Mick pulled them off with her teeth.

She entered her sweet core with one finger. The wetness she found was evidence that Logan wanted the same thing she did. "Oh, baby, you're as hungry for me as I am for you." She played with her clit and flicked her tongue against it.

"More." Logan bucked against the pressure.

"As you wish." Mick hummed against her opening and then added another finger. She played with her, rejoicing as she licked the sweet nectar. When she found the motions that made Logan purr, she repeated them again and again. As her walls clamped and spasmed around her fingers, Mick stole a peek at Logan's face. It was a picture of pure pleasure. Mick was elated that she had caused that look. She smiled as Logan grabbed at her hair.

Logan pressed Mick's face into her, guiding her, refusing to let go. "Right there... Right there! Oh, Mick...my God!"

"Yeah, right there?" Mick hummed again, falling into the rightness of being where she was.

"Yes, yes, yes... I can't believe...I'm coming again. Don't stop."

"That's my girl." Mick moved her fingers in a circular motion. The vise-like grip gave Mick a hand cramp, but she fought through the pain and tried a different action. Pressure on her clit and a deeper motion caused a third explosion. Logan practically hyperventilated. Mick slowed her movements and stroked Logan's stomach.

"Shhh," she whispered. "Easy there."

As Logan calmed down and her breathing returned to normal, Mick moved back to the top of the bed.

"You okay?"

"More than okay." Logan rested her head on Mick's shoulder. "That was wonderful."

"Glad you liked it."

Logan reached over and kissed her. "Can we take a break? I'm dizzy. But this is not over."

"Have you even eaten today?"

"No, they didn't feed us in the jail."

Mick should have thought about that. "Why don't we order room service before we start round two?" Mick suggested.

"Really?"

"Hey, I'll need my full strength to keep going."

"Okay, I want a burger and fries. I'm going to hop in the shower and wash the jail away."

Mick reached for the hotel book on the bedside table. "Not a problem. Go on."

Logan disappeared into the en suite as Mick picked up the phone. "Hi, can we get a filet mignon and a burger? Add truffle fries and scallops. Thanks."

Mick got up and put on a robe from the closet. Then she found two settings of silverware and placed them on the huge dining table. It was an extravagance to pay for a room for only an afternoon. Should she stay here and leave the Bradys to celebrate on their own? She really was embarrassed that she had taken their hospitality for granted. Besides, they might need time to settle things alone. She could stay here. It would hurt to not be with them, but she had time to decide.

She answered the door when their food arrived and tipped the staff member.

Logan looked like a new woman as she entered the dining room. "Wow! I keep saying that." Logan took the dome off her plate. "Looks good. What did you get?"

When Mick took off the dome on the place settings. Logan shook her head. "Geez, Mick, are you that hungry? I thought I was the one needing a second wind."

"It's just a steak and side. I got you truffle fries."

Logan picked up the menu and her eyebrows went up. "I would never pay these outrageous prices for a burger and fries."

"It's just money." Mick believed that if you had it you should use it. Besides, Logan should be given anything she wanted. "I like taking care of people."

"For someone who complains about money, you sure do throw it around a lot." Logan picked up a fry and made a sound of appreciation.

"I'm not complaining. I just don't like it when others think that's all I am good for."

The two ate in uncomfortable silence for a few minutes. Mick wondered if she'd overdone it somehow. Logan had seemed to be happy to get a room, but now she looked ill at ease. She couldn't seem to win.

Logan pushed her plate away. "I am grateful for your help today, my whole family is. This is nice, but I think I'm full."

"But you still have most of your burger and fries left," Mick said as she placed her fork beside her plate.

"I don't mean to sound ungrateful. But I believe you have a problem." Logan fiddled with a fork. "I didn't ask for this extravagance."

"You don't like it?"

"It's not like that. I don't want you to think I'm here because of your money. I'm not like everyone else you know."

Mick wasn't sure what had happened in the last few minutes, but she'd lost her appetite as well. The conversation had turned ugly. She had never opened up to someone like Logan, she *was* different. "Okay, tell me. What do you think my problem is?"

"Seems to me you have a poor little rich girl attitude."

"Oh, is that so?" She'd worked hard for everything in her life. How had she been so foolish? Mick had let in the Bradys with all their drama and now she wished she had never taken Donavan up on his offer or met his frustratingly beautiful sister. "You don't even know me."

"That's because you haven't let us in."

"You haven't let *me* in, little miss. What do you know about me?" It always came back to money. She'd let emotion creep in and now she was angry with herself. She knew better and now she was defensive. "What have you actually asked about me?"

Logan looked like she was going to say something, but Mick didn't let her.

"You or anyone in your family for that matter. Not one person has ever asked me about my life. Not what I do for a living. Not who I had in my life, or anything." She crossed her arms, closing herself off. "I knew I was invited here as an investor in your brother's game. Not as a friend, and don't think I don't know that. You and I started something, and you said you didn't care about my money. But you do, just in a different way. You're judging me for it instead of wanting it, and that sucks too, in case you aren't aware. I would gladly have paid your bail money, if I didn't think you'd have been pissed off because you're all so proud."

"The judge let us off with a warning!"

So she had, but Mick suddenly felt as if she had shared too much and allowed too much emotion into her orbit. She wanted to storm out and go back home. She should have never come here. Her philosophy of open mind, closed heart had worked for her in the past. She should've clung to it and not rushed forward with Logan.

"I'm going to get dressed. I think it's time we go home. I'm sorry if I'm a brat and out of line. I'm not used to having money, and none of my friends ever had it, so I'm not sure how to act when money is involved. I feel guilty when you spend your money on me, because I can't match it. Maybe I'm wrong, and you really don't see how differently we approach money. If so, sorry again." Logan looked hurt as she closed the bedroom door to get dressed.

Mick retrieved the card Jimmy had given her and picked up the phone. Logan was right. It was time they *both* went home.

Chapter Sixteen

"Miss?" the cabbie spoke over his shoulder to get Mick's attention.

"Yes?"

"Did you leave anything back at the hotel?"

Puzzled, Mick looked up from the text she was making on her cell phone. "No. Why would you ask?"

"There's been another cab following us ever since we pulled away from the curb. Looks like one of ours. Want me to radio and find out why they're following?"

Mick turned and checked for herself. "Unbelievable."

"Excuse me?"

"Stop the car. Just pull over. I'll find out what's going on."

Sure enough, when they slowed and stopped, so did the cab behind them. Mick tore out of her warm seat and stormed toward the other vehicle. "What in hell are you doing?" she demanded of Logan.

Logan jumped out as well, with tears streaming down her cheeks. "I wasn't finished talking to you."

Taken aback, Mick rocked on her heels as snow pelted them both. "You said you wanted to go home and I agreed. Logan, there's nothing else to say."

"Maybe not for you, but I need to talk."

Exasperated, Mick tapped on the driver's window, then fished into her coat pockets. "How much does she owe you?"

"No, you're not bailing me out." Logan pushed aside Mick's hand.

Mick jostled back and stuffed a large bill into the cabbie's hand. "I'll take it from here," she told him. Then to Logan, she muttered, "Get in the fucking car." When Logan refused, Mick took her arm and marched them both to the first cab. "Get in. We can't talk out here."

If Mick thought she'd run this conversation, she was mistaken. Before the cab even pulled back onto the highway, Logan pounced. "Why aren't you going back to Mom and Dad's with me?"

"I have to work."

"Don't give me that shit. Why?" Logan waved her hands wildly. "You have money, you have things. What neither of us have is the truth. I want to know why."

Mick's gut twisted. "We can talk about this another time. I have a flight to catch."

"When?" Logan demanded. "You're running away. I'm not going back to DC, so when are we to have this enlightening discussion?"

"Logan, I don't like your tone."

"Tough. Get used to it. I'm not the *baby dyke* you called me in Chicago. I'm an adult, even if I get a little crazy sometimes. And you're not going to run roughshod over me like you probably do everyone else in your life. Talk to me, Mick. I want answers."

Painful silence filled the cab. Their driver paid attention to the road, but his eyes kept darting to the rearview mirror, where he watched them carefully. In the silence, he finally said, "Do you still want to go to the airport, miss?"

"Yes, thank you." Mick kept her voice as even as possible. The poor man had likely seen his share of hysterics when he drove, but she didn't want him thinking she or Logan would endanger anyone.

Moments later, they pulled to Mick's drop-off point. She paid the driver. "This should be enough for my fare plus the trip back to Overland Park. Will you take her home? She can give you the address."

"I'll pay my own way, thanks." Logan stuffed her hands into her coat pockets.

"With what, Logan?"

"Maybe I'll hitchhike." Logan swiped at the tears on her cheeks. "If all else fails, I'll call Donavan for a ride. Either way, I'm not your responsibility."

"You're a pain in the ass. That's what you are." She shook her head and waved the driver off since Logan had jumped out of the cab and stood in front her, still talking.

"And you keep changing the subject. I'll follow you to your plane until you answer my question. Why leave early to go back to your job when I know you've taken off several days? What did we do that offended you so badly?" She swiped at her tears again. "What did I do?"

The entire time, Mick guided them inside, with Logan still ranting.

"What was it, Mick? Did we not pay enough attention to you? Did we not say thank you as often as you'd have liked? Or...or was it the fact that I wasn't prepared to come out to my parents on your schedule?"

Passersby stared. Mick responded by smiling a weak, uncomfortable apology. "Well, if you were worried about coming out, you seem to have lost your inhibitions." She guided them to a seating area where TSA wouldn't toss Logan for not having a ticket.

"Why don't you come with me?" Mick asked. "Then we can talk more. Once we arrive in DC, I'll treat us for dinner and we can..." She shrugged, unsure where it was they should go from here, or if there should be anything further between them at all. "Pick up where we left off at the hotel."

Logan's expression said it all. Fuming, she nodded. "Right. That will fix everything. You think all I want is your money, and I think all you care about is sex. Anything to distract you from answering and giving me truthful answers."

Surprised, Mick started to retort when Logan continued.

"You haven't even noticed that I quit smoking. I've only had one cigarette since we got to Kansas. But you're so busy nursing your hurt feelings or whatever it is you dwell on, that you haven't noticed. And this is a big deal to me."

Mick's jaw lowered. Logan was right. She'd been so self-absorbed that she hadn't noticed. "I'm sorry, Logan. You're right, and I'm sorry. Congratulations." She didn't know if Logan accepted her apology or not. All Logan did was nod and rise. "But not everything is about you, Logan."

Mick was tired. Maybe Logan Brady was a bad idea. They had too many issues they hadn't discussed. Mick was withholding, that was true, but she justified it because of the age and monetary differences. Maybe she could explain the walls she'd put up better when she was back on familiar turf. "Logan, I'll phone you once I'm home. Maybe we can talk then?"

"Don't bother. If you can't say it to my face, I don't want to hear it."

"Wait! I'll say it to your face. You and your family—you're wonderful, but you're all so damned dramatic. I'm used to no drama, no arguing. I've never seen a food fight in my life, much less the inside of a jail."

Logan nodded. "I'm sorry about all of that."

Mick shook her head. "Those are small things in comparison to what's going on between us. I'm out—you're not. I'm older and frankly, more mature than you are."

"You think I'm childish?"

Mick nodded. "At times, yeah. You overreact, and I haven't figured out why. I'm sure it has something to do with that chip on your shoulder about money and whatever keeps you from being honest about being queer. I think you're confused, and when you get cornered about anything, you get paranoid and you go off the rails. You say hurtful things without thinking about how they'll affect others." She pinched the bridge of her nose and closed her eyes. "I don't need someone flinging words at me like knives. Especially someone who doesn't know me or herself."

Logan snorted. "Childish and paranoid. Anything else you want to add before you get on that plane?"

"Yeah. I never said I didn't love you."

Chapter Seventeen

Christmas Eve had always been special for Logan. Enjoying her mom's hot chocolate and cinnamon rolls while the family made last-minute decisions on decorating. Boiling potatoes for the next day's mashed potatoes. Trying to guess what was in each present beneath the tree.

This year was painfully different. Something…someone… was missing. And she was exhausted. Food fight, jailtime, lots of sex, and a fight with Mick. None of this had been on her agenda.

"Hey, you!" Paul swept by Logan when she entered through the front door. He thrust a small cooler of boutique beers he carried toward her all nestled in ice. "Take one. You might want to change out of your bulky coat into a cozy sweater and join us in the garage. We're putting together Ben's new awning that Mick bought him. Where is she?"

Thankfully, Donavan shouted from the garage. "Where's my beer?"

The beer elf grinned at Logan and headed for the garage. "I'm coming."

Logan shook her head. "No, thanks. None for me."

She headed for her bedroom to shuck her coat and grab a sweater as Paul had suggested. Once she was ready to join the rest of the family, a wave of sadness washed over her. Logan sat on her bed and picked up one of her pillows. She didn't know whether to punch it or hug it. Logan brought the pillow to her face and inhaled. She murmured to herself, "It smells like Mick."

Tears filled her eyes. Pain pierced her chest, and her lungs seemed to quit functioning. She couldn't take a deep enough breath to satisfy her. "Talk to me, Mick," she sobbed. "I know you hear me. I feel your presence, so talk to me, tell me what I can do to make this right. I have to know."

A soft rap on her door shook her out of her pity party.

"Lo?" Doreen asked. "Are you okay? What are you doing up here all by yourself?"

"Feeling sorry for myself." Logan didn't know where to begin. Her lips moved, but no sound slipped past her throat.

Doreen immediately went to her, sat beside her, and wrapped Logan in a hug. "Oh, honey, what's wrong?"

Logan shook her head, still unable to speak for a few seconds. She buried her face in Doreen's shoulder and cried so hard that Doreen reached for a box of tissue and yanked out a handful and shoved them at Logan. It took several minutes for Logan to calm her racing emotions.

"Oh, Doreen, I'm pissed. Within a few hours I've been laid, played, and now I'm dismayed. Depressed to the max. And I think I've done something awful. Mick says none of us were really interested in her, and she said I was immature and mean when I freak out. I don't see it that way, but…feelings aren't right or wrong. They're just feelings. But what if what she said is true?"

Doreen kept hugging her. "Sweetie, you are one of the nicest people I've ever known, and I don't say that because we're sisters. Mick, and I do like her, probably has her own baggage. She has no family, so I'm sure she's built up all manner of walls. You know? It's probably difficult for her to connect with you, not because of anything you've said or done but because of those walls she's built to make her feel safe."

"Then what do I do?" Logan said between sobs. "I can't change just like that. She's out and I'm not. She's rich and I'm jobless. For God's sake, I can't force her to let me in. And maybe she's right. I'm not as mature, and I said some jerky stuff."

"Nope. That's up to her, and people say dumb stuff all the time. That doesn't mean you can't make things right and grow up a little." Doreen released her and sighed dramatically. "Logan, do you have any idea where she went?"

"Back to DC. Do you think I should follow her?"

"Do you want to leave? It's Christmas."

"I know!" A fresh bout of tears shook Logan to the core. "And no, I don't want to leave. I want Mick to come back home. I want a chance with her, but I probably screwed that up."

Doreen's lips creased into a sad little smile. "Maybe Mick will realize that she's welcome here and come back. Maybe you both need time for change." She sat back and studied her. "Logan, have you been happy being back?"

"Oh, yeah."

"No misgivings about leaving Washington?"

"No. I have friends there, sure, but this is my home." Logan's brows knitted. "Why? What are you getting at?"

Doreen shrugged. "I'm going to find an apartment next week. I didn't want to discuss this at Christmas, but it's time I grew up and lived on my own. I married and left home then moved back here after the divorce. I need to make my own way now, and I wonder if maybe you can't say the same."

"Me? Live with you?"

"No, dork. Get your own place, so you can get your stuff together. And have a place for privacy for if, no, *when* Mick comes back."

"Oh." Logan thought a moment. When had Doreen become wise? "That makes sense." She took a deep breath, at last feeling incredibly hopeful.

Doreen stood. "We'd better go downstairs and help with the awning...pergola...whatever it is." She extended her hand to help Logan from the bed. "Don't worry. Seriously. Do your best to get into the festivities here. It'll mean a lot to the rest of the family, and you might enjoy yourself. What do you say?"

"Maybe getting lost in the holiday wouldn't hurt." Logan dried her tears, took in a deep breath, and followed Doreen downstairs.

❖

With the kitchen now clean and her dad's porch covering in place, Logan waited for exhaustion to strike. When it didn't, she took a nice, warm shower and sat on the edge of her bed. Her laptop on the desk across from her beckoned.

"Damn it, I can't believe I'm snooping on her, especially when I know her secretary is the one who keeps her social media accounts going." She sat before the computer and typed. Seconds later, a page of links, all leading to information on Michaela Finnegan, greeted her. Photos of Mick's corporate skyrise in Washington, DC, even photos of Mick herself. Articles from the area's LGBTQ news magazine. Reports of her charity work reinforced Logan's good opinion of Mick and made her more ashamed of calling Mick a poor little rich girl. She was anything but. It went along with the conversation they had when playing the game her brother made. She was worth billions. Why would Mick even be interested in her when she had the pick of anyone? Gossip columns, in which catty reporters spoke of Mick's legendary reputation as a once-and-done lover, supported that fact.

Logan winced. How could she compete for Mick's affections when she didn't stick around long enough to form a relationship? Was she even worthy of her?

Someone had done an unauthorized biography on her—one of those tell-all narratives about the life of a rich and famous lesbian. The book didn't appear to have any favorable reviews, which of course said more about the author than the subject. Logan considered purchasing the book, then decided against it. No, she'd rather her knowledge of Mick come straight from Mick rather than some gossip hack who probably didn't know her. It crossed Logan's mind that the woman might have been one of Mick's one-night stands.

Logan closed the laptop. She wasn't writing about Mick, but wasn't her research just as bad? Intrusive? Wasn't this like spying? Granted, anything and everything was on the internet, out there for anyone to find.

Frustrated with herself, Logan gingerly opened the computer again. This time she clicked an article written by someone she'd heard of who contributed to one of the architectural magazines in Washington.

"Wow!" Logan's jaw dropped. Mick's loft shouted expensive. Along with the exquisite taste Mick obviously had, the apartment reflected shadows of something that disturbed Logan. The lighting was perfect, the place immaculate, but it seemed all for show. There were no personal effects, no paintings on the walls, not even a bowl of fruit in the kitchen or dining area. Nothing in any of the photos enticed the viewer to take a closer look, to explore. It was cold. Beautiful yet uninviting. Not the Mick she knew.

Now Logan was sadder than she'd been since Mick left as she pictured Mick in that sterile place, alone, on Christmas.

A knock on her bedroom door alerted her she wasn't alone upstairs. "Come in."

Donavan entered. "Are you decent?"

"Always." She rose and went to the bed, giving him the chair.

"So what are you doing? Aren't you sleepy?"

"I'm tired but can't seem to fall asleep." She indicated the computer. "So I looked up Mick on the internet."

"Ah, find anything interesting?"

"Yeah. I found out that snooping on someone I care about doesn't make me feel good about myself."

Donavan sighed. "And she's not here, is she? C'mon, don't sulk. You'll see her again."

"Oh, I don't know." Logan shook her head. Then she told him about hailing a taxi and following Mick to the airport.

"You did what?"

"Yep. I thought if I badgered her enough that she'd talk to me, but she didn't. She's a famous lesbian—I'm a closeted mess. I've got a lot on my plate, and I wasn't playing fair. Then to top it off, I pretty much told her talk to me then or never, because I'm not returning to Washington."

Donavan rose and went to sit beside her on the bed. "Oh, sis, I'm sorry. Not that you're moving home, but...oh, you know what I mean." He hugged her. "Mick can be insensitive, but that's not her fault. The second anyone gets remotely close, she backs off. I suspect it has something to do with her childhood, but there's nothing anyone can do about that but her."

Logan leaned against him. It'd been a while since he'd comforted her like that. "Don?"

"Mmm?"

"Are you going to leave your car here when you and Paul go home?"

He looked down at her. "Yeah, we could fly back, and Paul has a car. Why?"

Logan met his gaze. "I know somebody who needs wheels so she can job hunt. It's either that or go back to school, and I'm already an overeducated idiot. Besides, I need the money more than I need another degree."

"I'll leave the keys on my desk." Donavan kissed the top of her head. He got up to leave, then turned back.

"I really hoped you weren't right, but it seems like Mick only wanted a holiday fling."

"Hey, kid, you still got me."

She still had a lot of people in her corner. She forced a smile and said, "Yep, lucky me." Alone, she sat back and thought about her conversation with Mick and all she'd found out about her since. Mick had been up-front about who she was, and yeah, maybe she deflected conversations away from herself, but it wasn't fair to hold that against her. Maybe if Logan had grown up like Mick she'd deflect from conversations about her past too. And she was right; the family drama had leveled up this year, and Logan had definitely added to it. She needed to get her stuff together. It was time to figure out who she was, and who she wanted to be, with or without Mick. That was the only way to be the kind of person Mick deserved.

Chapter Eighteen

I love you, too." Logan's voice broke as she said it. "And I will. I promise." She turned to find her mom staring at her. "Look, I have to go. I know it's not for a few hours, but merry Christmas."

Her mom's expression held concern. "Was that Mick? Did you two make up?"

Logan shook her head. "No, it was Marcus."

"Oh. Your fake fiancé." Her mom busied herself measuring grounds for a fresh pot of coffee.

Logan blinked and her stomach dropped. "Somebody told on me."

Donavan entered the kitchen from the living room. "That would be me. Sorry, sis."

"I'd hoped she was talking to Mick," said her mom.

"Me, too." Donavan perched on one of the chairs at the table. "What did Marcus have to say? Anything going on in DC that you should know about?"

"And what did he want you to do?" asked her mom. "You kept reassuring him that you would do something."

Logan's chest filled with pressure of words not said, feelings not realized, energies not spent. "He told me why he refused to accompany me home."

Her brother and mother stared at her, waiting on her to come clean. Her dad, Doreen, and Paul filed into the kitchen.

"What's wrong?" asked her dad. "We're missing the game."

"Oh, hell, why not?" Logan shrugged. "I'm gay." No preamble, no build up to it, just wham, in their faces.

"Oh, that." Her dad poo-pooed her words with a wave of his hands. "We already knew that."

"I did, too" Doreen said. She took a deep breath before continuing. "Okay, when you told me, I thought it was just a crush, not that it was the real thing. It just wasn't openly discussed."

"Nothing ever is," her dad said, hanging his head. "And that's my fault."

"Our fault." Her mom stood next to him and took his hand in hers. "We grew up in a different world than you kids did. Nobody in our families talked about stuff like this."

"We thought you knew we loved you, regardless. All we want is for you to be happy. We should have talked about this years ago," her dad said.

Logan looked accusingly at Donavan, who held up his hands, as if to say *I surrender.*

"Don't look at me. I just blabbed to Mom about the fake fiancé."

"About damned time," Paul said.

"How long have you known?" asked Doreen.

Logan's exasperation bubbled over. "Oh, I don't know, since third grade? It's not like a pregnancy, Doreen. Nobody did this to me. I have green eyes—"

"Only one green eye," Donavan pointed out.

"And I'm gay."

Doreen punched her arm. "You could have said something sooner, damn it. I'm your sister, for Pete's sake. I told you my secret."

Her mom chuckled. "Not that your secret would have kept past another couple of weeks without everyone knowing."

The coffee dripped into the glass pot, and the aroma was delightful. Her dad and Paul stood in front of it with empty mugs in their hands. Donavan rose to stand in line with them.

"Ben, go watch your game. I'll bring you the first cup," said her mom. "You, too, Paul. Set your cup next to Ben's. Cream or sugar?" she asked.

"Both, please." Paul smiled in gratitude then left with her dad.

Logan's knees threatened to give beneath her. She looked up at her brother. "You really didn't say anything?"

"Swear to God." He bent to kiss Logan's forehead. "I never said a word."

"How did you figure it out?" Doreen asked their mom. "I mean, when it comes to guys who are gay, my gaydar goes ding, ding, ding, ding, ding. But if the gay is a female, I'm at a loss."

"It's a mom thing," she said as she poured coffee. "I'll be right back. Gotta take these two cups to the guys watching television."

Donavan sat in the chair their mom had vacated. "Logan, I never told a soul."

Doreen sulked. "You knew," she said to her brother. "You knew, and you never told me."

"Doreen, you know how tight-lipped the folks were after they figured out I was gay. I swear they hoped it was just a phase. Sexuality wasn't discussed. I wasn't about to bring it up. Besides, it was Logan's business."

"My fake fiancé was also my business," Logan said.

"Which reminds me…" Donavan leaned closer to her. "What did he want you to do while you're here? Why wouldn't he come with you? He knows our family."

"Marcus was upset with me that I hadn't come out to all of you. He said if he'd accompanied me, I'd have never done it. He didn't want to be part of that kind of lie."

"I'd say he was right, wouldn't you?" Her mom returned and pulled out another chair. "Now I can ask you questions. I've always wondered how this gay thing works."

Donavan choked on his coffee. Their mother rose, poured him a glass of water, handed it to him, then returned to her seat.

"Never mind, son, I didn't mean you. I know what you see in men—same thing that I do."

"Wh-what?" He choked again. "No, no, that's just wrong. I'm not talking to my mother about gay sex. I'd rather watch football."

"Who said anything about sex?" She grimaced. "And I just told you that I'm not that interested in what you'd have to say. I want to know about Logan and Mick."

Logan's tongue felt lodged somewhere between the roof of her mouth and the back of her throat. This was sooo not how she'd envisioned spending Christmas Eve with her family.

"Well?" her mom said. "How did you two know the other one was gay?"

"Mother!" Doreen cried.

"What?" Her mom stared back. "It's not like they had signs on their foreheads. *Lesbian seeking lesbian. Must have long tongue and short fingernails.*"

Doreen gasped. Logan buried her face in her palms.

Mom folded her arms across her chest. "Go ahead and laugh. There are no books in the little library I go to on the subject for parents. Ask me how I know that one. Besides, I wasn't going to have that nosy librarian asking me why I wanted to read about that. She'd have probably told one of our neighbors or someone I play cards with. If we haven't talked about sexuality here, how would I do so with others? It doesn't make me ashamed, it makes me uncomfortable. And if I brought a book like that home, I'd have to explain to your father. Well, that was before he and I discussed your brother."

Donavan quit choking on his coffee long enough to stare at her. "Y-y-you went to...?" He laughed until his face turned pink.

"The library, plus the little mom-and-pop bookstore I frequent. I even attended one of those twelve-step anonymous meetings held on the university campus to see if anyone there knew where to send me. I wondered if I'd pushed you away, son. And I didn't want to lose my youngest daughter because I didn't understand what she was going through. I wanted to be a part of your lives and thought perhaps understanding you might help."

Just when Logan thought the conversation about her parents' understanding or misunderstanding of gayness would never end, silence blanketed the room.

Don cleared his throat. "Mom, did they help you?" he asked.

"No, but I received two invitations to dinner that week from a couple of nice young men who wanted to get to know me. One of them said he wished his mother had taken an interest in finding out more about who he was."

"Wait." Donavan took another sip. "You mentioned a twelve-step meeting? I didn't know there was such a thing for gay folks. What's it called?"

Her mom blushed furiously. "I just went to the meeting and waited to introduce myself, then blurted out my question."

"Nope. Not so fast," Donavan said. "All of those groups are geared toward something. What meeting did you attend?"

She stuttered and stammered until she finally spit it out. "Oh, all right, it was a sexaholics' meeting. I'd thought it was alcoholics anonymous until the guy on my right stood and said clear as you please, 'Hi. I'm Pat, and I'm a sexaholic.' And then my tongue sort of stuck to the roof of my mouth for a moment. It seemed like an eternity."

For a moment, nobody said a word. Then they all started talking and howling with laughter and it grew so loud that her dad came into the room. "Pipe down, will you? We're still watching the game." He looked from face to face as if to make sure all was well before returning to the television.

Doreen leaned forward. "Oh, my God, Mom. What did you do?"

She shrugged. "I did the only thing I felt I could. I stood and said 'Hi, my name is Cora, and I'm an asshole. I'm at the wrong meeting.' Then before they could say anything, I added that while I was there, and they were there, I had a question. So I asked where I could find information for parents on homosexuality so I could better understand my kids."

Donavan set his mug and glass on the counter, wiped tears of laughter from his eyes, then hugged his mother. "Mom, libraries are full of books on LGBTQ issues."

"I know they're there. What I don't know is which to read first, what is garbage and what would tell me what I needed." She wrung her hands. "I get so confused as it is."

Doreen patted her hands and told Donavan to leave it alone. "Mom barely knows how to check her email and find recipes."

Logan looked at her siblings' faces and felt the love that connected the entire family. They were quirky as hell. They didn't have a lot of money, but they got by. A fleeting sadness engulfed her for a moment. She needed to call Marcus back and tell him she'd made a decision, that she'd be moving out of their shared apartment. Even if it cost her a relationship with Mick, Logan needed to do something to get her own life back on track.

Her mom drained what was left of her coffee. "I still don't understand why you promised Marcus you'd do something."

"I told him I'd come out to my entire family." Logan thought a moment. "And he was right. I'm glad I did this. I don't know what I was afraid of, or why it took me so long."

She patted her hands. "Honey, you did the right thing." She stood, placed her chair beneath the table, and told them to scoot while she prepared lunch. "Don't the rest of you need to complete the assembly of Mick's gift for your dad?"

Donavan snapped his fingers. "I'm on it. I'll get Paul to help me move it to the back so we can attach it to the patio. It's a shame Mick will miss Dad's Christmas evening feast."

Her mom placed her hand on Logan's shoulder. "Don't worry, honey. I'm sure she'll be back. We just have to be patient. In the meantime, it's Christmas."

Logan knew what that meant. People depended on her to do her part, to put on a happy face, to help set the table, construct the patio covering, clear away the debris their celebrating left behind. She wasn't about to let them down because she had her own crap to deal with.

She walked through the house to the garage, warming to the laughter of her family. She'd considered them dysfunctional as hell for years. She'd taken them and their generous spirits for granted. What with the virus infecting the entire world, and public transportation only available intermittently, Logan had imagined that spending time with her family would drive her insane. Instead, she discovered she'd missed them. She'd become fond of the idiosyncrasies that had irritated her. And she'd fallen in love all over again with the community she'd fled.

Life continued, but it sure would have been more enjoyable if Mick were with them.

CHAPTER NINETEEN

Mick woke on Christmas Day cold and exhausted. In the Dupont Circle area of DC, it felt nothing like home. She tossed and turned in the huge California king-sized bed. She not only missed curling up against Logan's warmth, she missed the crowded small bed with its heavy homemade quilts.

Mick stumbled from her starkly white bedroom. She remembered the blue velvet headboard in the presidential suite. Whatever made her think white was even a color? She'd once thought of this modern, sterile apartment as evidence of her success. Today, her surroundings seemed harsh, rigid and lacking. Once in her ultra-modern kitchen, she looked at the chrome accents, marble countertops, and glossy tile. The finishes she had taken care to select might as well have been cardboard. There was no character, no personality, no soul. With no smells of baking or sounds of chatter, nothing felt homey here.

Coffee, she needed large amounts of coffee. She opened her refrigerator. The contents were bare, just like her heart. As she filled her carafe with water, the phone rang.

She had avoided her phone on the plane. She wasn't sure if she dreaded or looked forward to a call from Kansas. A quick glance told her it was her secretary, Georgette.

"Hello."

"Oh good, you're home. How was your flight?" Georgette asked.

Why would she call on Christmas? "Georgie, is everything okay?"

Georgette chuckled. "That's supposed to be my line, boss. When you called wanting the company jet in Kansas City yesterday, I wondered why you came home early. Weren't you going to take off for two weeks?"

"Yeah, well, I needed to get back to work." Mick retrieved a small white china cup from the dishwasher. She thought of the huge brown mug that she used in Kansas. She absently poured coffee. "But don't worry, you won't have to come in till the fourth."

Georgette seemed to have covered the phone and mumbled something to someone in the background. "Did the meeting with the gamers go okay? And what's with the money you had transferred to your personal account?"

"Turns out, I didn't need it." She took a sip of coffee and winced at the pain. "Damn it all to hell!" The jerk reaction spilled hot liquid on the counter and splashed on her bare feet. "I just spilled my coffee." Her lip, where Logan had bucked against her, had swollen. The bruise reminded her of the best part of yesterday.

Georgette brought her back to reality. "I could come by later, if you want." More muted conversation commenced before she returned. "Really, Mick, whatever you want."

Mick didn't know what she wanted. But she certainly wouldn't ruin another family's holiday. She mopped at the coffee with a kitchen towel. "No, you go on back to your company. Enjoy the holiday." She remembered Georgette had people coming in from out of town. Seeing life outside of work at the Bradys' had made Mick realize her life was limited. Had she taken advantage of Georgette's life outside of work?

"You still there?"

"Yeah. Thanks for calling and thanks for getting me home. But don't worry about me."

"Easier said than done. You've never cut a business trip short before."

It was Mick's turn to laugh. "It wasn't *all* business."

"Oh?" Georgette's voice pitched high with curiosity. "Did you meet someone?"

Yeah, a whole family of someones. Mick didn't think she was ready to share how she'd messed up again. Georgette would listen and gladly commiserate with her. Her loyalty was something Mick could always count on. With little prompting Georgette would drop everything in a heartbeat. Mick refused to let her this time. "We'll talk later. Go have a merry Christmas. And, Georgie, thanks again."

"Merry Christmas, Mick."

The empty apartment's vibe suddenly went from cold to frosty.

Mick had to get out of there. So what if it was Christmas? She'd go to the office and get lost in what she did know. She quickly got dressed.

When Mick checked her phone again before she left the apartment, there were no texts, emails, or voice mails. The absence of any communication was a sad reminder that Mick was alone again for another Christmas.

And whose fault was that?

Mick reflected on what her life was like before she had money as she walked toward the Metro. At the first street curb, she took in a deep breath. The smell of moisture in the air spoke of snow that could begin at any time. If she increased her pace, she'd get a mini workout, clear her mind, and beat the weather. She pulled the scarf tightly about her neck and took off. As she came to an antique store, she couldn't help but stop as she was inundated with thoughts of Logan.

The display of books in the window impressed her. On top of the stack, a well-loved copy of *The Wonderful World of Oz* enticed her to enter. Instinctively, Mick grabbed the handle and pulled. The door didn't budge, of course, since it was Christmas Day. *Damn! What a perfect gift for Logan.* The sign said *closed* in bold letters. The hours posted noted they would open later that week. Mick resolved to return if she had time.

Determined again to distract herself, Mick shook her hands and limbered up again. She jogged the entire two blocks to the nearest Metro station. Red and green tinsel were draped in store windows. The poles of streetlamps were covered in red and white ribbon to look like candy canes. Christmas cheer displayed on the streets devoid of people made Mick feel like she did every year on this day, alone and forgotten in the world.

The Metro Red Line was nearly vacant. She exhaled as her racing heart slowed and she regulated her breathing. Puffs of air showed like clouds of fog. The only other person in the car seemed to be a sleeping bum. Mick couldn't tell the sex of person, and she wondered if the huddled mass was asleep or dead. The thin gray blanket pulled up to their knit cap couldn't have given much warmth.

Memories of Mick's past overcame her. How many times had she huddled in an empty car trying to catch sleep? If the library closed back then, it forced Mick to take refuge anywhere she could find. God, she had hated holidays, when not only was she cold and sleeping rough, but she was most decidedly alone.

A bell chimed, signaling a stop, and the figure moved. The brilliant green eyes that turned Mick's way reminded her of Logan's. The young girl looked around. She pulled the blanket closer around her and stood at the door. She paused for a fraction of a second. "Merry Christmas," she said. Then she stumbled onto the platform.

"Wait!" Mick went after her.

The ragamuffin turned, her eyes full of confusion. "You talking to me?"

Yes, she was, and suddenly Mick knew why. "I am." Mick strode toward the girl with confidence. *What had she wanted at that age?* Anyone to care. Mick reached out her hand to touch the girl's. "My God, you're ice cold!" She promptly dug into her pockets for her gloves. "Here." She held them out as an offering.

The Metro bell sounded again, and the doors closed.

"You'll miss your ride." The girl pointed to the subway as it disappeared in the tunnel. "You don't ride the Metro often, do you?"

"Why do you ask that?"

"Because your sense of timing sucks. You jumped like you were surprised when those doors closed."

"I did? Why don't we get some hot cocoa?" Had Mick seen hope in the girl's expression?

"Why?" The question came in a shaky whisper.

Mick wanted to give her more than just a handout. "It's Christmas. I don't need a reason, but it looks like maybe we could both do with some company."

The girl tugged on the gloves as she shuffled alongside Mick, and she moved as if walking through a fog. Her oversized galoshes scraped against the floor with every heavy step.

"Where in the world are your people?" The shrug sent Mick's way didn't answer her questions. "I know there's a convenience store near this stop. Come on."

At the top of the escalator, Mick waited. Huge soft flakes of snow fell, wetting her hair. She put her arm around the girl, who immediately stiffened. The kid reeked and needed a bath. Mick gave her a slight squeeze anyway. Then Mick quickly directed her to the storefront.

"Thank God, you're open." Mick smiled at the guy behind the counter.

"Yeah, merry Christmas." The disinterest of his tone said the opposite of merry. He returned to reading the paper.

Mick took in the whiff of burned coffee. She busied herself making two hot cocoas at the drink station. What could she do? She had to do something.

The girl plopped onto a barstool at a narrow ledge that looked out onto the street. The kid looked as if she was going to bolt any second. With her back to the wall, she watched Mick's every move like an animal watching their prey.

Mick grabbed two pastry snacks and paid for her purchases.

"I can never pass these up. I love junk food," Mick said as she placed the sweet in front of the girl.

The girl ripped into the wrapper and nearly inhaled the snack. With her mouth full, she mumbled, "Like I said, why?" She took a sip of cocoa. "You've done your good deed for the day." She began to bundle up with the thin gray blanket. "I'll just be on my way."

"Not so fast, little lady," Mick said, hoping to keep her from disappearing into the snow beginning to fall outside. The heat of the cocoa scorched the roof of Mick's mouth. She ignored the pain. "I need to talk with you."

"If you're into little girl sex, I don't roll that way. Sorry."

"What?" Mick shook her head. "No, God no, not at all." She gave what she hoped was an empathetic smile. "You asked why. I'd like to tell you."

The girl's eyes were glued to Mick's pastry.

Mick pushed it over and nodded. "Go ahead, eat while you listen." She took another drink of cocoa and a deep breath. "It's something I avoid talking about. It's going to take a moment."

Mick had been interviewed tons of times. Sound-bite answers for questions concerning her past wouldn't work today. The cold, hard truth was called for.

"I've been where you are. I slept on that same train years ago." Her hands began shaking. A hitch in her voice made her stop. "How old are you?"

"Sixteen."

Mick cleared her throat. "Really?"

"Okay, almost fifteen." The girl took another bite.

Mick nodded as she thought back to those years. "At fifteen..." Her voice quivered. This conversation felt more important than any Mick had ever had. "I slept in doorways, under bridges, and knew all the safe alleys in the area."

Was the girl listening? She'd slowed down eating and the blanket hung loose on her shoulders.

"It gets better. You just have to focus."

"Easy for you to say. You have fancy clothes, an expensive coat, and you're gorgeous." The child caressed the gloves on her hands. Wide eyes pleaded for answers. "How did *you* do it?"

Mick found it hard to breathe. "It's not easy. But it's also not impossible." Nothing was impossible if you were focused. But the kid didn't need platitudes. She wanted specifics. "You need an address. Just a P.O. box will work." Street life was hard and there was so much Mick wanted to share. "Oh, and don't drop your schooling."

"Yeah, stay in school. I've heard it all before."

"No, you haven't." Mick loosened her scarf and rubbed the back of her neck. "Looking back, I wished I'd listened. It's hard to find work and stay out of the system at your age. It's even tougher to get your GED at the same time."

It appeared the kid had heard. The smirk on her face morphed into a scowl of concentration. Was she thinking about the words Mick said or the fact that her cocoa was drained?

"Do you have a safe place to stay? There's a church a couple of blocks from here. Father Robert would take you in."

The girl nodded. "I know the place."

"Good. When they trusted me enough to let me volunteer was when it came together for me. Soup kitchens have more than food. The benefit of returning to the same one is crucial. They know shelters with room and programs to help you."

The kid looked interested now.

"I did dishes and they let me take home leftovers. Two meals in one day, not a bad trade."

The girl stood and took off the gloves. "Thanks," she said.

"You keep them." Mick put her thick scarf around the teen's neck. "Take care of yourself. And let people help you."

"I will, and thanks. Really." She walked out the door in the direction of Father Robert's church.

Mick followed her out to the sidewalk and shivered. She had gone from a loner kid to loner adult without letting anyone get close. That was no one's fault but hers. She took in a gulp of air. All she could think of was something Father Robert had told her years ago. *The truth will make you free.* The temperature should have chilled her, yet she was warm inside. She walked toward a gleaming high-rise in the distance.

❖

Once in her office, Mick settled down to business. The interaction with the young homeless girl had spurred her on. She'd make a donation to every mission and homeless shelter in the area.

She'd been making calls and transferring funds for hours, when her stomach growled. She meandered to the break room and pulled open the refrigerator door.

She had to laugh. Sitting on the shelf was a familiar circular tin. She would never think of fruitcake again without the memory of the Bradys haunting her. She snacked on the treat, which paled in comparison to Cora's.

Christmas had been like a swear word to her in the past. Why hadn't she accepted any invitation to a holiday gathering till now? Donavan's family had snuck into her heart. She could finally see the blessing a family could be. She wanted that blessing more than any amount of success.

When she turned on the TV, a story about kids crazy about some new tech game greeted her. That brought to mind Donavan and Paul's game. The game would be great. *Finnegan's Treasure* could be a way to show people how to be of service to others. It could spur a whole new phase of giving, community, and purpose to lost souls. Like herself, and the girl from the subway. It could be so much more than a game. Mick still wanted to finance it.

But had she already burned that bridge, too?

CHAPTER TWENTY

Mick had fallen asleep on the couch in her office. She woke with a pain in her neck, stretched, and massaged it. She had dreamt of Logan, of course. Never before had she experienced such instant responses to her caresses. The way Logan moved under her hands had Mick thinking this was special. No, she knew she was, and wanted more. Better yet was the emotional connection between them. Yes, Logan had issues, but who didn't? And yeah, there was an age difference between them, but so what? They could overcome that.

But she had ruined that. She'd gotten pissed off at the accusations that were no doubt true. Offended, and like a brat, she had gone home. Suddenly, Mick felt like Scrooge, disoriented. Had she slept through the whole Christmas holiday? If so, this wouldn't be the first time. What she hadn't revealed to Logan during their argument at the airport was that she had never shared the holiday with a significant other. Somehow loneliness during the holiday was her norm. Mick told herself that it was best she didn't have to worry about someone else.

She had a friend who had been married and divorced more times than she could count. Once when LeAnn had been drinking, she confessed that if she divorced prior to December thirty-first she could file single on her next year's income tax forms. Afterward, Georgette referred to LeAnn as a tax bride and seemed to cringe every time LeAnn visited.

Now, she examined things in her life she'd not considered. If this relationship with Logan was to work, one of them needed to relocate. Logan was comfortable in both DC and Kansas City, but she couldn't presently afford DC's higher cost of living. Cost wasn't a factor for Mick, but she'd need to change her primary place of employment if she was the one to relocate.

Mick gathered her things together to head back to her apartment. She decided to get off the Metro a few stops early and walk home to clear her head. She could make this right. First, she had to get Georgette on board. She opened her phone and texted.

Can you get away and meet me today?

Three dots signaled an answer being typed. It appeared instantly.

Whenever you want.

Good old Georgette. If she could help, she would.

This was Mick's city. She loved the Bohemian style, the scattered park benches with permanent chessboards, where everyone from the homeless to the aristocracy felt comfortable to sit, chat, and enjoy a game or two. Mick winced at the thought of not seeing her favorite Beaux-Arts architecture. She'd also miss the June festivities of the annual Gay Pride Parade and the October hysterics of the High Heel Race as a bevy of drag queens raced three blocks or so wearing their outlandish garb and the highest heels they could find. But she and Logan could visit the city often if they chose. Mick could even keep her apartment so they'd have a nice getaway location should they need it. That was if Logan even wanted to be with her. Mick was confident she did, even with no proof. She could feel it in her heart that felt like it was finally coming to life.

A couple of blocks later, she stood outside a neighborhood bar just off Dupont Circle. She rapped on the window.

Someone inside was sweeping. The man paused, looked up, and shook his head. "We're closed," came from his lips, though Mick couldn't hear the words. She dug into her purse, pulled out a fifty-dollar bill, and pressed it against the glass. She rapped again harder.

The guy's eyes got wide as he came to the door. "I'll get in trouble if anyone knows I let you in before noon." He opened the door long enough to snatch the bill from Mick's hand.

She added another fifty, which made him pause again. This time he looked around. The streets were vacant, so he motioned her inside and closed the door after her.

"My watch says its twelve o'clock." Mick glanced at her bare wrist and laughed.

"Nice watch." He chuckled. "What can I do ya for?"

Mick pulled out her wallet again, this time to hand him her business card. "Who can I speak to, if I want to rent this establishment for the day?"

"I can call the owner. For the whole day, you said?" He took the card Mick held out. "Ms. Finnegan. *The* Finnegan?" Surprise and recognition dawned on his face.

"The one and only," Mick said with pride. "I have a need to be undisturbed."

"Right this way." He walked toward the back of the room. "It ain't much, but you won't be disturbed. I'll make that call and be back in a second." He motioned to a room with a poker table littered with remnants of a game still scattered around.

"Perfect." Mick entered then turned. "And your name is?"

"Garret. I'll send someone to tidy up as soon as he gets here."

Mick pushed aside red plastic cups and crumbs. She placed her laptop on the edge of the table, then pulled up a chair. She couldn't take the chance on even one security guard at her office finding out her plans. No one would think of her doing business here. She sat and texted Georgette the address. She quickly added ASAP before hitting send.

She couldn't wait to get started.

Hours later, Mick got caught daydreaming as she sipped her tea. "What did you say?"

"I said that you're different." Georgette patted Mick's hand. "Whoever this Logan is, she's gotten you all turned around. Tell me about her."

She's beautiful, caring, and special. How was Mick supposed to explain that? Instead she tried another tactic. "It's not just her. The whole family is great. There's also her brother's venture and other things to consider. I just think it's best for me to be there."

Georgette shrugged. "I thought you said she lives here? And what am I going to do if you're hundreds of miles away?"

A man who looked really familiar returned with a tray. Earlier, he'd cleaned the room and taken their order. "Can I get you anything else?" He set the tray in the center of the table.

"No, thanks." Georgette took some fries and smiled. "This is great." Turning to Mick, she asked. "Why move all the way to Kansas?"

Mick caught a surprised look on the server's face. He stopped at the doorway to the kitchen, as if he'd seen a ghost.

"You okay?" she asked.

"Yeah. But that's weird. My roommate told me she was moving to Kansas." He looked embarrassed. "I wasn't eavesdropping, but how strange. I have to keep her stuff till she gets a new place. I can't even rent her room, that's why I took this job. But Kansas... what are the odds?"

Garret stuck his head in. "Everything okay, Ms. Finnegan? Marcus isn't giving you any trouble, is he?"

Mick knew the server looked familiar. She must have seen his picture on Logan's phone or in one of the albums in her room. "You're Marcus?"

"Yes, Marcus Dupree. Why?"

Mick reached out and pulled up another chair. "Your roommate's name isn't by chance, Logan Brady, is it?" She patted the seat.

"It is!" Marcus moved into the seat. His eyes narrowed. "You're Mick?"

"I am." Was he going to hit her? What had Logan told him?

"I spoke with Logan a couple of hours ago. I think we have a little something we should talk about."

Mick nodded. "I'd say we have a *lot* to discuss." She turned toward Georgette. "Get his information and make an appointment as soon as possible."

Georgette didn't miss a beat. She clicked the keys of her keyboard. "Name and address?"

Marcus slowly gave his information, the whole time scowling in Mick's direction. "Are you the reason Logan is dumping her belongings on me? I mean, I love the girl, but this puts me in a bind having to come up with her share of the expenses."

Georgette, the well-oiled machine, knew how Mick thought. She didn't even have to ask what she needed. "How much is Logan's half of the rent? And how much space would you say Miss Brady's belongings take up, Mr. Dupree?"

Mick took the opportunity to grab a bite of food as she watched her associate's precise interactions. Georgette would make a great vice president. She felt secure that Georgette could take over in DC. Mick looked at the man being questioned. However, she wasn't sure where Marcus fit in. "Aren't you the guy who bailed on Logan?"

He crossed his arms and huffed. "She needs to come out to her family. If I went along with being her fiancé, it would never happen. Like I said, I love her, but the girl has issues, and I didn't want her to use me as an excuse not to face her folks."

She nodded. That was true. Maybe now that Donavan and Paul had come clean, Logan would too. Mick had to hope Logan felt something strong enough for her to make it happen. It might help if Logan didn't have to worry about how Marcus would take her decision to leave DC. Logan wouldn't have to come back if her stuff wasn't here either. Mick rubbed her chin as another idea came to her. "I can find a place for you, as well."

"What?" Marcus stared defensively at her.

Georgette answered for her. "Oh, I've seen that look before." She picked up a pen and pad beside her laptop and started scribbling.

Mick remained silent as she pondered her options. "How would you like a job?"

"I'm all over it, boss." Georgette gave the pad to Marcus. "I'll need your social security number and brief work history."

Marcus looked confused by the turn of events, but he seemed to change his mind quickly. He shrugged and took the pad and began writing.

This could be a chance to get back into Logan's good graces. It all depended upon whether Logan could accept help, rather than think Mick high-handed, as she'd called her in Chicago when she'd taken Logan's cigarette from her and tossed it into the snow.

Mick smiled as she watched the scene. She knew in that moment, she could and would do whatever it took.

CHAPTER TWENTY-ONE

Mom, your Christmas brunch gets better each year." Doreen patted her full stomach and looked longingly at the remnants of the two nine-by-six-inch stoneware dishes on the table. One had contained a French toast casserole with pecans, cinnamon, and vanilla. The other had held a scramble-and-bake of eggs, breakfast sausage, onions, peppers, and spicy cheeses. A selection of her homemade syrups and a bottle of popular hot sauce sat next to them.

Donavan picked up the bottle of hot sauce and smacked his lips. "I put that shit on everything," he said, mocking a current television commercial about that very condiment.

Their dad chuckled and whacked him gently on the back. "You think that will set your throat on fire? Wait till you taste tonight's supper I'm grilling." He leaned to look out the nearest window. "And by the looks of that snow coming down, I'm glad I have that awning out back. Wish Mick was here to enjoy it with us, and so I could thank her. That's a mighty thoughtful present."

Logan thought of that moment later after they'd opened presents. The family usually took down the tree sometime between the day after Christmas and New Year's Day, but something told her this year would be different. If she knew her mother, that tree would be there, along with all the unopened gifts beneath it, until Mick came home.

"Put your coat on and come outside." Donavan smacked her butt.

"Hey."

"Just do it. You, too, Doreen. And both of you wear your mittens and scarves."

They did as requested and met the guys in the front yard. Logan eyed the uneven patches of snow suspiciously. The moment she realized what was happening, it was too late. Donavan and Paul pelted them with snowballs big enough to drench her and her sister from nose to navel, and there was nowhere to hide. Donavan and Paul took refuge behind the cars in the driveway. Their mom and dad stood giggling at the front door, and when she turned, she heard it lock.

Screaming, protesting, and hollering like schoolgirls, Logan and Doreen packed snow in their hands and fired back until they were breathless.

"I'm out of shape," Doreen said. She smacked her knit mittens against her thighs to shake off the snow.

"You're also pregnant." Logan gave her a once-over. "You okay?"

"Yeah. Just tired and ready to accept defeat." Doreen smiled after she said it.

Logan let out a sigh of contentment. *My big sister is having a baby. Twins. And my adult siblings and I just had a snowball fight to rival any we'd had as children.* Logan sighed with contentment. If Mick had been there, it would have been completely perfect.

The garage door opened, and her mom stood just inside, holding a bunch of towels. "You kids sit on the bench by the door and take off your shoes. Hang your coats out here to dry. Don't want to track snow back inside."

It didn't occur to Logan until long after the snowball fight took place that their neighbors might have phoned the police to complain of noise again. Wouldn't *that* have been something, to be locked up twice in one holiday week? The thought made her laugh.

"Do." Their dad nudged her. "Wish Abe could have been here for brunch."

Doreen hugged his arm as their dad bent to lay his head on her shoulder briefly. "Me too, but with the twins coming, he's volunteering for double time holiday pay."

Their dad grinned broadly. "This time next year we'll have a much bigger celebration. Are you ready for that?"

"I don't have a choice." She laughed. "But yes, I'm ready and eagerly looking forward to it." Doreen glanced toward her mother and Logan. "Abe asked me to marry him this morning when I called to say merry Christmas. I told him I'd think about it."

Nobody said anything for a few seconds. Her dad nodded, and her mom sniffled.

Doreen rushed to give them an all-encompassing bear hug. "I'm lying. I said YES, of course."

More tears, laughter, hugs. Donavan and Paul came into the circle in the garage.

"What's going on?" Donavan asked, hugging tightly.

After Doreen told him, Don looked extremely nervous. He congratulated her and hugged her, then took off his gloves and put a hand in his pants pocket. He pulled out a small jeweler's box.

Paul beamed while Don paled. He glanced toward Logan and gave her a thumbs up.

"Son?" asked their mom.

"Oh, what the hell. Paul asked me to marry him." Donavan took out the ring and placed it on his ring finger, left hand. "And I said yes, too."

"Oh. My. Gosh." Logan swallowed a lump in her throat. This had been a Christmas of surprises, and she'd known about this one, but it still felt overwhelming. "Congratulations, Donavan." Logan hugged first her brother then Paul. She placed a kiss on both their cheeks, then waited.

Their mom and dad didn't disappoint. They hugged the boys in turn, with their mom crying and laughing at the same time.

"Doreen, I'm sorry. I don't mean to horn in on your big moment with the folks." Donavan shrugged. "I just didn't know how to broach this, and I saw what looked like an opportunity. I hope you don't mind." He swallowed, and his eyes welled with tears. "You're the one I worried most about telling."

Doreen, to Logan's amazement, burst into tears and fell into their brother's arms. "I love you so much, and I want you to be happy. Of course, this is okay. It's better than okay. It's wonderful!" She cracked up laughing. "I was afraid you'd turn out to be the old maid, not me."

Don feigned shock. Everyone else laughed. Doreen then hugged Paul.

After Doreen released Paul, their dad shook his hand. "Welcome to the fam-damily, Paul."

Logan rushed into the house, hoping no one followed. The thought that she'd considered passing off a fake fiancé to this bunch saddened her and made her ashamed. She tore off blindly for the stairs, chastising herself. How could she possibly have lied to them? They were her family—and they were a good one. She had thought them all dysfunctional, but they were accepting and kind and wonderful. *And I'm truly an asshole.*

She threw herself on her bed, facedown, and cried as if her heart had broken. She had no excuse for staying away and not being honest with her family. Mick had no family and had been nothing but kind. In most people's world, money solved everything. Judging Mick for having it was wrong, especially when she was so down-to-earth and helped so many other people with what she had. With every beat of her heart, she reached out silently for Mick. *I'm truly sorry, and I need you now. Can you forgive me?* Mick was right, Logan didn't know her well, and now she probably never would. *You can get through this. Just breathe.*

Logan had no desire for a pity party, so after a few moments, she dried her face and took a few deep breaths.

Heavy footsteps on the stairs leading to the bedrooms announced her father's presence. He knocked on her doorjamb and poked his head inside. "Hey, squirt. You okay?"

"Yeah, I'm fine."

"In that case, come downstairs and help me prepare dinner." His face reflected his excitement. "It's now my turn to cook, and your mom bought me a present so I'd keep warm." He chuckled and held out his hands. "Dress for outdoors if you want to go outside with me."

Logan saw what he meant when she followed him to the kitchen. On the deck not far from the grill was a new outdoor electric heater, one of the tall ones that didn't take up much floor space.

"Isn't she a beaut?" He sighed dramatically. "A guy could feel spoiled."

"You deserve it," said Logan.

He rubbed his hands together and turned around. "Remember how I showed you how to stack a kabob last summer?"

"Yep."

"Well, this year, we're doing the shaved beef on the long metal skewers. We're having fajitas with that." He patted a new package of wooden kabob spears. "And we're putting the Hawaiian stuff on these. From bottom to top, they'll have chicken, bell pepper, pineapple, then shrimp. These, too, will be fajitas. Got it, my little sous chef?"

"Got it, master chef."

"Wait here while I run get the veggies roasting on the grill." He donned his boots and coat, grabbed a couple of potholders, and opened the sliding glass door. Within seconds, he came back carrying two wire baskets stuffed with cottage fries, strips of onions, and small ears of corn.

Logan handed him two large cake pans lined with foil. "That smells wonderful, Daddy!"

He smiled his appreciation. "I figured we might want something on the side that won't fit in the tortillas." He emptied the baskets into the cake pans, covered them with foil, then shoved them into the oven and set it to warm.

Logan wondered when they'd have the father-daughter talk, which was a tradition. Every Christmas Day while her dad cooked, he'd ask Logan about her plans for the upcoming new year. She wasn't sure yet what she'd say this time.

"Okay, grab your coat and let's take these to the grill. We'll have to stay out there and watch these, make sure that the pineapple and shrimp don't char."

He grabbed a cookie sheet lined with kabobs and left the second sheet for her. He unloaded his first then reached for hers. While the food cooked, they sat opposite one another in deck chairs.

"How about that?" He warmed his hands near his new outdoor heater.

Logan did the same. "This is great."

"We have so many cardboard boxes in the garage," her dad said with a chortle, "the service that collects our garbage will think either Santa broke the bank this year or a new family moved in."

Logan agreed.

"Are you okay with what went on earlier?" he asked.

"Sure. I'm happy for them." Logan warmed her hands next to his. "How about you?"

He nodded. "The boys are playing video games downstairs with Abe. He got here while you were upstairs and Don and Paul absconded with him right away. Your mom and Doreen are planning weddings. I just wanted to make sure you didn't feel left out. And I wanted to talk to you about your plans for next year, like we always do. Do you mind?"

"Not at all. But I don't have anything in mind yet. I have to find a job—that's number one on my list."

"Not moving out?" he asked.

"After I find work, but I can't afford to move yet. I hope that's not a problem."

He hugged her. "Honey, your mom and I have missed you. You're welcome here as long as you like." He paused. "Have you heard from Mick?"

She shook her head. "We haven't talked since she left. I have no clue what she's doing or what she's thinking. I wanted to text her to at least say merry Christmas, but I don't have her number. Besides it feels weird since she's probably alone. Maybe we'll just be friends, you know? Call and write, that sort of thing."

"Your brother said you're not interested in going to school. What if you stayed home and didn't go out to work? I mean, this virus thing may not be over, and we can afford for you to stay here. You'd be a great help for your mom. Hell, I probably won't see much of her once those babies are born. I'm sure she'd love your company and to have you help with the grandmother and aunt stuff that'll be coming up."

"Daddy, I can't just stay here and not do anything. I appreciate the offer, but—"

"I was remembering how you always wanted to write but didn't have time. Well, daughter, you have the time now. And I've got the money to support you while you do it."

Logan was so surprised she nearly slid off her seat. She watched him as he lifted the lid on the grill and turned the kabobs over. "Daddy, what on earth would I write? I mean, I'd have to spend time doing nothing but thinking, planning."

"Nonsense. Writers write, don't they? They put their butts in a chair and type. What do you need to plan?"

"But what would I write?" she asked again.

"You could start by working on your Christmas gifts to everyone next year. How about a cookbook with recipes we've used this holiday season? Of course, you could always put more in there besides Christmas eats, but I for one would like to have a family cookbook."

The wind shifted, and snow fell softly against her cheeks.

He told her to get up and move closer to him. "I've been watching stories about how several businesses have closed during this pandemic, but because seating and space is limited in theaters and gyms and things, people are reading more." He thumbed toward the house. "The kids are playing more video games, which is good news for your brother."

"You've given this some consideration, haven't you?"

"Yep. This Brady bunch is pretty self-sufficient. I've been thinking of ways we can do more of what we enjoy and make money doing it." He pointed to a patch of the backyard near an old storage shed. "For instance, your mother loves gardening. I'm thinking of working the ground over there, turning it, mulching it, and helping her grow whatever she wants. She used to can, you know? She made some of the best pickles, and we had sugar snap peas and pole beans, everything. What do you say? Could you help her with that this next spring?"

Logan nodded enthusiastically. Her father's plans took hold, and the fear, worry, and dread she'd felt earlier dissipated. In what she considered a Scarlet O'Hara moment from *Gone With the Wind*, she remembered a famous line from the movie and applied it to her own life. Mick was gone now, but she'd ask her brother for her number. With any luck, between the two of them they could think of a way to bring her home.

After all, tomorrow was another day!

The clock sent its old-fashioned bong into the stuffy office, jerking Mick from another daydream. She had been working nonstop for days now. Two more and the clock would be ringing in the new year. How had the chimes gone from dream to reality?

Georgette began to stretch and pace. "You think we get to have a life after all this reorganization?"

"Huh?" Even with all the paperwork and legal details to address, Mick found it hard to keep her mind on work. "I don't know." She didn't know much of anything except her heart was halfway across the country. The graphs and financials couldn't hold her attention. She'd been caught daydreaming again. Mick had hardly heard a word said to her in the past few hours. It was a wonder Georgette hadn't strangled her yet.

Georgette would wear ruts in the drab carpet soon. Mick thought about the fun part of having a new office. No cold modern edges in Kansas. She'd have Logan pick bright colors and cheerful decorations. She'd loved the way Logan had decorated her room with her unique style.

"What did you say?"

Georgette shook her head. "I said, you've never done this before."

Mick tried to ignore her. She riffled through the stack of papers on her desktop. "Can we just get back to work?" She should at least attempt to concentrate on the business at hand.

Georgette wouldn't let her inquisition die. "Usually when you meet someone you push them away. I've seen the pattern repeated often enough through the years when it comes to your lovers."

Mick had asked a lot of Georgette. She was perhaps her closest friend. She deserved the truth. Mick shrugged, unable to admit her real feelings.

"What's different this time?" Georgette rolled her neck again.

Logan Brady was the difference. The entire Brady family was special. Mick couldn't help but love them all. The thought of becoming one of them both excited and terrified her.

Georgette stood there now with her hands on her hips waiting for an answer.

"She makes me…" Her cheeks were on fire. "Want more," Mick confessed.

Georgette looked surprised. "Finally." She sighed. "I'm happy for you. You do realize you're going to disrupt an entire company for a woman."

"No, for a future." Mick pushed the pile of work to the side. "You had family visit for Christmas, didn't you?"

Georgette nodded.

"Well, for the first time in my life, I experienced what a family could be," Mick explained. "You know what else? They care nothing at all about my money. And Logan makes me want to open up. She makes me want to be there, every morning, every night. That, my dear Georgie, is the difference."

"That's a good difference." Georgette looked satisfied as she returned to her chair and the details on her laptop screen.

Mick picked up her phone and checked again for the hundredth time for any messages. After, she texted Donavan with her charitable contacts in DC so he could begin filtering that information into the game's programming. She wanted to fund the game and get things moving. Would they still name it *Finnegan's Treasure*?

Her phone pinged with his response almost right away. *How dare you think I can be bought? You hurt Logan. Forget about us.*

Mick fired off an email, since a text wouldn't suffice. Hopefully, he read it.

Donavan,

I've never said this before, but you're like a brother to me. I've deposited $50,000 to start your project into this account. (see attachment) If you don't use it, it will go to various homeless shelters in Kansas City. Your choice.

I've changed, because of your kind invitation to Kansas. Please be patient. The new year is going to start with a big bang. I believe the game will be a big hit. I hope it helps so many others. I have seen myself as others do. I got defensive because I didn't like what I saw. Don't give up on me. I never did on you, Don. You are on the verge of greatness. I admire you. I promise to make everything all right,

Michaela Finnegan

She hit send and closed her phone. When she glanced up at Georgette, she had her eyes closed and looked exhausted. Christ, she'd kept her working all week. Way to go. "Hey, you're right. Let's go home. I've taken enough of your life for the day."

"Really?" Georgette perked up and smiled. "Thank you. You know I'll do whatever it takes, but I'm so exhausted one more detail may send me into a coma."

"How about just one more?"

"If it's only one, then name it."

"Do we have the jet pilot scheduled for New Year's Day?"

"Yes, and Marcus will meet you at the airport."

Mick was determined to start the new year right. Georgette and now Marcus were both in her corner. They'd gone above and beyond to help make the transition to Kansas City go smoothly. She had to make one last attempt to get the Bradys' approval as well.

If Mick really wasn't wanted, it would hurt. But she would keep herself busy. It would take another three months to undo all she had put into place the last few days, but she'd do it if she had to. But she was going to give this her best shot ever. "You better get some rest. We have a lot to do before I leave."

Another grueling day of details. Mick tripped over the welcome mat as she opened her apartment door late on December 30. The word welcome came across as ironic to her since she hadn't made anyone feel welcome here. She threw her keys on the console and plopped on the couch. The ring of her phone made her open her eyes. She hurriedly dug into her bag to answer the phone before it went to voice mail. *Too late!* The 913 area code made her heart leap with anticipation. Mick swiped right and gasped.

The text read *COME HOME* and nothing else.

It hadn't come from Donavan's phone. She didn't recognize the number and deduced it could only be one of the other Bradys. Either way, it must be important.

Mick hit redial and was surprised when she heard Cora Brady's voice.

"You've reached Cora Brady." Her shaky, uncertain tone stalled before she continued. "Please leave a message and I will try to return your call if I can."

What's wrong?

She pictured Cora squinting at the buttons on her tiny phone. It must have taken at least twenty minutes to text those two words. If she remembered right, the Bradys had joked about how Cora didn't know how to text. She was stuck in the last century and still had a flip phone. Should she call Marcus and get him to call? No. Hell, she would ruin the element of surprise herself.

Mick texted back immediately. *Be there ASAP tomorrow.*

CHAPTER TWENTY-TWO

Mick stood by the skycap station at the airport waiting for her newest employee. Her eyes widened when Marcus stepped out of the cab. The spectacle before her was worlds away from professional. She shook her head.

The bright orange faux-fur coat Marcus wore stood out like a stoplight. He struggled to roll two huge matching gold suitcases in her direction. A large canvas bag that precariously balanced on one case threatened to spill.

Mick took in a quick breath as adrenaline zapped her, and she rushed to help him.

At the same time, the strap on his leather backpack slipped from his shoulder. Marcus tripped. The canvas duffel fell from its perch, and Marcus looked as if he would land face-first on the sidewalk beside the bag.

Luckily, a handsome airport employee caught Marcus before he landed. "Whoa there. Let me help you folks."

Marcus took the hand offered as if he were a princess in a fairy tale. "Thank you, dear man." He fanned himself with his free hand, taking time to regain his footing.

"Which one is your departure gate?" the skycap asked. He grabbed a case and bent to get the canvas bag.

"Careful with that," Marcus said sweetly. "Mick, you'll want to take that."

"Private jet terminal." Mick read the name tag on his vest. "Thank you, Peter." She took the bag and followed him to the desk.

"I'll get you a car." Peter attempted to use his walkie-talkie. Marcus had looped his arm into the crook of Peter's elbow and held on for dear life.

Mick let out a heavy exhale. "Marcus, let go of Peter so he can do his job." She didn't want any more drama. Every minute of delay made her anxious to get back to Logan. "Did you get what I wanted?"

"Of course." Marcus nodded toward the canvas bag. "I am a man of my word."

Worried the spill may have damaged her gift, she peeked inside. "Perfect." Mick sighed with relief. A deep violet velvet box sat cushioned safely with tons of lavender tissue paper. "Logan's going to love this. Thanks."

"You're welcome. Her biggest present will be me, of course." Marcus laughed at his own wittiness.

Mick couldn't help but join his infectious mood. "I'm not certain of that." She chuckled. "But she will love you, too!"

"She already does. What's not to love?"

Indeed. Marcus was definitely a character Logan loved. His quirky attitude was growing on her, and she knew she'd made the right decision in bringing him along on her business adventure.

The car arrived and Peter assisted in moving the luggage to the trunk.

"Geez, you think you packed enough?" Only half-joking, Mick added a smile. "We can send for your belongings later."

"Oh, there's plenty more where this came from." He handed Peter his backpack.

"I'll bet there is." Mick saw Marcus place something discreetly into Peter's hand.

"You folks have a nice flight." Peter closed the door and tapped on the roof.

As the car pulled away, Marcus turned in his seat and waved good-bye. "I'll be back."

Mick rolled her eyes. What kind of relationship could come from a random meeting at an airport? She stifled a laugh. She had met Logan at an airport. Butterflies fluttered in Mick's stomach. Was she nervous or afraid? She looked at Marcus. Either way, she was headed to the Land of Oz with a very colorful surprise.

❖

Logan stared at the blank page on her computer screen. Even though she'd had a book in her hand and read voraciously even before kindergarten, who was she kidding. *I can't write a book.* Stringing words together to make any sense was daunting. The blinking cursor mocked her.

"Knock-knock." Donavan stood at the door. "You busy?"

Logan waved him inside. "No, unfortunately."

"What are you doing?" Donavan moved the extra pillows on her bed and sat.

"Not writing a book." She huffed. "And I am doing a great job of it." She pointed to the blank screen.

"Dad told me you might write. I think it's great."

Logan crossed her arms and scowled at him. "You think it's great? That I'm failing at something else?"

"No. That you *will* write a book." Donavan jumped up to stand behind her. He rubbed her arms. "You can do this. I can see you as a success. Why not just start with journaling?"

"That's a great idea!" If she could get her thoughts down it could be therapeutic. No one else had to read it.

"Start with a question," Donavan suggested. "What are you passionate about? What was your most embarrassing moment?"

Logan held up her finger. She immediately thought of her first encounter with Mick and smiled. "Oh, that's a good one." She quickly placed her fingers on the keys. The clicking sounds found a rhythm. Words spilled onto the screen as smoothly as butter. Her most embarrassing moment was easy.

"Ahem." Donavan cleared his throat. "You're welcome. But I did come up here for something else. I thought you'd be getting ready for Misty's party tonight. Won't some of your old friends be there?"

Logan lifted her hands from the keyboard and hit her forehead with her palm. She'd forgotten the New Year's Eve party. She turned back to her brother. "I wasn't. I don't have a present, and we were never close."

Donavan nodded. "Yeah, but if you are staying in KC you need to reacquaint yourself with old friends. Wouldn't hurt to make new ones either. Get back out there. You can ignore Misty completely."

"If you're saying Mick's not coming back, I don't believe you."

Donavan shrugged. "I'm not saying that. It's just that Paul and I are going to Missy-B's later tonight. It's New Year's Eve, so the place should be packed to the rafters." He paused. "Isn't Missy-B's where Misty's party takes place? So we'll all be in the same building."

Logan considered it. She could also come out to her friends. She didn't know when another perfect opportunity would present itself, and this way she'd know who the real friends were and who she could leave behind. "It might be fun. Her party starts at seven thirty, before the drag show." She glanced at the time on her PC. She had an hour to get ready. "Okay, I will. Can I borrow your car?"

"Sure." He dug in his pocket and tossed her his keys. "Dad can drop us off and we can all come home together."

"Okay, get out of here so I can get ready," Logan pushed him out the door playfully. Donavan really did want the best for her and had been a big help in keeping her mind off Mick for the last few days. She stuck her head into the hall. "And thanks, Don."

He had a stupid grin on his face and shrugged. "What are big brothers for?"

After she shut the door, she closed her laptop, dropped the car keys onto the desk, and went to the closet. Hanging next to her jeans and bohemian-styled tunics hung Mick's clothes, which she hadn't bothered to stop and get when she'd headed to the airport. Her heart sank. Her dream of spending the new year getting to know Mick was fading. Mick's designer apparel made Logan's clothes appear as rags. She'd felt like that since the first glimpse of Mick at the airport. She pushed the three-piece suit to the side and discovered a brilliant emerald green silk blouse. She'd clean it before she sent it back, and Mick would never know.

Logan placed her finger on her lips. "Hmm." She chose a pair of dress slacks and her silver vest. She could make it work.

After she showered and dressed, she put on her makeup. She leaned close to the mirror. She could barely see for the tears in her eyes as she applied mascara. *Pull it together.* She shook her hand to steady the shaking. She had to give up the dream of ringing in the new year with a kiss from Mick at midnight. A knock on the door startled her. She almost poked her eye with the wand.

"Logan, I have a wedding gift wrapped and ready for your party," her mom yelled through the closed door.

Her mother always came through. "Mom, you're the best!"

When Logan descended the stairs, she paused to take in a deep breath. Her parents and Donavan stood at the bottom gazing up with strange expressions on their faces. This moment reminded her of her prom.

"You look beautiful!" her mother cooed.

She felt beautiful, and a bit foolish. "You think Mick will mind if I borrowed her clothes?"

"You clean up good, sis," Donavan said. He kissed her cheek when she reached them. "Got the keys?"

She dangled them in front of his face. "Yes, and I'll see you and Paul both before the clock strikes twelve, right?"

"You bet. You'll have two Prince Charmings at your service," Donavan said. He bowed low in her direction.

Her dad opened the front door. "Don't drink and drive." Logan heard the concern in his voice.

"I'm the designated driver tonight. I'll get her back safe and sound after we meet her at the bar," Donavan told him.

Logan grabbed her handbag and the present. "Thanks again, Mom."

"It's one of the quilts I had in my stash." Her mom followed them to the door. "We just want you to have fun, honey."

Logan said softly, "I will. I promise."

She stepped onto the front stoop. A chill in the air made her shiver. Before she headed to the car, she could hear her mom inside.

"Donavan, have you heard anything from Mick?"

Logan wasn't sure if she wanted to know the answer or not. Damn it, even without Mick she would have the night of her life.

She cranked the heater and headed toward Missy-B's.

Mick's heart pounded as her driver, Jimmy, parked in front of the Brady residence. She needed to get out of the car but couldn't force herself to move.

"This is the right address?" Jimmy asked as he turned to face her. "Right?"

She didn't know how they would react. "I truly hope so," she answered. "You'll wait for me, right?"

"I'm your man all night, Ms. Finnigan. I brought a book, so don't worry about me." He turned and settled in with his novel.

"Good. It may be a while." Other than getting Marcus set up at the hotel, with instructions for later, she'd done nothing but travel all day. From cabs, planes, and now a stretch limo, her limbs ached from lack of movement. She opened the door and stretched her stiff legs.

Before she reached the door, it swung open. Cora and Ben stood with open arms.

"Oh, thank God you're here." Cora engulfed her in a hug.

Ben's strong arms came around her next. "You're a sight for sore eyes."

Cora and Ben released her, and she stepped into the house. The fragrances of baked bread, pine, and cinnamon filled her lungs. *God, I love this place.* "I got your text, Cora. I came as soon as I could. What's wrong?" Mick asked.

The volume of the TV in the living room decreased. Heavy rapid footsteps approached. Then Donavan came into the entryway. "Mom texted?" He laughed then added, "We'll get you into the twenty-first century yet." He rubbed Cora's back then turned to Mick. "Hiya, 'bout time you got here. I'd almost given up on you."

"Almost?" Mick asked.

"Yeah, but then I read your email," Donavan answered. "Figured I'd give you the benefit of the doubt."

"Let's give Mick a minute to settle in. I'll get her some hot apple cider. It's chilly out there." Cora disappeared into the kitchen.

"I'll give you guys a moment." Ben excused himself then followed his wife.

"I don't rate a hug?" Donavan held his arms wide.

Mick didn't hesitate. She squeezed him hard. Gratitude for his invitation filled her heart. When her eyes began to tear up, she pushed away. "I was so worried that you hated me."

"Was a bit miffed, but I got over it. I could never hate you, Mick. Come in and sit a spell." He directed her to the cozy living room.

The tree in the corner still had presents beneath it. Had they not opened them? "Didn't you celebrate Christmas already?"

"Those are yours." Donavan motioned to them.

"For me? Why?" *I don't need anything but Logan.* "Where's your sister?"

Paul made his entrance, taking all of Donavan's attention. Understandable because the tuxedo blazer and crisp blue bowtie made him look every inch like a *GQ* magazine cover model.

"Wow!" Donavan said. "I'm a lucky man."

"Mick!" Paul shook her hand and gave her a friendly half hug. He sounded relieved. "Oh, thank God. Logan's been sulking around all week. Glad to see you're back."

"Thanks, it's nice to be...home." She gave him a smile.

Cora and Ben came back into the room. This was her chance. "Where are Logan and Doreen?"

Cora handed her the brown mug full of steaming apple cider. "Doreen took Abe to the station. Every available cop is on duty tonight. She's waiting for him at his place and won't be home till tomorrow."

"Logan's at Misty's bridal shower," Ben said.

"She did come out, so you can relax," Donavan said.

Mick sat in the recliner next to the tree. She scanned their expressions and saw only acceptance. Not a surprise, really. She took a sip of cider. The sweet and spicy drink helped calm her. What did that mean for them as a couple? Maybe she should go to the hotel and come back tomorrow.

Ben put in his two cents. "She also told us she cares about you. And we love our kids, no matter who they're with."

"We do pay attention," Cora said. She knelt by the tree and dug out a large box, then presented it to Mick. "Open this one."

Mick took another drink and set her cup on the side table. She couldn't remember the last time she'd received a gift that wasn't something practical from an employee. "Okay." She took the box and untied the ribbon. She excitedly ripped into the paper with the gusto of a child. "Oh...my!" Her eyes widened in surprise. Mick stroked the soft, maroon and autumn-colored quilt. She rubbed it against her face. Ridged fabrics of corduroy and velvet caressed her cheeks. "It's beautiful. How did you know my favorite color?"

"Like I said, we pay attention to our kids. You wear jeweled tones most of the time. I hope you like it."

"It's perfect!" Mick hugged the quilt again. "Can I ask a question?"

"Of course, dear," Cara said.

"How do you feel about me having a thing for your daughter?"

Cora and Ben shared a look and nodded. Cora reached for Mick's hand. "Honey, we'll keep the quilt for you. Come with us."

Why didn't they answer my question? Maybe they don't want Logan involved with me. She stood and placed the beautiful quilt in the chair then followed them back to the entryway. Instead of going into the den where Mick fully expected to receive a private lecture, Ben opened the front door. Her stomach lurched. *Are they kicking me out?*

Cora prodded her toward the front porch. "We both think..." She placed a kiss on Mick's cheek and smiled. "It's about time you go get your girl."

CHAPTER TWENTY-THREE

L ogan watched Misty open presents, joining in with what she hoped were appropriate oohs and aahs. Silverware, a gravy bowl, and other various items made time move in slow motion. Logan turned away to observe the Missy-B's waitstaff set up the other side of the room. Bright-colored decorations encased in glitter, along with noisemakers, were being placed just so on each table. She imagined these men were the evening's entertainment, out of drag. They certainly argued and rearranged with the drama of true queens. The midnight celebration felt years away, not hours.

A burst of applause and overzealous oohs returned Logan's attention to the party.

Misty's bright-red face caused Logan to clap harder. She hadn't believed Misty could be embarrassed. Misty fanned her face with one hand and held up a skimpy negligee with the other. The black lace, open-crotch contraption was not Misty's style.

Logan joined in with enthusiasm this time. "Wow!"

Misty tried to recover as only she could. "I believe," she said playfully, "this is a gift for Richard more than me." She cocked an eyebrow. "It's definitely not on the bridal registry list."

Laughter erupted among the women.

"What's the fun in that?" Misty's maid of honor, Betty, teased her.

Logan's face was probably as red as Misty's, as she imagined Mick looking at her in the kinky garment. Mick had seemed classy. Would she like something like that in private? She sure would like the chance to find out.

"Open the big one next," a girl suggested.

"Yeah," Betty added. "I'm dying to know what Logan brought you."

"It's not on the list either," Logan mumbled.

The group added another smattering of applause. "Open it. Open it," Betty started a chant, and the whole party took it up eagerly.

A handmade item, not on Misty's list, would be just another thing Logan had done wrong in Misty's eyes. "Go ahead," Logan said and sighed. She was used to the embarrassment. Already tonight, she'd had the lowest scores for the bridal shower games.

"Okay, I will." Misty grabbed the large silver-wrapped gift and ripped off the paper.

The room went silent with anticipation.

After a long pause, Misty lifted the quilt from its box to show them. She glanced at Logan. Hints of respect replaced Misty's familiar looks of judgment. "Oh, Logan, I don't know what to say." She passed the quilt to the woman next to her to admire then rushed to the end of the table where Logan sat. She bent down and wrapped her arms around Logan's shoulders. The squeeze, as well as Misty's sentiment of joy, startled her. "It's beautiful," Misty said. "I don't deserve it. But thank you, so very much."

Logan was speechless. Misty actually approved?

Misty whispered in Logan's ear. "This is the best gift all day."

Logan gave Misty's arm a friendly pat. "You don't know that. There are still presents left." She smiled and waved Misty back to the head of the table.

Misty returned to her original position and resumed unwrapping. The smile sent Logan's way confirmed their relationship had changed. With Misty's approval, Logan could finally relax and enjoy the party. As she took a sip of punch and nibbled at her dry cake, she listened to the chatter of the women, but as usual, she felt like an outsider looking in.

"You know that is the wedding ring pattern, right?" Betty informed the lady next to her. They fawned over the quilt, petting and inspecting it, and then passed it down the line.

"I've seen this pattern before," Julie or Jenn said. Logan could never remember her name. "Quilts like that are listed for as much as two thousand dollars in craft shows."

The gift reached Logan, and she examined it for the first time. The weight of it would definitely keep someone warm. When she unfolded one corner, her eyes widened. She discovered scraps from her prom dress, Donavan's old Sunday-best suit, and Doreen's favorite peasant blouse sprinkled throughout. How many quilts did mom have in her stash? Logan studied the stitches and let her fingers run along the seams. Had her mother been so lonely and bored, she turned to such intricate details just to keep busy? It must have taken months, maybe years, to finish the quilt. Logan gently touched a square she recognized. One of her grandmother's old kitchen aprons had been added.

Betty magically appeared at Logan's side and interrupted her thoughts. "It's also hand-quilted," Betty said. "So classy, girl."

The comment startled her. Never considering herself classy in any sense of the word, Logan looked back to Misty.

"I love it," Misty said. "I love all of them," she added hastily. "You girls are the greatest. This has been so much fun. The new year is looking pretty good right now."

Out of nowhere, Betty bellowed, "Who is going to stay and help with the cleanup?" Betty always had to be in charge. "The drag show is to die for, I hear. How many chairs will we need?"

Some of the girls shrugged and exchanged confused looks. The party was over.

Only minutes ago, Logan had wanted this event to be done. Now that she had gained a sense of fitting in with the cool kids, of course, it was over.

Betty herded a few of the girls outside with stacks of gifts to put in Misty's car. When they came back in, Jenn said, "There's already a stretch limo across the street waiting for the bar to open."

Logan hurriedly stuffed paper plates and cups into a trash bag. After the group of girls took the trash out the back, Logan was alone with Misty.

Misty put her hand on Logan's arm. "Did you see a square of our cheerleading uniform in the quilt? I can't wait to show that to Richard."

Logan must have missed the uniform scrap. "No, but mom keeps everything, so I'm not surprised."

They busied themselves scooting chairs and tables apart. Within minutes, Missy-B's transformed from an intimate bachelorette party and bridal shower to a New Year's Eve extravaganza. Betty came from the back with a massive centerpiece for their table. "The party's not over, yet. The drag queens gave us a bouquet of candy penis lollipops." She stuck one in her mouth and pointed to Misty. "What flavor do you want?"

Misty laughed and chose a long chocolate shape out of the bouquet. "Logan, what kind do you prefer?"

Logan rolled her eyes. "I am so not into sweets." *Nor penises.*

The group of girls sat and watched as people dressed to celebrate New Year's Eve arrived. Music with a strong bass beat began, and Logan felt it pound through the floorboards.

Misty raised her voice. "Is your gorgeous Mick coming tonight?" The sickening flirtatious tone she usually used was absent.

Logan didn't answer and feigned interest in a commotion behind the curtain of the stage. She needed to speak her truth and tell her the person she'd introduced her to that day wasn't Mick at all. She raised her head to meet Misty's eyes. "Well, that's another reason I came tonight. I need to tell you something."

"You two haven't broken up already?" Misty sounded genuinely concerned and interested in Logan's answer.

As if she'd wished them there, Donavan and Paul walked through the door. He waved at Logan and walked in their direction.

"Speak of the devil." Misty jumped from her seat and rushed to greet them. She wiggled between them, took each by the elbow, and escorted them to the table nearest the stage. "I have the best seat in the house reserved," she bragged. "Join us. Logan and I were just talking about you."

Logan shared a look with her brother. Relieved she wasn't alone, she kissed Donavan on the cheek. It was the right time.

Donavan nodded to encourage her. "You got this. Go on, sis."

Logan took in a deep breath and pointed at Paul. "His name isn't, Mick, it's Paul," she explained.

"Okay." Misty looked confused. "He's still gorgeous."

This wasn't going according to plan. "You see, Paul's—"

"Misty!" A high squeal pierced the air. "You shouldn't have." Jenn returned to the table at that moment. "You hired two fine hunks to escort us tonight?" She clapped her hands with excitement.

Logan looked around for a server. Was it too early to get drunk? She rubbed her temple and lowered her chin to her chest. When she lifted her head to meet Donavan's gaze, he rolled his eyes. "Okay, I'll help. Misty, Paul's with me." Don held up his left hand to show her his new ring. "We're engaged."

Misty's hand went to her mouth. She cleared her throat before she replied. "Congratulations, Donavan." She smiled toward Paul. "All the best looking men are gay." Misty then turned back to Logan. With her hands placed on her hips, she awaited an explanation. "Then who the hell is Mick?"

Paul leaned close to Logan. "Hon, rip off the bandage. Now. Just do it."

Everyone from the party, along with Donavan and Paul, watched for Logan's response. If she was going to have friends in Kansas City, they needed to know who she really was. She rubbed the back of her neck with her sweaty palm. Was this her moment of truth?

A burst of cold air came through the door. Logan turned to find her answer. The truth stood staring her in the face. The silhouette of a figure that had haunted her dreams for a week stood in the doorway.

The boys must have known, given their smug smiles.

Mick Finnegan stood looking back at her.

❖

For the second time today, Mick couldn't move. This time, it wasn't because of sore muscles. She was stunned.

Logan was here all right. Beautiful didn't come close to describing how good she looked. Logan filled the designer threads in ways Mick's lean frame never could.

Suddenly, Donavan waved his hand in front of her face. "Hey, Mick, you there? Come on. Logan needs you."

That snapped Mick back to reality. She looked at Donavan and studied him. "Is she okay?"

"Yeah, just scared."

"Of me?"

"No. She's coming out tonight to everyone she knew in high school. Follow me." Donavan took her hand and weaved his way toward the stage.

Mick had no intentions of including a drag show in her festivities. "I told you my plans for tonight, Don."

He shrugged off her comment as if it meant nothing. "Yeah, well, you also told me you would wait for my text before coming in. We see how well that worked."

He had a point. While she had waited in the limo, Mick had checked her phone every few minutes since they dropped the guys off. It felt as if she'd been sitting there for a month.

When they got to the table, Donavan twirled her around like a ballroom dancer and dramatically bowed. "Misty, and party members, allow me to present—"

"Ladies and gentlemen…" A deep voice boomed from the speakers.

Dizzied by Donavan's twirl, Mick giggled. She steadied her footing and tried to get her bearings. When she raised her head, Logan stood in front of her.

"Our New Year's Eve Extravaganza will begin in five minutes." The announcement on the speakers ended. Servers hurried to take orders and people scrambled to get a good seat.

In all the commotion, Mick tried to focus on Logan. She must have worn heels because they were nearly eye level. Mick cleared her throat. She should say how nice Logan looked or how sorry she was for leaving. Instead, she said softly, "Hello."

Logan laughed. "Well, hello yourself." She stood only inches away.

Mick's heart raced. She'd give every cent she owned to kiss her.

As if Logan could read her thoughts, she placed one palm against Mick's cheek and yanked her close then pressed their lips together. Mick leaned into the warmth of her touch. Butterflies made loop the loops in her stomach. As their tongues reacquainted and Mick deepened their embrace, she heard applause. It was hard to breathe, but she didn't care.

Someone tapped her shoulder. Then, as quickly as the kiss began, it was over, and Logan pulled away.

"Okay, girls, you can get a room later," Donavan said.

Mick had let the world melt away. She'd forgotten where they were, but the announcer came back to remind her.

"Get ready for the time of your life!" the voice boomed overhead.

Mick was already having the time of hers with Logan. She barely perched on the edge of the seat she was ushered into.

Retro music began, and colored lights flashed over the audience then beamed onto the stage. When Mick turned her attention back to the group, Don and Paul were smiling, and the girl at the head of the table, who Mick had met at the restaurant the week before, stood with her mouth agape.

"Misty, *this* is Mick!" Logan yelled over the thundering music.

Misty appeared speechless. But Mick didn't care what anyone from the group thought. She wasn't staying here a minute longer.

The lights dimmed and a colorful drag queen dressed in Tina Turner fringe came onto the stage. "Rolling on the River" began slow and dirty.

"As the song says, let's roll," she told Logan, hoping like hell she'd made the right decision and searching Logan's eyes for the answer she needed. She took Logan's hand, and relief came in an instant when she felt no resistance as she pulled her toward the door.

CHAPTER TWENTY-FOUR

Mick climbed into the limo, relieved to be out of the cold and safely tucked in the privacy of the car. She rubbed her hands together more from nervousness than the need to keep warm.

"You came back," Logan said almost in a whisper.

She reached for Logan. "I couldn't stay away." Neither could she keep her hands to herself. Mick drew Logan close. Her heart pounded, and she couldn't catch her breath as their kiss deepened. She threaded her fingers through Logan's hair. When she pressed their bodies together, she could feel Logan's breasts against hers. She silently cursed the fabric that separated them.

A knock on the glass between the driver and passenger section intruded.

Mick pushed the speaker button.

"I don't mind," Jimmy said. "But you're fogging up the windows, Mick."

Mick laughed and pulled away reluctantly. "Sorry, Jimmy."

"No. You're not." He pointed at his watch and shrugged. "But you told me to do whatever it took to stay on schedule."

Mick gave Logan's addictive lips a quick peck and let out a huge exhale. "You're right, Jimmy, of course." She nodded to the driver. "Okay. Stop number one, here we come." She wanted the night to be perfect. The car pulled away from the curb.

Logan cocked her head, looking curious.

"I have three surprises planned before midnight."

"You walking into Missy-B's was surprise enough for me," Logan said.

"We don't have much time, but I think we should talk."

"Finally." Logan pulled her seat belt around and clicked it in place. "I'm listening. All I ever wanted was to know the real you."

Mick smiled and fidgeted with her jacket. "I don't understand that." She got her phone from her inside pocket and glanced at Logan sitting beside her. "I got no texts, voice messages, or emails. I wasn't sure you wanted me back."

Logan crossed her arms. "I meant what I said. If you can't say something face-to-face...wait—" She looked surprised and hurt all at once. "Do you have to do that while we're talking?" She pointed to the phone that Mick was tapping on. "Besides, you never gave me your number. And I didn't want to ask Donavan."

"Well, stupid me. That explains a lot." Mick frantically texted Marcus. "I'll put it away, I promise." She spoke the words as she typed. *Be there in ten minutes. Love, Mick and Logan.* She made an elaborate gesture to return the phone to her pocket and her attention to Logan. "Now, I'm all yours."

"Who is it that's hiding behind all your money?" Logan turned toward her and rested her hand on Mick's thigh.

Mick ran her finger along the leather trim on the armrest. How could she explain? "I'm uncomfortable talking about my past." She rubbed the armrest back and forth.

"You're avoiding my question." Logan took her hand and held it, then forced Mick to look into her eyes. "Who is Mick Finnegan?"

Mick remembered the girl from the Metro. That child's search had just begun, Mick's had ended. She'd found the place she wanted to call home. And that meant letting people in.

The car slowed down, and the intercom came to life. "We're here, Mick."

"Okay, give us a sec." She addressed Logan. "I want to try to explain. A few days ago, the universe, God, or whatever sent me a sign."

Logan held her gaze intensely. "Really, what happened?"

"Christmas Day, on my way to work—"

"You went to work on Christmas?" Logan shook her head, but the look of disappointment on her face told Mick she believed her.

Ashamed, Mick nodded back. "Yeah, I had a lot to do and nowhere else to go. Anyway, on the subway, I met someone who reminded me of where I came from."

Logan seemed interested, but something outside the window had caught her attention. Her glance over Mick's shoulder confirmed it. "I don't mean to interrupt, but that's strange."

Mick turned to follow Logan's gaze and saw the bright orange fur at the driver's door.

"I have a coat just like that," Logan said.

The window lowered, and Marcus placed his arms on the ledge. He slowly bent down to look inside. "Hey, pretty ladies."

Recognition dawned on Logan's face. "Marcus!" she yelled. She jumped out of the car and hurriedly ran around the front.

Mick got out and leaned against the limo to watch the scene. She'd give damn near anything in the world to see that smile on Logan's face every chance she got.

Marcus's orange-furred arms engulfed Logan. He picked her up off the ground in an enthusiastic hug. "Now that's a hello that makes one think you missed a queen," he said.

Logan hugged him again. "I didn't know when I'd see you again." Still flustered, she turned back to Mick. "Is this my surprise?"

She hoped Logan reacted to the others the same. "Marcus is number one."

"Of course, I am." Marcus took off the orange coat and placed it over Logan's shoulders then addressed Mick. "We should go inside," Marcus said. "And we need to hurry because I have a date."

"Of course, you do," Logan groaned. "You've been here, what, two hours?"

Mick laughed and happily followed them into the vacant lobby.

"It's not much to look at yet." Marcus waved dismissively at the walls and walked past the reception area. "Oh, and, Mick, you have an appointment to tour the Scarritt Building and Arcade on the third at two p.m."

Logan stared first at Marcus then Mick. "What did you do?"

Mick stood by Marcus and placed her hand on his shoulder. "I hired the best research man in DC to help move my company to KC, and he's going to stay and help me make it work. This is the beginning." She motioned to the building around them and gave Logan a satisfied grin. She'd do it again to see the joy on Logan's face. The quicker Mick could get business done, the faster she and Logan could continue their night. Mick turned back to Marcus. "Tell me about Scarritt. How big is it?"

Logan disappeared to peek down hallways and into empty rooms as they talked.

Marcus's demeanor had changed the instant he transferred the coat to Logan. Not only was Marcus all business, but he looked fantastic. In a dapper, silver tuxedo with tails, Marcus flipped through his planner and rattled off statistics. "The Scarritt is one hundred fifty-eight thousand square feet. It was built in 1907." He scrolled through the screens. "It has twelve floors and an annex of another four, the Arcade. Put on the National and Kansas City's Register of Historic Places—"

"Enough about work." Mick held up her hand to stop him. "Thanks, and we'll get back to that next week. Did you bring my gift?" She softened her tone, worried about Logan's response. "You promise she'll like it?"

Marcus pointed toward the front door. "Already gave it to James." He returned her smile with one of his own.

Mick nodded. "Good."

Logan returned from inspecting the surroundings. "This could work. It's nothing like the Scarritt, but nice. And what gift?"

"You heard all that?" Mick asked.

"The place is empty. It echoes in here."

Mick placed her hands together as if in prayer. "I promise, Logan, no more business till the third of January."

Marcus started walking to the entryway. "Mick, she'll love it. And besides, you need to go because—"

"You have a date," Mick and Logan both said in unison. Laughter echoed as the three of them returned to the door.

Logan paused to give Marcus another hug. "I'm so glad you're here."

"I'll see you this weekend. And, Logan, remember it's the thought that counts."

Logan waved and said, "Okay?" She drew the word out as more question than answer.

Jimmy waited by the open limo door.

"Love you," Logan said to Marcus and ducked inside.

"Good night, James," Marcus said to the driver.

"Happy New Year, Mr. Marcus." Jimmy tipped his hat at Marcus, who waved and then hurried back inside.

Jimmy turned to Mick. "James. I think I like that. Sounds more official."

Mick chuckled. "Well then, James, onward to stop two."

James bowed and motioned to the car. "Yes, ma'am."

Mick slid into the warmth of the back seat.

Jimmy leaned down and whispered, "Your gift is under the blanket." He closed the door and returned to the driver's seat. The limo turned the corner, and they headed for stop two. This surprise, Mick looked forward to the most. Logan would love it for sure.

She shivered more from nervousness than temperature. She reached for the blanket on the floorboard. When she placed the thick gray throw on her lap, Logan's gift lay unveiled. The deep purple velvet box tied closed with an elegant white bow awaited.

Logan raised her eyebrows. "I don't have your present. It's at home under the tree."

Mick reached over Logan and gently pulled her seat belt around. "Yeah? What did you get me?" she asked with a flirty undertone. What Mick wanted didn't fit under a tree. Logan naked and under her would be her ideal present.

"Like I said last week, it's something simple and practical."

"There's nothing wrong with practical." Mick didn't care what Logan had gotten her; it would be perfect. "Time with you is all I need." She had that now, and she would remember this night forever.

Mick sent up a silent prayer that Marcus was right, and Logan would love the gift. She bent to pick up the box and placed it gently on Logan's lap. Mick gazed into the eyes she'd come to love. With all the sentiment bottled in her heart, she whispered, "I hope you like it."

Logan couldn't believe the way her night was going. Neither could she believe anything else could make her happier. Mick and Marcus were staying in Kansas City.

Logan pulled the fuzzy collar of her coat against her cheek. She'd only regretted leaving two items in DC. The orange coat was a favorite, and Marcus knew that. She could still smell his expensive cologne. She glanced at Mick and then at the box on her lap.

"Are you going to open it?" Mick asked.

Logan touched the soft velvet box. "How much did this cost? The box itself is exquisite." She wondered how much Mick knew about her since they met. It hadn't even been two full weeks.

"Please? Marcus helped a lot," Mick asked, wincing a little.

Logan quickly untied the white silk bow and lifted the box's cover. The other of her precious items from DC lay inside the box.

A raggedy paperback copy of *The Wizard of Oz*, complete with a rubber band to hold in the loose pages, lay nestled in lavender tissue paper.

"Oh, Mick!" Logan knew the thought behind it. She'd reread the book so much she could quote from it. When Logan had gotten homesick during the quarantine, Marcus caught her crying. Back then, she had wanted desperately to go home, just like Dorothy, but there'd been no one to whisk her away. She pressed the book lovingly to her chest and smiled at Mick. "I do love it."

"What?" Mick's eyes narrowed and her eyebrows furrowed. She grabbed the box and inspected it. "That was Marcus's touch." She sighed as if full of relief. "My gift is underneath." She returned the box carefully to Logan's lap. "Keep going."

What in the world? Logan moved the lavender tissue paper and gasped. "You didn't." The iconic green hardback of *The Wonderful Wizard of Oz* lay encased behind heavy clear plastic. "Is this…?"

"Is it a first edition?" Mick smiled but still looked apprehensive. "Yes."

"You shouldn't have."

"Why? I really thought you'd like it." Mick looked a little dejected.

"Damn. It must have cost a fortune." Logan pouted, although she was deeply touched. "This is too much. All I got for you was bubble bath, candles, and a guide to the Kansas City area."

"My gosh, that's amazing!" Mick looked as if she was excited, and she meant it. "An experience is better than a gift anytime. I can't wait."

"Really?"

"Are you kidding? What we could do in a Jacuzzi tub and it would be memorable."

Logan grinned. She imagined Mick up to her neck in bubbles and what could happen after the bath. "That is a pretty good gift, isn't it?"

Mick's shoulders relaxed. "It's the best." She looked out the window and pressed the intercom. "Jimmy, are we going to make it in time?"

"Yes, ma'am, ahead of schedule," he answered.

Logan returned both books to the box and closed the cover. She still had no idea what the rest of the night entailed. "Where are we going?"

"The Plaza," Mick replied.

Logan grinned. "Oh good, I love the lights. We didn't get a chance to see them before."

"The holiday season in Kansas City is magical on the Plaza." Her excitement grew. Mick didn't know what adventures awaited her in Kansas City. Along with the guidebook, Logan had compiled a folder of the area's charitable organizations. Satisfied that she still had one surprise for Mick, Logan peered into the night to catch the first glimpse of lights.

The car slowed, and Jimmy's voice came through. "Mick, we're here." He parked the limo and opened Logan's door. Holding his hand out, he bowed and offered assistance. She glanced at Mick, who was busy refolding the blanket.

Logan took Jimmy's hand and got out. She looked around. They weren't on the Plaza. "Where are we?"

"Only a quarter of a mile away, Miss Brady," Jimmy explained.

Mick got out next, with the blanket still draped on her arm. She had the silliest smile on her face and pointed to the other side of the street.

"Your carriage awaits, my princess."

Logan turned her head and raised her hand to her mouth. Tears stung her eyes. The pumpkin-shaped carriage had twinkling lights wound through its frame. A large sign on the back said, RESERVED.

"The Cinderella carriage!" Logan didn't care if the whole world watched. She grabbed Mick, gave her a huge hug, and kissed her in the middle of the street.

Mick was right. Experiences like tonight Logan would remember forever. She grabbed Mick's free hand and rushed to the waiting carriage.

It was as magical as she'd always thought it would be, and she loved every second. They'd been riding for a while and had circled the Plaza twice. They'd talked about Mick's encounter with a homeless kid, and her troubled past she'd tried hard to forget. Mick refused to accept Logan's compliments during the talk.

"But this is really great," Logan said. "I mean, I wish you had shared things like this with me earlier."

"It's difficult when people jump to conclusions." Mick's voice held a small quiver.

"You're right, and I'm really, really sorry about that. I was putting my own baggage on you. It's impressive how you turned your life around," Logan told her. "What about your future here?"

"The company will be great." Mick looked completely certain. "I could have hired a firm to do the work, but what with the pandemic we've all gone through, the first two businesses I called said they didn't have the manpower. Donavan and Paul are helping with renovations to whatever building I decide to buy. The game the guys made will be a big success. I've been thinking a lot about it and how it can help you understand yourself. It helped me see myself as others might, the more I thought about the doors you can choose. Did you know that in their game, the more you interact with other players, the more details you can see?"

"No, how is that?" Listening to Mick open up, seeing the vulnerability in her eyes, made Logan's heart ache in the best way.

"First, you only see shapes and walls. Then the more you cross paths with another gamer, you see colors and wallpaper in their houses. If you continue, you can see their treasures. I mean, like details as intricate as knick-knacks on tables and titles on the spines of books in their rooms."

Logan didn't know much about the gaming world, but she nodded. Mick reached for her and wrapped the blanket around them tighter. "When people get to my room, they'll see pictures of you and your family. People who changed me, who showed me what life can be." She blushed and took a shaky breath. "I'll be quiet now. I'm so glad you liked your surprises."

They both sighed, contentment palpable between them. Logan mulled over all Mick had told her. She'd assumed, incorrectly, that Mick was all about money. In fact, she was truly the woman she'd hoped she'd be. Strong, empathetic, ambitious, and hardworking. How she could have misjudged her so much she didn't know, but it was a lesson she wouldn't forget.

The carriage slowed to a stop in front of Mill Creek. The water reflected the beautiful stars overhead. The sound of fireworks erupted, and a church bell rang in the distance.

"Happy New Year!" they both said at the same time.

Mick reached for her, and they kissed, soft and sweet at first. Logan counted the rings of the bells as the kiss deepened. When the bells stopped, they pulled apart, and Mick grinned at her.

"I've found my treasure," Mick said. "I love you, Logan Brady."

Logan maneuvered to snuggle her back against Mick's chest, and her head cradled on Mick's shoulder. "I love you too, Mick Finnegan. I'm happy to be your treasure."

With Mick's arms wrapped around Logan under the blanket, the coldness of winter melted away. As they both gazed into the beauty of the night sky, Logan believed their love to be her treasure, and it shone brighter than the stars above.

EPILOGUE

One year later

"I can't believe there's no snow this Christmas." Logan's mom scanned the sky from the Brady backyard.

"It's Kansas. Give it fifteen minutes." Her dad stood behind her mom and put his arms about her shoulders. "Did you bake fruitcakes for the annual food fight?"

She gouged him in the stomach with her elbow. "That still shocks me. How could such a thing have happened?"

Logan giggled. She and Mick watched and listened from their seats on the swing set that Ben had erected a few yards from the back porch.

"Happy?" Mick asked quietly.

Logan nodded. "We've all come a long way since this time last year." She smiled. "Doreen's boys are, what? Six months old now? Donavan and Paul will celebrate their one-year anniversary in a couple of weeks."

"And us?" Mick teased her.

"We are the miracle I still can't explain, not even to myself."

Mick wrapped her fingers about the chains connecting her seat to the metal bar above and pushed off. "As my future father-in-law once told me, sometimes we just have to accept what's before us without putting a label on it."

Logan paused before asking, "Like the word wife?"

"Yeah. I was angry at first when you refused to marry me. Hurt, really. But now I understand. You couldn't say yes until you got on your feet, as you put it."

Logan watched as Mick's swing took her higher. "What if I told you I was on my feet now?"

Mick slowed then stopped swinging and stared at her. "Are you serious?"

Logan nodded. "I needed to know that I could live off my own merit."

"Baby, you know that if anything ever happened to me, you'd be set for life. Right?" Mick took her hand.

"It's not about the money."

"Now you're just full of crap. It's always been about the money with you. I've told you that it doesn't matter who pays for dinner or a vacation, as long as we're together."

"Until now." Logan sighed and squeezed Mick's hand.

"So what's changed?"

"I did. You did. I'm not the scared little closeted *baby dyke*, as you called me. You're no longer the corporate exec who can't relax."

Mick narrowed her eyes. "Nah, something happened. Tell me."

Unable to keep from laughing and being so serious any longer, Logan gave in. "Know that heavy box you carried in for me and placed beneath the tree?"

Mick jumped from the swing and pulled Logan to her feet. "You received your books?"

"Yep. Marla sent them overnight, and she said that the pre-sales are better than expected."

Mick hugged her. "That's great!" Then she stood back. "Ah, so it *is* still about the money."

Logan punched her shoulder. "No. It's about my self-confidence. I set a goal last year and accomplished it. The girl who always did as she was told—well, she took charge."

"Yes, she certainly did. Now tell me what your editor said about sales. Be specific."

Logan cleared her throat. "Okay. Marla said I have two new reviews, one from…get this…the *New York-freakin'-Times*. A review on a self-published cookbook! They compared me to that new girl on the Food Network channel. Only I'm an anomaly. I've only been cooking about as long as I've been writing. Most of their cooks are chefs who later get into writing."

Mick burst into laughter and hugged her again. "I told you that Dad gave you a great idea last year."

"I heard my name." Her dad sidled up to them while her mom went into the house.

Mick repeated what Logan had told her.

He whistled softly. "Baby daughter, that's great. When do we get to see the cookbook?"

"There's a large box of them beneath the Christmas tree," Mick said, "and I have the bad back to prove it."

"What are we waiting for?" He strode toward the sliding back door.

"Breakfast?" Logan asked. "Brunch?"

He opened the door for them and stood aside. "Hurry before your mother yells at all of us. I'm not waiting to eat. I want to see it now."

Sure enough, her mom met them as they headed toward the den. "Where are you three going? We're about to sit down to—"

"Cora, my love, our daughter's first book is out, and it's here in our house."

Everyone gathered excitedly around the tree. Doreen and her bunch, Donavan and Paul, all of them. Logan couldn't have been more excited and prouder if she'd tried. Being able to celebrate this accomplishment with her family and the woman she loved was the best thing ever.

Her dad had barely unwrapped the box before everyone had a hand outstretched, waiting for their copy.

Donavan opened his book and gasped. "You didn't." He showed Paul the table of contents and crowed delightedly. "The Queens' Quiche, page sixty."

"I love it, this one's mine." Paul clutched the book to his chest.

"You all get a personal copy," Logan said.

"Cora's Christmas Casseroles. There's an entire chapter devoted to them." Her dad pointed to page eight. Then he gave a whoop. "Ben's Backyard Kabobs. Oh, thank you, honey!"

"Thank *you*—all of you." Tears misted Logan's eyes. "I could never have done this without you." She sniffed. "Mom and Doreen taught me how to cook. You told me to write. Mick has supported me the entire journey."

Abe peered over Doreen's shoulder as she pointed out something to him. He looked at Logan. "You included my parents' recipes?"

"You're family, Abe, and so are they," Logan said simply.

"Oh, which reminds me…" Her mom snapped her fingers. "Abe, I invited them. Your folks and your younger sister will be here around two this afternoon. I don't know where we'll put them, but I figured we'd find room."

"They can stay with us," Doreen said. "Abe and I have the space, just not the beds."

"Logan and I go camping often, so we have an air mattress if you need it," offered Mick. "And his sister is welcome to stay with us. She'd have her own bedroom and bathroom."

"Perfect." Doreen scooped the wriggling twin her husband held and handed him off to her mom. "Abe and I can use the air mattress in the kids' room and give our bed to his parents."

"Oh, and…" Logan cleared her throat. "Mick's going to be family too. We're getting married," Logan added.

Mom and Dad rushed to give them both a hug. Her mom put down the twin she was holding as everyone joined in another group hug.

Mom pulled away first. "She already was family." She kissed Mick and then Logan on the cheek.

Her dad winked at her as everyone talked at once.

Logan leaned against Mick and basked in the warmth enveloping the room. *My family. My beautiful, wonderful, wacky family.*

About the Author

Diana Day-Admire, with the support of her spouse of twenty-five years and her writing group, has self-published two nonfiction collections and is included in *Kansas City Story*, a historical fiction anthology. Diana has won awards for an LGBTQ genre series as well as a sci-fi romance trilogy she plans to finish.

Lyn Cole is one pen name of a multi-published author who writes everything from mainstream women's fiction to erotic romance. She's a perpetual student, a world traveler, a horrid cook, a voracious reader, and a lover of fur babies and British television shows. Her favorite British shows are *Doc Martin*, *New Tricks*, and *DCI Banks*. She's also a Marvel Comics maven who wept when Thanos snapped his fingers.

Books Available from Bold Strokes Books

A Fairer Tomorrow by Kathleen Knowles. For Maddie Weeks and Gerry Stern, the Second World War brought them together, but the end of the war might rip them apart. (978-1-63555-874-6)

Holiday Hearts by Diana Day-Admire and Lyn Cole. Opposites attract during Christmastime chaos in Kansas City. (978-1-63679-128-9)

Changing Majors by Ana Hartnett Reichardt. Beyond a love, beyond a coming-out, Bailey Sullivan discovers what lies beyond the shame and self-doubt imposed on her by traditional Southern ideals. (978-1-63679-081-7)

Fresh Grave in Grand Canyon by Lee Patton. The age-old Grand Canyon becomes more and more ominous as a group of volunteers fight to survive alone in nature and uncover a murderer among them. (978-1-63679-047-3)

Highland Whirl by Anna Larner. Opposites attract in the Scottish Highlands, when feisty Alice Campbell falls for city-girl-about-town Roxanne Barns. (978-1-63555-892-0)

Humbug by Amanda Radley. With the corporate Christmas party in jeopardy, CEO Rosalind Caldwell hires Christmas Girl Ellie Pearce as her personal assistant. The only problem is, Ellie isn't a PA, has never planned a party, and develops a ridiculous crush on her totally intimidating new boss. (978-1-63555-965-1)

On the Rocks by Georgia Beers. Schoolteacher Vanessa Martini makes no apologies for her dating checklist, and newly single mom Grace Chapman ticks all Vanessa's Do Not Date boxes. Of course, they're never going to fall in love. (978-1-63555-989-7)

Song of Serenity by Brey Willows. Arguing with the muse of music and justice is complicated, falling in love with her even more so. (978-1-63679-015-2)

The Christmas Proposal by Lisa Moreau. Stranded together in a Christmas village on a snowy mountain, Grace and Bridget face their past and question their dreams for the future. (978-1-63555-648-3)

The Infinite Summer by Morgan Lee Miller. While spending the summer with her dad in a small beach town, Remi Brenner falls for Harper Hebert and accidentally finds herself tangled up in an intense restaurant rivalry between her famous stepmom and her first love. (978-1-63555-969-9)

Wisdom by Jesse J. Thoma. When Sophia and Reggie are chosen for the governor's new community design team and tasked with tackling substance abuse and mental health issues, battle lines are drawn even as sparks fly. (978-1-63555-886-9)

A Convenient Arrangement by Aurora Rey and Jaime Clevenger. Cuffing season has come for lesbians, and for Jess Archer and Cody Dawson, their convenient arrangement becomes anything but. (978-1-63555-818-0)

An Alaskan Wedding by Nance Sparks. The last thing either Andrea or Riley expects is to bump into the one who broke her heart fifteen years ago, but when they meet at the welcome party, their feelings come rushing back. (978-1-63679-053-4)

Beulah Lodge by Cathy Dunnell. It's 1874, and newly engaged Ruth Mallowes is set on marriage and life as a missionary... until she falls in love with the housemaid at Beulah Lodge. (978-1-63679-007-7)

Gia's Gems by Toni Logan. When Lindsey Speyer discovers that popular travel columnist Gia Williams is a complete fake and threatens to expose her, blackmail has never been so sexy. (978-1-63555-917-0)

Holiday Wishes & Mistletoe Kisses by M. Ullrich. Four holidays, four couples, four chances to make their wishes come true. (978-1-63555-760-2)

Love By Proxy by Dena Blake. Tess has a secret crush on her best friend, Sophie, so the last thing she wants is to help Sophie fall in love with someone else, but how can she stand in the way of her happiness? (978-1-63555-973-6)

Loyalty, Love, & Vermouth by Eric Peterson. A comic valentine to a gay man's family of choice, including the ones with cold noses and four paws. (978-1-63555-997-2)

Marry Me by Melissa Brayden. Allison Hale attempts to plan the wedding of the century to a man who could save her family's business, if only she wasn't falling for her wedding planner, Megan Kinkaid. (978-1-63555-932-3)

Pathway to Love by Radclyffe. Courtney Valentine is looking for a woman exactly like Ben—smart, sexy, and not in the market for anything serious. All she has to do is convince Ben that sex-without-strings is the perfect pathway to pleasure. (978-1-63679-110-4)

Sweet Surprise by Jenny Frame. Flora and Mac never thought they'd ever see each other again, but when Mac opens up her barber shop right next to Flora's sweet shop, their connection comes roaring back. (978-1-63679-001-5)

The Edge of Yesterday by CJ Birch. Easton Gray is sent from the future to save humanity from technological disaster. When she's forced to target the woman she's falling in love with, can Easton do what's needed to save humanity? (978-1-63679-025-1)

The Scout and the Scoundrel by Barbara Ann Wright. With unexpected danger surrounding them, Zara and Roni are stuck between duty and survival, with little room for exploring their feelings, especially love. (978-1-63555-978-1)

Bury Me in Shadows by Greg Herren. College student Jake Chapman is forced to spend the summer at his dying grandmother's home and soon finds danger from long-buried family secrets. (978-1-63555-993-4)

Can't Leave Love by Kimberly Cooper Griffin. Sophia and Pru have no intention of falling in love, but sometimes love happens when and where you least expect it. (978-1-636790041-1)

Free Fall at Angel Creek by Julie Tizard. Detective Dee Rawlings and aircraft accident investigator Dr. River Dawson use conflicting methods to find answers when a plane goes missing, while overcoming surprising threats, and discovering an unlikely chance at love. (978-1-63555-884-5)

Love's Compromise by Cass Sellars. For Piper Holthaus and Brook Myers, will professional dreams and past baggage stop two hearts from realizing they are meant for each other? (978-1-63555-942-2)

Not All a Dream by Sophia Kell Hagin. Hester has lost the woman she loved and the world has descended into relentless dark and cold. But giving up will have to wait when she stumbles upon people who help her survive. (978-1-63679-067-1)

Protecting the Lady by Amanda Radley. If Eve Webb had known she'd be protecting royalty, she'd never have taken the job as bodyguard, but as the threat to Lady Katherine's life draws closer, she'll do whatever it takes to save her, and may just lose her heart in the process. (978-1-63679-003-9)

The Secrets of Willowra by Kadyan. A family saga of three women, their homestead called Willowra in the Australian outback, and the secrets that link them all. (978-1-63679-064-0)

Trial by Fire by Carsen Taite. When prosecutor Lennox Roy and public defender Wren Bishop become fierce adversaries in a headline-grabbing arson case, their attraction ignites a passion that leads them both to question their assumptions about the law, the truth, and each other. (978-1-63555-860-9)

Turbulent Waves by Ali Vali. Kai Merlin and Vivien Palmer plan their future together as hostile forces make their own plans to destroy what they have, as well as all those they love. (978-1-63679-011-4)

Unbreakable by Cari Hunter. When Dr. Grace Kendal is forced at gunpoint to help an injured woman, she is dragged into a nightmare where nothing is quite as it seems, and their lives aren't the only ones on the line. (978-1-63555-961-3)

Veterinary Surgeon by Nancy Wheelton. When dangerous drugs are stolen from the veterinary clinic, Mitch investigates and Kay becomes a suspect. As pride and professions clash, love seems impossible. (978-1-63679-043-5)

A Different Man by Andrew L. Huerta. This diverse collection of stories chronicling the challenges of gay life at various ages shines a light on the progress made and the progress still to come. (978-1-63555-977-4)

All That Remains by Sheri Lewis Wohl. Johnnie and Shantel might have to risk their lives—and their love—to stop a werewolf intent on killing. (978-1-63555-949-1)

Beginner's Bet by Fiona Riley. Phenom luxury Realtor Ellison Gamble has everything, except a family to share it with, so when a mix-up brings youthful Katie Crawford into her life, she bets the house on love. (978-1-63555-733-6)

Dangerous Without You by Lexus Grey. Throughout their senior year in high school, Aspen, Remington, Denna, and Raleigh face challenges in life and romance that they never expect. (978-1-63555-947-7)

Desiring More by Raven Sky. In this collection of steamy stories, a rich variety of lovers find themselves desiring more, more from a lover, more from themselves, and more from life. (978-1-63679-037-4)

Jordan's Kiss by Nanisi Barrett D'Arnuck. After losing everything in a fire, Jordan Phelps joins a small lounge band and meets pianist Morgan Sparks, who lights another blaze, this time in Jordan's heart. (978-1-63555-980-4)

Late City Summer by Jeanette Bears. Forced together for her wedding, Emily Stanton and Kate Alessi navigate their lingering passion for one another against the backdrop of New York City and World War II, and a summer romance they left behind. (978-1-63555-968-2)

Love and Lotus Blossoms by Anne Shade. On her path to self-acceptance and true passion, Janesse will risk everything—and possibly everyone—she loves. (978-1-63555-985-9)

Love in the Limelight by Ashley Moore. Marion Hargreaves, the finest actress of her generation, and Jessica Carmichael, the world's biggest pop star, rediscover each other twenty years after an ill-fated affair. (978-1-63679-051-0)

Suspecting Her by Mary P. Burns. Complications ensue when Erin O'Connor falls for top real estate saleswoman Catherine Williams while investigating racism in the real estate industry; the fallout could end their chance at happiness. (978-1-63555-960-6)

Two Winters by Lauren Emily Whalen. A modern YA retelling of Shakespeare's *The Winter's Tale* about birth, death, Catholic school, improv comedy, and the healing nature of time. (978-1-63679-019-0)

Busy Ain't the Half of It by Frederick Smith and Chaz Lamar Cruz. Elijah and Justin seek happily-ever-afters in LA, but are they too busy to notice happiness when it's there? (978-1-63555-944-6)

Calumet by Ali Vali. Jaxon Lavigne and Iris Long had a forbidden small-town romance that didn't last, and the consequences of that love will be uncovered fifteen years later at their high school reunion. (978-1-63555-900-2)

Her Countess to Cherish by Jane Walsh. London Society's material girl realizes there is more to life than diamonds when she falls in love with a non-binary bluestocking. (978-1-63555-902-6)

Hot Days, Heated Nights by Renee Roman. When Cole and Lee meet, instant attraction quickly flares into uncontrollable passion, but their connection might be short lived as Lee's identity is tied to her life in the city. (978-1-63555-888-3)

Never Be the Same by MA Binfield. Casey meets Olivia and sparks fly in this opposites attract romance that proves love can be found in the unlikeliest places. (978-1-63555-938-5)

Quiet Village by Eden Darry. Something not quite human is stalking Collie and her niece, and she'll be forced to work with undercover reporter Emily Lassiter if they want to get out of Hyam alive. (978-1-63555-898-2)

Shaken or Stirred by Georgia Beers. Bar owner Julia Martini and home health aide Savannah McNally attempt to weather the storms brought on by a mysterious blogger trashing the bar, family feuds they knew nothing about, and way too much advice from way too many relatives. (978-1-63555-928-6)

The Fiend in the Fog by Jess Faraday. Can four people on different trajectories work together to save the vulnerable residents of East London from the terrifying fiend in the fog before it's too late? (978-1-63555-514-1)

The Marriage Masquerade by Toni Logan. A no strings attached marriage scheme to inherit a Maui B&B uncovers unexpected attractions and a dark family secret. (978-1-63555-914-9)